BROKEN

HOI T. PHAM

First edition January 2021
Published in Hong Kong by Hoi T. Pham

ISBN 978-988-75358-0-5 (paperback)
ISBN 978-988-75358-1-2 (ebook)

hoitpham.com

JOIN THE HTP CREW

Sign up for the *HTP Crew* newsletter to receive updates from the author, including his writing journey, writing resources and tips, tidbits about his life, info on new releases and much more.

hoitpham.com

To Gio, for your infinite patience whilst I was writing this book.

To Seoul and Leia, for keeping me young at heart.

1
____

Unlike for her brother, Sophia couldn't find an acceptable excuse for her colleagues' stupidity. She kept her head bowed, propping her forehead in her hand as her thumb and forefinger gripped her temples. The door swooshed open, sucking the air out of the room as an IT technician hurried in. The nine others in the room sat motionless, watching how the stony-faced woman at the head of the table would greet him.

Sophia looked up. "It's been working for the last forty-two minutes," she snorted.

"You still have eighteen minutes then," the IT guy replied.

She opened her mouth, on the verge of saying something about not appreciating his tone, but he cut her off.

"Hello? Is this working?" He turned to the two people on screen. As they leant forward to respond, the room held its collective breath, but the virtual attendees shook their heads, shrugged, and tapped their ears.

"Seb," Sophia sighed. "Sebastian!" She raised her voice when he didn't respond. "Is this going to be fixed today?"

The technician dead-eyed her for a second longer than necessary before running his finger down his notepad again: *mute off, volume up, internet connected, microphone on.* He repeated what must be the most common greeting in any video conference. "Can you hear me?" His voice was muffled as he spoke into the microphone. "One-two. One-two. Two-two."

The people on screen responded with the same shaking of heads and tapping of ears.

Seb shrugged. "Looks like it's the audio cables. Gotta raise a work order."

Sophia knitted her eyebrows and raised her wrist for a closer look at her watch in case he hadn't realised how displeased she was. "So, you've taken six and a half minutes to do precisely nothing."

"Just use the phone." Seb gave a dismissive wave as he walked out of the room.

She shot a reply as fast as she could, pretending that his obvious suggestion hadn't caught her off-guard. "I was going to say if you can't fix it, I'll just use the phone."

She dialled the two remote attendees from the conference speakerphone and turned back to the woman staring at her laptop at the other end of the table. *At least pretend to listen this time.* "What were you saying?"

"So," May replied, looking up, her eyes wandering around the room. Anywhere but at the person grilling her. "We'll have the first cut of numbers in three business days. It'll take another—"

"That was the same update you provided a week ago," Sophia interrupted. "No. Nine days ago."

May sat up straight, leaning forward as she folded her arms and drilled a stare into Sophia. "You only requested it yesterday..." But her voice gave way as Sophia mirrored her forward posture and dug her elbows onto the table, propping her chin in her hand.

May cleared her throat and composed herself. "And I was out of the office, sick. I'll chase them again."

Sophia sat back in her chair. "Guys, do I need to repeat what I said at the kick-off? I don't care about your—"

"If you're talking to me, the name's 'May'. *Senior Manager of Strategy.*"

Sophia trained her stare at the woman who dared to talk back before diffusing it around the room. "Guys, I don't care about your *personal* issues. Work is work." She raised her voice so there could be no mistake she was speaking to everyone. "The Chairman will deliver a flawless update on our results, so Project Panda needs to be ready by the fourth or I hope you have an up-to-date CV."

Sophia paused, letting the message marinate in the silence. She tried to catch the eyes of those in the room, but all found better places to look. As she opened her mouth to continue, the vibration of a phone interrupted her. Taking a deep breath, she counted to three in her head, trying to restrain herself, but it didn't prevent the pencil from snapping in her hand. The attendees exchanged nervous looks. Some darted their eyes to their phones idling on the table, whilst others patted their bodies to locate the noise. "Why can't—" Sophia started before spying a message on her phone.

Lunch? :-)

She rolled her eyes. Not again. The necks of the attendees might have been saved this time, but she wondered about her own.

THE WAITER CLEARED THE BOWL OF PEANUT SHELLS AND replaced it with a fresh supply. Sam looked up from his mindless thumbing of the menu and politely smiled – the fake kind where he scrunched his face and pursed his lips. He checked his watch again, deshelled another peanut and popped it into his mouth. For the fourth time, he flicked the menu back to the front cover.

Heels tapped rapidly towards him against the wooden floor. Sophia caught her breath as she pulled out a chair opposite.

"Sorry, I thought you meant Yaki. The one next to Saint James," she said, scanning Yoko, a small bustling restaurant that was a mix of modern and traditional Japanese – a good balance of East meeting West. Without so much as a glance at him, she picked up the menu, leafing through it. "Have you ordered?"

Sam swallowed his peanut starter. "Uhh... hello, I'm good, and yourself?"

"Sorry I couldn't make drinks the other night. I had... this... thing."

"Thing?" He raised an eyebrow; he wasn't born yesterday.

"Anyway, Project Panda's a nightmare." She shook her head, not wanting to talk about it.

"Lucky I have the best person on it."

"I told you, I'm only helping out for another five weeks."

But it wasn't the response he was after. "So, how's things?" he asked, changing the topic.

"I haven't even started Project Lithgow," Sophia said, still scanning the menu.

Sam plucked the menu from her and placed it on the table. "I've already ordered."

As if on cue, a bento box of prawn tempura, miso soup,

rice and assorted sushi and sashimi served on a charcoal platter arrived.

"Always remind me of school lunch boxes," Sophia said, pointing to the compartments in the box that demarcated each food as she tucked into the salmon sashimi. "Didn't have breakfast."

He looked at her wondering if she had an off button. "You're welcome," he said sarcastically. Not getting a reaction, he dug into the sushi and tried a different angle. "I spoke to the CEO."

She looked up from her lunch. He always knew how to get her attention.

"And?"

"Well, you know we have cost pressures, so every promotion is being scrutinised. Our investors have been vocal about our performance over the last quarter, so it wasn't an easy conversation. I mean, I've had several discussions with Henry, and then with HR to justify the cost increase. Once I got through that, the CFO asked what this was all about, so I had to—"

"Sam! Is it a yes or no?" Sophia demanded, her mouth agape, ballooning with food. Her eyes grew bigger as his pause grew longer.

"Congratulations." He flashed his white teeth. "You're going to be the youngest programme director in Eastle's history."

"Yes, yes, yes!" She pumped her fists, drawing stares from neighbouring diners. She lowered her voice but still struggled to contain the screams in her head that tried to burst out. "Thanks, Sam. You have no idea what this means to me."

"I think I've got a good idea. You mention it almost every day."

"I'm not that bad." She chomped on the ginger garnish.

"Seems like your plan for world domination is finally coming together. Now you can put a deposit on that place in… in… where is it?" he asked, clicking his fingers.

"There's nothing on the market," she responded a little too fast before reining in her reply. "I mean, I've been too busy to look."

"Well, now you don't need to worry about if you should have extra pepperoni on your pizza or choosing between standard or next-day delivery for your online shopping." Sam chuckled at his poor attempt at a joke, but Sophia had already zoned out, glancing at the time on her phone, sighing. "Relax," he said, "enjoy your lunch first. Project Panda will still be there when you get back."

He expected more energy from her given she had finally landed her coveted role, not to mention the trouble that he had gone through to secure it. His long-winded explanation about justifying her promotion to the Chief Executive, Chief Financial Officer and Human Resources was partly in jest but all of it was true. It was a significant step up even for the best of performers, but no one was more deserving than Sophia. Her emails and messages to him at odd hours in the evenings and weekends were regular reminders of the hard work and dedication she had shown since she joined the firm as a management trainee straight out of university.

However, desperate conversational times called for desperate measures, so he reached for the tried-and-tested conversation starter. "So, any plans for the weekend?"

All he could elicit from Sophia was her going through the motion of eating and synchronising her nods with *ah-has* and *mm-hmms*. It was the start of a faltering conversation, during which the silences stretched ever longer. The remainder of the lunch felt longer than the forty-five minutes they had left but soon enough, they were standing at the counter.

"You must've been hungry," Sam said to Sophia as he waved his credit card at the cashier.

"What?"

He frowned. "Everything okay?"

"May's going to be pissed off," she said, glancing at her phone.

He tracked her gaze through Yoko's French doors, and wondered when the downpour had started. "How long were we here for?" he asked. Sophia peered out for a taxi, which were usually in abundance but just like toilet paper in a public lavatory, her ride wasn't there when she needed it most. "Meeting?"

"In twelve minutes," she said, checking the Uber app. Her jaw hit the ground when *3.5x* flashed across her screen.

"You've got to be kidding. The surge is three and a half times the price?" Sam asked. Uber sure knew how to maximise its marginal utility, or, in plain language, screw passengers over. "Just cancel the meeting."

"Can't. It's with May. It's been rescheduled twice already, and we need an answer on our target customer segments ASAP."

"Do you want me to call her?"

Sophia blew out a resigned sigh before accepting the price of the Uber. "It's fine." She tracked the car on the app like a hawk, willing the little icon to move faster. As the downpour became a deluge, brake lights lit up synchronously, and slowed traffic to a crawl. With every passing minute, the lines on Sophia's face folded deeper as she wringed her hands to relieve the anxiety.

"I'll give May a call," Sam insisted, pulling out his phone from his pocket. As he dialled, a car tooted its horn. He looked over to Sophia, but she was already making a dash to the car. He trailed behind her, slamming the door as soon as he dove onto the seat. As the car pulled away, Sophia turned her phone to selfie mode to check how much of the little makeup she was wearing had smudged.

"It's your fault!" she cried.

Sam laughed, brushing the water off her clothes to emphasise the triviality of it all. "It's nothing."

The windscreen wipers squeaked, flapping at full speed. Visibility was poor, compounded by the condensation that had accumulated in the car despite the air conditioning trying its best to evaporate it away.

He grabbed her hands, clasping them into his. "You're freezing!" he said, rubbing her arms. "Driver, mind if you switch on the heater instead?"

Sophia recoiled, surprised by his contact, but she had more urgent things on her mind. "Come on," she said under her breath, willing the driver to slice through the traffic faster.

After a ride that took two and a half times longer than usual, the Uber pulled up at the headquarters of Eastle Financial Group, a sleek fifty-five-storey glass building that projected power and wealth. She opened the car door and ran towards the office but stopped before making it to the entrance, soaking up the rain. She looked back at Sam, surprised that he was still in the car. She turned out her palms, shrugging, but he stayed put. He waved to her and slammed the door shut.

"Let's go for another spin," he said, catching the eye of the driver in the rear-view mirror.

A pair of hazel eyes stared back at him. "You mean, come back here? Okay, but it'll be extra."

Sam smiled, the fake kind where he squinted his eyes and pursed his lips. "It won't break the bank, I promise."

Sophia disappeared into the building lobby as he reminded himself that he shouldn't be seen with Sophia in an Uber together, particularly after lunch, wet from the rain. Imagine the rumours. No. He was a professional.

2

The woman decreased the setting to thirty-seven degrees on the digital thermostat, tapped it up to thirty-eight, down to thirty-five, before punching it all the way to forty-three degrees. Chutes of water washed onto her hair as she massaged in the conditioner. She let out a giggle. "Love it!"

What a difference it made. Unlike home, there was no need to wrangle for water pressure, especially when someone else was using the other shower. She savoured the silky curtain of water that draped her from head to toe. Steam fogged the room, but it was a small price to pay for this luxury. She shook the bottle of moisturising shower cream and slathered it on her legs before gliding the shaver from her knees down to her ankles. It wasn't long before she was sloshing in a shallow pool of water. She felt the tiles, bumbling for the grate and pulled out a tangled wad of hair. She tossed it to the corner, but the stream of water washed it straight back into the drain. However, that wasn't her problem. She was a paying customer, after all.

With the water now lapping against her ankles, she slapped off the tap and slid the shower door open but stopped. She almost forgot. She turned back to the shower cubicle and grabbed the bottle of Kings Hotel Vanilla Scented Moisturising Body Wash, and the sample-sized Rosemary and Mint Shampoo and Conditioner. She smiled as she stepped out of the shower, her feet forming soapy outlines on the mat. If only all her mornings were this satisfying...

She let out a shriek, dropping the toiletries. "What the... who the..." she stuttered at the figure standing in front of her. She grabbed the larger-than-usual towel, wrapped it around her body and retreated into the shower cubicle, splashing in the water that still hadn't drained, cornering herself in. Pushing the door closed, she took stock of what was in front of her: a tall young man, sporting a fringe that dipped into his eyes, and a protruding tummy like a child who drank too many fizzy drinks. Whilst his eyes met hers, the focus was somewhere behind her. His irregular blinks and occasional face pulls were more awkward than threatening.

"Get out!" she yelled.

Despite her panic, the young man squirted disinfectant onto the basin and started to wipe it down. Which part of *get out* didn't he understand? Perhaps a profanity would drive home the message, but that wouldn't be lady-like.

"Out!" She flung her arm to the side, pointing a sharp finger towards the door, just as another Kings Hotel employee skidded into the bathroom.

"Oh shit!" the employee said, catching sight of the woman. He spun back out, giving himself a crick in the neck. He called out by the door. "Lewis? You can't just... you got a minute?" But Lewis continued to spray and wipe down the basin as per the instructions in the hotel procedure manual.

3

———

Vegetables were strewn in the sink waiting to be washed, on the chopping board waiting to be sliced, and in pots waiting to be blanched. Gayle, the orchestrator of the coordinated chaos in her tiny galley kitchen, slapped the steaks onto another cutting block, flicking back the strands of short greying hair from her eyes. Frowning at her expanding waistline, she loosened the tight apron as she poked her head out to the living room, decorated with copious amounts of cushions covered with images of her smiling family. Her favourite was the one of the family all together. In contrast, the walls were plain and dented – no, punched in – but there was no use fixing something that constantly needed repairs. Some of the cavities were the size of a basketball whilst others were as small as tennis balls.

"I said, 'clear the table', Robert," she called out to the motionless body slumped on the sofa, mouth agape and snoring, but the man in the orange high-visibility vest didn't even make the slightest of movements. She sighed. She should have known better after thirty-five years of marriage, but that didn't stop her from trying. At least he was home every evening these days.

As she ducked back into the kitchen, Lewis continued to shadow her, making an already cramped kitchen feel even more claustrophobic. He towered over his mother, and because of that, she had always felt safe when he was with her, even if it was him who needed the care. Gayle ducked back into the kitchen and pointed Lewis toward the toaster. "Make sure you have it on number three. We don't want it too crunchy."

Lewis nodded. "Number three." He held his breath. His eyes popped with anticipation. He tried to control his involuntary twitches and irregular blinks as he held his hands out over the toaster, readying himself. He had come a long way since he was a boy, when the movements were more animated and abrupt but that's what made him special.

Gayle slid the eggs and tomato halves from the pan and onto a plate. "How's the toast going?"

Before she could finish asking her question, two slices of bread sprang out from the toaster. Lewis slapped his hands together, but it slipped through his fingers. "Toast going?" he parroted, picking up the fallen toast and dumping it onto the plate with the eggs and tomato.

"We put the toast here," Gayle said, sliding it to the right, "and eggs and tomatoes on the left so everyone can see it."

Lewis rearranged the two slices, fidgeting with it until it was just so. "Toast on the right."

"Perfect, Lewis!"

"Lewis perfect."

Gayle beamed, "Yes, you are." She poked her head out of the kitchen again, but Robert was still asleep. She turned to her son. "Can you tell Daddy dinner is ready?"

"Dinner," Lewis repeated under his breath and headed out to the living room. He poked at the high visibility vest, pressing onto his father's chest. "Dinner," he whispered cautiously to ease Robert out of his slumber. When there wasn't any reaction, he pushed his face into his father's, their noses almost touching, but he jerked back, pegging his nostrils from the bad smell wafting back. Lewis scratched his head, looking around before the string around Robert's neck made him pause. He held his finger in the air, tracing the thread back to his father's ears. Lewis leant over for a closer look, pinching the line before yanking the earplugs out. "Dinner," he repeated. This time, Robert shifted but it wasn't enough. Unsure of what to do, Lewis paced on the spot, twitching his fingers then bit at his fingernails before striking inspiration. He stepped back, knocking over the open can of Guinness on the floor. He swept his arm up and swung it back down.

Smack!

His hand flew across Robert's face, rudely jolting his father out of his nap. "Daddy's awake!" Lewis shouted towards the kitchen.

ROBERT OPENED AND CLOSED HIS JAW, GENTLY MASSAGING IT. He gingerly chewed on his steak, testing the strength of his teeth.

"You sure you don't want some of this?" Gayle asked Lewis, motioning towards the vegetables.

He screeched but she didn't take the bait; she could read all her son's idiosyncrasies. With limited vocabulary, the screeches, grunts and cries were Lewis' instinctive reactions to the world around him. The screech was loud but flat, without a hint of desperation. Gayle exchanged a look with Robert.

"Look at your mum when she's talking to you," Robert instructed his son.

Lewis shook his head and kept his focus on his phone, not wanting to break his attention from *Fortnite* – an addictive combat survival game where players fought each other and zombie-like creatures.

"Put it away..." Gayle began, but the breath she took to raise her voice dissipated. The dining table was a place for family bonding, not arguments, and after toiling away for the past hour in the kitchen, the last thing she wanted was to aggravate him – she was too tired. Besides, what difference would half an hour of play make?

"Anyway," she said to Robert, "guess what happened at work today?"

"At childcare?" Robert asked, without looking up from his dinner.

"You wouldn't believe it."

Having only paid scant attention to the countless stories Gayle had relayed about her work, Robert decided on a vague yet safe option. "Uhh... did that kid hit the other kid again?"

"No, Leo was well-behaved today. Mustafa brought milk for play break again."

"Who's Mustafa?"

"Every time he brings it, he has the worst diarrhoea."

"Oh," he nodded, "the lactose-intolerant kid."

Gayle tried to contain her giggles. "Sometimes he can't make it to the toilet quick enough."

"We're having dinner," Robert protested with a sigh as he thrust another piece of overdone steak into his mouth.

"Like today!"

Robert shook his head. "Tell the parents not to pack it."

"His dad works at the corner shop, so he gets it for free."

"Did he make it to the bathroom this time?"

She shook her head. "And he didn't bring a spare change of clothes. All we had was the nappy from Little Big Ben. He was naked except for a borrowed nappy!" Gayle chuckled, but her laugh was broken by the swing of the front door. Sophia walked in, typing away on her phone. "You're early," Gayle said, wiping her jovial tears. "Did you get my message?"

"Don't worry, I didn't get sacked," Sophia replied.

"Good timing. We're talking about poo." Robert rolled his eyes.

"Yum." Sophia kicked off her heels and dropped her handbag by the shoe rack.

"Soph's home," Gayle said to Lewis but *Fortnite* still absorbed his attention.

"Dinner's in the kitchen," Robert said to Sophia.

Gayle directed the conversation back to the table. "Anyway, I did some searches during my break again."

"Any luck?" Robert asked.

"It's about $25 a week more if we want to be within walking distance of the hotel."

"Nothing closer?"

"Yeah, but it's $100 more a week," Gayle said.

"What's $100 more?" Sophia asked, bringing her dinner to the table. She tried to sit next to Lewis but was obstructed. "Move," she ordered her brother.

"Soph!" Gayle snapped. "Lewis, can you move in a little?" Sophia pushed past behind him, almost tipping him over in his chair. Gayle turned her palms out. How many times did she have to see this play out again? "Soph!" she repeated.

Sophia shrugged. "He didn't move."

Robert's eyes ping-ponged between his wife and daughter. His teeth ground the steak a little too hard, making his tense jaw muscles pop out. He shifted along the table, creating space and waved Lewis towards him. "Come on."

Sophia seated herself and returned her focus to her phone.

"Oh! Before I forget." Gayle sprang up to fill the silence. "Lewis got an invitation."

"Really?" Robert asked.

"Yeah, an award. From Kings. Isn't that right, Lewis?" But he was still cocooned in his game.

"When is it?"

"Friday. Next Friday," Lewis said with a grin.

"He prepared an average of fourteen rooms a day. Others typically only do ten." Gayle beamed.

Robert patted Lewis on the back. "Good on ya, mate. First time for everything, isn't there?" But like a flip of a switch, Lewis was lost in his own world again.

"Lew, finish your dinner first," Gayle said.

"Why don't we have a look at Homebush?" Robert said to Gayle.

"It's a little closer to Kings but smaller."

"Let's just see it first."

"Bowlpinch is cheaper but..." Gayle trailed off as Robert frowned. She nodded in agreement. Yes, the lower rent came with higher safety concerns.

Sophia put her phone down and looked at her parents. "What's $100 more?"

"Homebush. It's a better area," Gayle said.

"I thought you said we won't move for at least another six months," Sophia replied.

"It'll be closer to Lewis' work. There's a direct bus to Kings from there," Robert chipped in.

Sophia put her knife and fork down. "Didn't we already talk about this? It'll take me another thirty-five minutes to get to *my* work."

"You know it's not the same," Gayle said.

"It's never the same," she said sarcastically.

"Not again, Soph. Not now."

"Then when? When, Mum?"

"Why can't we just have a normal dinner for once?"

"Because you keep brushing it off. You keep lying to my face!"

Gayle looked at her daughter, frozen, disbelieving the turn in the conversation. "What's gotten into you?"

"Gotten into *me*?"

"Is work that stressful these days?"

Sophia let out a puff of contempt, incredulous at the poor attempt to patronise her. "Don't turn it into my problem. My work is fine."

"Why do you always... that's not what I meant."

"I'm so sick of this. And you wonder why I'm hardly home for dinner."

Robert placed his utensils down and folded his arms. His gaze was low, analysing Lewis for any reaction. As bad as the gaming addiction was, thank goodness it was taking his attention away from what was playing out in front of him.

"Why can't you see he's different? Everyone sees it except *you*." Gayle paused, unsure about whether to continue but Sophia didn't push back as expected. "You used to want the world for your brother," Gayle continued. "You used to tie the skipping rope to the clothesline so he could jump rope before school, so he could at least remember he had some fun when he was by himself during break time."

Sophia opened her mouth to respond but the past gave her cause to reflect.

Sensing her soft approach was working, Gayle ploughed on. "When his classmates said, 'He's stupid, he's dumb, don't touch him or you'll get infected too,' you said you'd protect him." Gayle paused, shaking her head. She crunched her fists into balls, smiling as she reminisced. "We even had to persuade the principal not to suspend you."

It all seemed so long ago, almost another lifetime. "When your friends were playing in the playground, your teachers said that you'd sit with Lewis because no one else would. And when he had to change schools, you came home crying for two weeks because you couldn't see him at school anymore."

The room fell silent. Even Lewis looked up from his game, darting his eyes around the table, puzzled at why the conversation had stopped.

"Do you remember how you kept wondering what he would be doing at his new school, or if he had any friends to sit with? Do you?" Gayle searched for the old Sophia that she once knew, hoping it wasn't too late to find her again.

Sophia dropped her head and nodded faintly. "Yeah, I remember. I remember no matter what I did, it was never enough. There was always more to do. I was there for him. But where were you and Dad for me?"

Gayle rubbed her temples. What else could she say to get through to her? "Lewis isn't the same as you."

"This is exactly what I'm talking about," Sophia said, shaking her head and jabbing her finger onto the table to underline her point. "I'm talking about *me*, and you're just focussed on *him*. You've focussed so much on him that I used to think that was normal. That everyone had a disabled brother and we all had to queue up at Human

Services to beg for his disability benefits every three months!"

"Is this about recognising what you did?" Gayle asked. "We know what you did but you know it wasn't... isn't... easy for any of us."

"Of course, I know! Do you think I've forgotten the birthday parties I missed, the sleepovers I wasn't invited to, the movies I wasn't even asked to go to? How do you think I felt when all my friends just stopped asking 'cause it was too awkward every time I told them I couldn't go?"

Gayle dropped her head, her plan of reminiscence falling flat on its face. Lewis trembled as he rubbed his earlobes, swaying his head from side to side, grinding his teeth. Gayle studied her son from across the table, examining his body language in case it was the start of another episode.

Robert looked up to meet his daughter's gaze. "We all have to make sacrifices." He clenched his fists, popping out the veins on the back of his hands. Was he going to slam them down on the table again?

"Yeah?" Sophia looked at the open can of Guinness. "Sacrifices like when you—"

"Soph!" Gayle tried to interrupt.

"—walked out on us when I wasn't even two because you couldn't – *didn't* – want to deal with a special-needs kid because Saturdays was golf, and Sundays was your pub day. Or, what did he say, Mum? 'That retard boy'?"

"That's enough!" Gayle yelled.

Lewis jolted up from his seat, clutching his arms to his chest as he rocked back and forth. His irregular blinks were more pronounced as he paced on the spot, trying to release the built-up anxiety. When that didn't work, he marched towards the TV and smashed his head against the plasterboard behind it, puncturing another crater through it. Gayle rushed to him, but Sophia wasn't fazed. She nodded at Robert.

"Yeah, that's right. You think I didn't know?"

Robert unclenched his fists and splayed them on the table. "You keep bringing up the past. Did your Mum also tell you that we worked five jobs between the two of us just to pay for our marriage counselling, all of Lewis' doctor's appointments, and to put you through school? Yeah, that's right. We've never made any sacrifices. Not like you."

Sophia took a moment to process the revelations. "What? You think you deserve a medal now?" she said finally, rising from her chair. "You think that justifies all your neglect of me?" She stormed past Gayle, who was nursing Lewis' head and rubbing his earlobes, then turned back. "Before you ask again, I got that promotion. Can't wait 'til I leave this shithole!"

4

———

May already didn't like the texture in her hand. She squeezed the ham, cheese and lettuce sandwich again, grimacing at the wet mush that was a poor excuse for bread. She quivered in disgust as she brought the sandwich to her mouth before taking a big bite.

"I keep telling you, just wash the lettuce the night before," her colleague Amora lectured. "It'll be dry by morning."

"Who's got time for that?" May took another bite.

"Then don't put lettuce in it. Better still, pack another sandwich!" Amora said, gobbling mouthfuls of her creamy mushroom spaghetti.

"Anyway, did you get the forecast from Finance?" May raised her voice so she could be heard amidst the crowd in the vast staff canteen.

"Not yet. They got the shits when I said it was urgent."

"Not surprised. Sophia only asked for it at three yesterday."

Amora shook her head. "She always does this."

"So, do you reckon you can get it before close of business or not?"

"Trying."

May sighed. "I've got a meeting with her next week to walk through our customer segments again because she was late to the last one. She didn't even apologise." She stared at the last bite of her sandwich. Even that was a more pleasant prospect than the thought of meeting Sophia again.

"I don't know why you don't talk to Sam. He's your boss too."

May glanced away. If only her workmate knew. "I'm catching up with him after lunch," she said as she sat taller, waving to a confused figure in the distance holding his lunch tray, scanning the hall full of tables.

"I don't even know how she got the job."

May raised her eyebrows. Surely everyone knew. "How old do you think she is?" she asked, changing the subject.

"Dunno."

"Early thirties maybe," Seb said, inviting himself into the conversation. He planted his lunch tray with a clang, spilling rice off the tandoori chicken and onto the table as he sat next to them.

"Took me seven years to move up the ladder and she's already..." May said, trailing off.

"Did you start bitching about our favourite friend without me again?" Seb interrupted.

"She's already what?" Amora asked, leaning forward, ears pricking up.

But Seb interrupted. "Did you hear what she said to me the other day? 'You gotta fix the video conference. It was working just a minute ago.' Yeah, well, not my problem if she can't use the phone."

"Seriously? She said that?" Amora replied perfunctorily

before turning back to May. "Like I said, why don't you tell Sam about her?"

May looked across to Seb, unsure whether she could tell Amora in front of him. She flicked her eyes back to Amora as she took the last bite of her sandwich, weighing what her response should be. She looked at her watch to buy more time, but it was already one o'clock. May pushed her chair back, squealing it against the polished concrete floor. She stood up and took a deep breath, readying herself.

"I gotta go," she announced, her face long from the dread of yet another meeting with *him*.

5

Sophia's face was stiff with determination, her eyes locked onto his office. She strode with purpose, at a pace that would topple an unaware bystander. As she reached for the handle, the door swung open and the closed venetian blinds clanked against the other side of the glass. May pushed past her, head bowed, one hand shielding her reddened eyes and the other adjusting her blouse. Sophia watched her colleague hurry away and disappear around the corner.

The abrupt opening of the door caused sheaves of paper to rustle on Sam's desk, where he studiously hammered out an email. He slapped the papers firmly back down before they could escape. Sophia dropped into the chair opposite him. As she waited for him to finish, she turned to the door behind her, curious about what May's excuse was this time around.

Despite having been in her boss' office countless times before, she surveyed it again. A large map of Australia hung behind his desk, punctuated by dozens of red drawing pins like a bad case of acne. A collection of team photos taken at various company events adorned the bookshelves, sitting next to several awards, patiently collecting dust. Everything was the same boring corporate office, except for the selfie of a photogenic woman radiating from a photo frame, and another of the same woman holding a four-year-old girl in a paddling pool. The child was rubbing her tearful eyes, clearly not enjoying her first experience in the chlorinated water.

Sam jabbed at the mouse. "Sent." He looked up at his visitor, but she beat him to the punch.

"I don't care what she just told you, but you have to tell May that she can't keep changing her mind *after* she's confirmed the target segments," Sophia fumed.

Sam leant forward and squinted. He took a moment to calculate his response then reclined in his chair, smiling. "You should try to relax. You might even make some friends around here."

Sophia glowered at him, waiting for him to make another misstep. Now wasn't the time or place to be making light of her hard work. "We're already five days behind, and *you* have to present this at your conference three weeks before the Chairman announces the results."

She was about to unload the next round of pent-up anger, but her mouth flapped in vain, unable to find the words to articulate her frustration. A low rumble punctuated the silence.

Sam raised an eyebrow. "Skipping breakfast again?"

Sophia didn't need to be reminded of the night before. She ignored the pangs of hunger and kept the conversation on track. "You gotta do something."

Sam leant forward, squinting again, studying her. "Why don't we take a break?"

TWO FLIGHTS UP A NARROW STAIRCASE SAT A BATHTUB FILLED with soil and a variety of sprawling plants, gracing the entrance of Cycle Up. Inside, antique bicycles hung as wall art, nineteenth-century Singer treadle sewing machines doubled as tables, and disused books brought a trendy, yet understated chic to the place. Sophia sat beside Sam on a second-hand sofa that was as out of place as the rest of the mismatched furniture. The yellow glow from the lights provided a dim yet comfortable ambience as she walked him through the project timeline covering the table.

"Are we on track with what *we* need to do?" Sam asked.

She nodded. "We've even started the Q and As for the Chairman in case some analysts throw tricky questions at him. I'm busting the team to make sure this is delivered on time, and it pisses me off that May doesn't respond to anything. And even if she does, it's always late!"

"She's got a lot on her mind."

"We're talking about a presentation for the Chairman! If she can't—"

"You know what they say about walking in someone else's shoes. I'll see if there are resources we can pull in from other areas."

Sophia jabbed her pen at the project timeline and circled the seventeenth of the month. For good measure, she underlined it several times, almost ripping through the page. "There's not much time left."

"You're doing a good job." Sam patted her knee, but it did little to relieve her frustration. "Excuse me," he said, flagging a passing waiter. "Can we get the Rainbow Decadent?"

"Are you expecting more people?" the waiter quizzed.

"No, just the two of us."

The waiter's eyes darted from Sophia to Sam and back to her, sceptical. "It would be an excellent choice for a party of four."

Sam smiled, tilting his head towards Sophia. "Someone didn't have breakfast."

The waiter flashed a tight-lipped smile. "Great choice."

Nine minutes later, an oversized ice-cream bowl slowly approached them, obscuring the head of the waiter carrying it. "One Rainbow Decadent," the waiter announced as he placed it on the table.

"Better?" Sam asked Sophia.

She wasn't sure what she was looking at. It was a mountain of a technicolour dessert that was almost as tall as her forearm was long. It was large enough to put a bear into hibernation and threatened to knock her out with one hell of a brain freeze. There were at least four scoops of each of the six flavours: classic chocolate cookie and cream, strawcherry (a mix of strawberry and cherry), peanut butter caramel, pineapple and banana, green tea, and whatever limited-edition Peppermint Snow was. Shaved ice was sprinkled over the ice-cream tower along with a handful of pomegranate seeds, oozing deep red juice which snaked its way to the bottom. If that wasn't pretentious enough, a waffle cone was jammed into the side of the mountain, looking as out of place as a hibernating bear having a brain freeze. It was an Instagram-worthy shot, screaming out to the world, *Take a photo of me, now!* which was just what Sophia did. She turned to Sam. "I hope you're going to finish this."

A waitress passed. "Together?" she asked, motioning at them.

Sophia waved her away. "It's okay."

"Sure," Sam said, overruling her. He slid over and threw his arm around Sophia.

"That's great," the waitress said, encouragingly. "Three, two, one, Kimchi."

Sophia scrutinised the picture and immediately found a cause for concern instead of appreciating the well-balanced photo of the Rainbow Decadent in the foreground, and the cosy photo of Sam and her in the background. "My hair's a mess."

"We should do this more often," Sam said.

"Uhh..." Sophia replied, almost choking on the ice cream.

"I mean, drinks. You're always too busy."

"Umm... yeah." Sophia searched for a better response – something that would let him know that she wasn't interested, but not too strong that it would cause offence. No one wanted to be in their boss' bad books. "It's hard to get the whole team together. It's just so busy."

"I mean, you and me."

"You know how crazy-busy Project Panda is."

"It'll destress you."

"I'm not a big drinker."

"Just come out for one."

She paused. Repeatedly turning down her boss was a high-stakes game, and risked retaliation and ostracism. It wouldn't necessarily mean that he would sack her, but she may not be considered for the next role or initiative. It was unnecessary psychological distress that she didn't need. "Uhh... let me check my diary."

"Great. I'll have Angela organise something." He dug into the massive dessert. "Who would've thought we'd be sharing ice cream!"

"Who would have thought..." Sophia said, trailing off.

"Ah!" Sam scooted closer and patted her on the knee again.

Sophia recoiled and tugged the hem of her dress to cover her legs. Had she overreacted? It was just Sam. "What?" she replied as nonchalantly as she could.

"Henry supports the recommendation. You'll get above market pay for your new role even though you have limited experience as a programme director."

"I've been doing this for over a year. If it wasn't for me—" she burst out, offended at the suggestion of her alleged limited experience.

"It's all good." Sam held up his hands in surrender.

"When do I get the paperwork?"

He pushed closer to her and slid his hand under her dress and up her thigh. "That's up to you."

Sophia's pulse flickered like faulty fluorescent lights. Paralysed by shock, a confusing array of emotions hit her at once. Apart from the physical reaction, what repelled her the most was the violation of trust. Sam had always been touchy-feely, and he was like that with everyone – male and female – but the barrier between two work colleagues had been broken. She looked around quickly, but she wasn't in luck. No one was nearby; not even the waiter. Was it a coincidence that they were sitting in a dimly lit corner, conveniently tucked away from prying eyes? Had she overreacted or misunderstood? He was married with a kid, after all. Did "that's up to you," mean how quickly she would agree to the salary, holiday entitlements and other mundane administrative details? Whatever it meant, she wanted to get out of there.

"Stop it!" she hissed urgently, plucking Sam's hand and tossing it away. "Waiter! Bill please," she called out, a plea to anyone who could hear her – waiter or not.

6

____

Robert surveyed the cityscape for familiar landmarks and ducked his head for a glimpse of the buildings on the left before turning back to the right.

"Don't worry. We've got plenty of time," he assured his son as he inched the car forward in the slow traffic. "We'll even have five minutes to spare, just how you like it." But it was a fib to reassure himself. Just as well his son was more fixated on the embroidered icon on his favourite shirt.

Lewis ran his fingertips over the four-piece puzzle that was arranged in an almost-square on the left breast of his shirt. Three pieces fitted neatly together, however the bottom left quadrangle was shaped slightly differently and sat atop the other pieces, askew, as it didn't fit the square. It was a simple yet powerful image: all the pieces were there, but the last piece was simply arranged a little differently, just like him.

Robert checked the address on the envelope again: Hotel H, 55 George Lane. Ignoring the stilted voice on his phone, instructing, "In. Ten. Me-tres. Pro-ceed to ex-it two. At. The round-a-bout..." he turned left into a narrow lane instead. It was worth a try given that he had already circled the area three times except for this lane. He would have been in the middle of a shopping centre if he had followed the GPS instructions.

"We're proud of you," he said, feeling the need to fill the silence. He craned his neck to catch the numbers on the buildings: 35, 37, 39... finally at 55. His relief at finding the restaurant was short-lived. The steep flight of steps at the entrance to the non-descript building wasn't exactly the flashiest location for a company event but any recognition for Lewis was a good one. Robert scanned the street for parking bays, but all were occupied. A car tooted its horn, irritated that they had double parked, blocking traffic.

"Do you think you can go up the steps by yourself?" he asked Lewis, pointing to the restaurant. "It's there. Just go up the steps."

"One, two, three, four." Lewis counted the pieces on the embroidered logo.

Robert rubbed his son's earlobes and flicked his hair into place. "You look good. If there's seafood, eat that first. It's more expensive."

Honk. The car sounded from behind again.

Robert looked over his shoulder and raised a hand to the driver to let her know that he wouldn't be long.

Hoonnnk!

He turned to the front, leaning over to the passenger side and pecked Lewis on the cheek. "You better go before the granny behind us has a heart attack. Oh, remember, Soph will pick you up."

"Sophia pick me up," Lewis nodded. He reciprocated his father's kiss and got out of the car.

Robert watched through the windscreen, flashing two thumbs up at his son and pointed to the top of steps, encouraging him to make his way up to the restaurant, but Lewis was content to wait next to an attendant.

"Can I help you, sir?" the concierge asked.

Lewis looked at her before forcing a blink and extended his invitation to her.

The concierge took a moment to read the card. She scrunched her face tighter and read it again (Kings Hotel Appreciation Night), flipped the card to the other side (nothing), checked the date on her watch (it matched the invitation), and returned it to him (he was blank). "Sorry, there's no booking under 'Kings Hotel'."

Lewis smiled and forced another blink.

"Up the stairs, Lewis," Robert shouted from his car, pointing to the top of the steps.

Honnnkkk! The car behind him sounded again.

Robert waved another apology to the driver behind him. He sped off, lest he received another reprimand, and watched Lewis shrink from his side-mirror view.

                               7
                         ———————

"No worries, Henry. It's already reserved for two. I'll
keep you posted," Sam said on the phone before
hanging up. He turned back to his senior team of eight,
squashed around the meeting table in his office.

"Why don't you send him a carrier pigeon?" quipped a
woman at the table.

"What?"

"'Keep you posted'? When was the last time you used
snail mail?"

"Call me old-fashioned," Sam chuckled. "How's everyone's day been? I know it's seven-thirty and some of you had
dinner plans. Unfortunately, the Chairman wants another
summary of our strategy. So, I do appreciate you making the
time." He flashed his straight white teeth. "I've got my own
plans tonight, so let's see if we can wrap this up in an hour."
His charisma was almost enough to make this unannounced
meeting bearable. "Have we got every—" The door swung
open, interrupting his flow. All heads turned towards it.
"—one?"

"Sorry I'm late," Sophia announced to no one in particular, scanning the room for a spare seat, avoiding Sam's gaze.

The eyes in the room gravitated to the empty seat next to the boss that was two strides away, however she betrayed their expectations and threaded through a row of chairs along the wall, mechanically apologising to each person she squashed, and wedged herself between the two people at the corner of the table.

Sam sniffed his armpits. "I even showered today."

There was a polite smatter of laughter around the table, but Sophia wasn't in the mood for his banter. She opened her laptop and bashed away at the keyboard, unaware that all eyes in the room were on her. They shifted to the boss, waiting to see what he would do next. Sam turned to Sophia, trying another angle to lighten the mood. "Is it your turn to take minutes today? We haven't even started."

She shot a steely look at him that told him not to push it.

He recognised her one-woman protest for what had happened at Cycle Up, but it was all a misunderstanding: as he shifted on the sofa at the café, his hand had slipped, making inadvertent contact with her. He looked at Sophia as he attempted to start his impromptu meeting again.

"So, who wants to provide their update first?" Before he finished his sentence, he turned to his left. He couldn't give Sophia the satisfaction of ignoring him.

The Head of Branch Network cleared her throat. "Well, branch sales are 3.4 per cent up from last week off the back of the mobile campaign we launched last week."

"Good to hear, Alisa." Sam nodded in approval. "But we need to ramp up to eight per cent by month-end."

"We can do another customer incentivisation programme and can probably roll it out in two or three days. What do you think?"

"That's up to you." Sam stole a glance to his right. The tapping of the keyboard stopped; Sophia's fingers hung above the keys. A second passed before she resumed typing but that was enough to know his message had registered. Yes, the café incident was all her misunderstanding as Alisa had no problems with what he had just said.

By the time Sam looked at his watch again, it was an hour and a half later. He stood next to the whiteboard that was graffitied with barely legible scribbles.

"If we don't control *this*," he said, circling a graph that showed increasing bad debts, "then *this* won't matter." He drew a red outline over the declining revenues graph and paced in front of the whiteboard. His tie was loosened, and one hand was cradling his elbow as his other hand was tucked under his chin. He stared at the floor, contemplating, expecting his senior team to jump in with a bright idea on how to improve the firm's performance, but some stared blankly at the board, whilst others tracked him as he paced from left to right and back again. Clearly, they wished they were someplace else too, but Sam pushed on. "Our credit policy must keep up—"

"Pizza, pizza, pizza!" demanded a little girl.

Sophia looked up from her screen and out through the glass door. "Damn it," she said under her breath as she closed the lid of her laptop. The other managers turned towards the commotion as a woman and her six-year-old daughter headed in their direction.

Sam spun around, his face dropping. "Give me one second," he announced to the table before greeting the two visitors outside his office.

"In a minute, sweetie," the woman said, trying to placate her hangry daughter.

Sam crouched to meet the girl's eyes and ruffled her

cheeks. "Hey, princess. Amy's a little hungry, is she?"

"She's been a handful since we left home," the woman replied.

Sam stood up. "It's not today, is it?"

"We can wait if you need more time."

"I'm so sorry, Teri. I thought you meant next Tuesday."

Teri looked at her husband, forgetting to blink as she tried to hide her disappointment.

"You could've... Anyway. So..." she said, waiting for him to announce his intentions.

"Come on, Daddy. Pizza!" Amy cried, tugging at her father.

"I've got this thing after this. It's... Henry wanted to... the two tickets have already been reserved."

"But it's our..." Teri looked down at Amy, disappointed for her too. "It's okay." She shook her head. There was no need to explain.

Sam rubbed the back of his neck, his face twisting in pain. "I'll make it up. I promise," he replied. Amy tugged at her father again, prompting him to crouch to her eye level again. "Sorry, sweetie. Daddy has to work but we'll do something on the weekend, okay?"

"Anyway," Teri said to Sam, deflated. "See you at home."

"I'll make it up, I promise," he repeated as if the more he said it, the more it would make it better.

"Okay," Teri dismissed.

"I'm really sor—"

"Don't be too late," Teri replied before he had the chance to finish his sentence.

The office door swung open. Sophia rushed past them, laptop in hand and slinging her handbag over her shoulder. "Sorry, I have to run," she said, turning back to Sam. "I'm on my mobile if you need me."

8

The honks competed with the profanities as the car weaved through the slow-moving traffic at dangerous speeds. She could barely see in front of her through the downpour.

"Come on!" Sophia muttered. She wiped the condensation off the windscreen with her hand whilst the wipers flapped at full speed. For the third time that month, she reminded herself to get the heater fixed. She impatiently tapped the dashboard – the frantic kind where every second counted, like when crossing her legs tight, hoping her bladder wouldn't give out at any moment. Or the kind when she was already twenty-five minutes late.

With condensation fogging the car, Sophia lowered the passenger window, allowing the rain to spit onto the seat. Catching a better view of what she was looking for, she slammed the brakes and jerked to a stop. A drenched figure at the foot of a flight of steps, head bowed, stared at the ground. She shook her head. It couldn't be anyone else. Reversing, she provoked further rebuke all round, but it didn't even register.

"Lew!" she shouted, waving her arms, but the storm was too loud. She tooted the horn, then a longer honk. It provoked as much of a reaction as screaming at a mannequin in the rain. "Bloody hell!" she cursed.

She turned her hazard lights on and got out of her car, striding towards her brother. She grabbed Lewis by the wrist and dragged him into the passenger seat. "Why were you just standing there?" She slammed the door as he got into the car. "You're getting the seat wet! Why didn't you go inside?"

She wiped the fog on the windscreen and looked over to her brother. His tall frame was hunched over into a tight ball as water dripped off every part of his body. He was silent except for his teeth chattering. Even with his fringe flattened by the rain and covering his eyes, the tears were hard to miss. The hurt was more visible the more he tried to hide it. Sophia softened, deflating before she could erupt further. A wet passenger seat was no longer her concern. She wriggled out of her cardigan, blotting Lewis dry. "Heater's not working," was her attempt at an apology.

"IT WOULD BE HISTORIC FOR AN ASIAN TEAM TO BEAT THE South Americans in these finals. It hasn't been done in the last seventeen World Cups," the commentator announced on TV. "Now, Jung has the ball and is looking dangerous. He dances around Martinez, and Jung is in with a chance! And... and... no! He's fallen. He's fallen! South Korea is appealing for a penalty. Colombia cannot believe it. I cannot believe it. Can *you* believe this?!"

"No!" Robert sprang to his feet from the sofa.

"Lewis wants some juice tomorrow. Can you get some

tomatoes and beetroot after work?" Gayle asked from the floor on a pink yoga mat, catching her breath.

Robert dropped onto the sofa again, watching the slow-motion replay like a hawk. The two players jumped up to headbutt the ball, but it was Jung who was successful. Martinez collapsed on the ground and withered into a foetal position, covering his head with both hands as if an axe had split it open. "You gotta be kidding!" Robert bellowed at the TV.

"Can you get it or not?"

"Get off the pitch, princess!"

"Too loud!" Gayle yanked her earphones out, removed the basketball between her knees and placed it next to her. She sat up, winded and flushed. In the silence after the outburst, the key sliding into the lock was unusually loud. The door flung open, reverberating against the doorstop, almost bouncing back into Lewis' face.

"Take off your shoes. Don't go inside yet," Sophia instructed her brother as she followed him in. She turned into the bathroom and emerged with a handful of towels, throwing one around his shoulders and another at his feet. "Stand on it so the floor doesn't get wet."

"What happened?" Gayle asked, rising to her feet.

Lewis disregarded his sister's instructions, and walked to his mother, hugging her in his wet clothes, shaking his head in anguish. "Everything will be okay," Gayle assured him.

"It's all right, mate," Robert said from the sofa.

"Soph, what the hell happened?" Gayle asked.

"He was just standing there," Sophia said, in between drying herself.

Still immobilised in Lewis' embrace, Gayle snuck her head around her son's shoulder. "Where?"

"What?" Sophia ruffled a towel through her hair, responding after a pause. "On the steps."

"What steps? Why didn't he go inside?"

Another pause. "Why are you asking me?"

"They didn't provide cover? Soph! Where was everyone else?"

There was another pause from Sophia as she continued to dry her hair. It was only a few seconds, but it was a few seconds too long for an impatient and concerned mother. Gayle tsked in frustration and peeled herself away from Lewis, whipping her head around, searching. When she found her phone next to the yoga mat, she jabbed at it, almost spearing her finger through it.

"The Kings Hotel, my name is—" said a soothing male voice over the phone.

"Lewis was standing outside on George Street all night. In the rain!"

"Hi Gayle," the operator replied, dropping his corporate tone. "What can I—"

"Lewis received an invitation for an awards night. From the company!"

"I'm not aware of any awards night."

"Brian, he received the 'Best Customer Experience' award. And he was waiting. All night! In the *rain*!"

"Sorry, Gayle, we don't have any awards thing."

"What do you mean you don't—" Gayle screamed down the phone, then it dawned on her, making her blood boil. She hung up. How could anyone do this to such a vulnerable soul? It wasn't just a prank. No, it was corporate bullying. There was no other way of interpreting it. For a child to be taken advantage of was bad enough but this was Lewis, her precious baby. She stood in silence, stewing over what she should do next.

"Don't worry about it," Robert said, his eyes still fixated on the game.

"I can't believe you!" Gayle snapped, hammering her fists down by her side, incredulous at her husband's apathy.

"He's fine. These things happen."

"Dad, you can't—" Sophia started but couldn't finish.

"If you let them!" Gayle lectured her husband. She grabbed the remote control and switched off the TV. Sophia could only watch with wide eyes at the rapid escalation, standing silent.

"Do we have to?" Robert pointed to the TV. "In the middle of —"

"Why did you leave him at the steps? Why didn't you walk him in?"

"It's my fault now, is it?"

"Yes! It is," she replied resolutely. "He wouldn't have stood in the rain, getting soaking wet."

"*I'm* supposed to know that he got a bogus invitation?"

"No. You were supposed to walk him in."

"Yeah, because the city's *so* full of car parks," Robert said sarcastically. "Why is it always my fault? What are *you* going to do?"

Gayle threw her hands up in frustration. "I'm going to... complain... talk to the big boss... I don't know!" Lewis shuddered at the escalation, closed his eyes and rocked back and forth, making unintelligible noises. Gayle drew him close and rubbed his earlobe.

"And it worked so well the last ten times you've done it."

"Shut up! At least I'm trying, Robert. At least *I'm* trying." She hurled the remote control at her husband, hitting his thigh.

Robert picked up the control, aiming it at the TV. Sophia shook her head at him for a long second, standing in front of him, blocking his view. She hesitated, choosing her words carefully. "Umm... I don't want to ruin the mood," she said sarcastically, "but you haven't forgotten about the seventeenth, have you? Should do something for a change."

She shrugged. It would be a near miracle if he did anything since birthdays, festivals and other celebratory events had never been a big deal to him. Life, in his view, was more about survival than unnecessary indulgences.

"We'll see," Robert said, which was his way of saying no. He waved the remote control to shoo her out of the way.

"We can do a double celebration." She lowered her voice as she cocked her head towards her mother. "My promotion, and *someone's* birthday."

He shrugged, which was his way of saying that he was open to the idea.

9

Despite the venue being standing-room-only, with barely enough space for the waiters to edge their way through to each table, it was as quiet as the reference section in a library. All eyes were glued to the TV screens around the room, and all ears tuned in on the World Cup commentator: "I know it's a school night and I'm sure we'll have some weary eyes tomorrow morning but can Park Chul Son break the four-four deadlock? Here we go now." The pub crowd held its collective breath, some inching closer to the screens for a better view. "It's Park with a short run up," the commentator continued, "he boots it into the corner. And... he's done it! South Korea advances to the quarterfinals!"

The cheers on the screens were drowned out by those watching in the pub and the TVs obscured by half the room jumping in excitement and punching the air, whilst the other half yelled profanities in disbelief.

"I told you. Didn't I tell you he'd do it?" Sam yelled across the table, competing with the noisy celebrations.

Henry, a shorter man with stiff hair that gave him the

look of having an involuntary buzz cut, leaned across the table. "What?"

Sam wanted to recoil from the smell, a mixture of sweat from being trapped in a room with eighty other football enthusiasts and a cologne that may have expired a couple of years ago. Instead, he held up his pint of beer, then lowered it so Henry could clink it. "Cheers!"

"We were robbed," cried Henry, "I don't believe it!" He pushed his glasses higher on the bridge of his sweaty nose. "Did you know that cheersing originated back in medieval days so when they bumped their glasses, a bit of their drink would spill into the other so they could check if the drink was poisoned?"

"Don't change the subject." Sam shook his head, wagging his finger. "Our $50 bet still stands."

The room erupted again in raucous screams, whistles and applause as the screens replayed the penalty shootout. Henry moved closer to Sam, shouting into his ear, "Do you want to head back?"

Sam held his breath and gritted his teeth. It was a school night but... "You're the boss."

THE GLOW FROM THE MOBILE PHONE MADE TERI'S HEAD appear decapitated given the rest of her was under the duvet. She clicked on the email from the school again: *Don't forget to pack Amy's hat tomorrow. No hat, no play.* Her mouth stretched into a gaping yawn as her eyes became heavier. She buried her face into the pillow and closed her eyes; her phone still illuminating her face. It was way past her bedtime.

As she faded to sleep, the faint click of the front door

jolted her back awake, her eyes springing open. She snatched her phone – 1.43 am – and wedged it under her pillow. The floor creaked sporadically as the approaching footsteps gently made their way to the bedroom. Despite the temptation, she snapped her eyes closed. *Relax. Pretend to be asleep.*

The wardrobe rustled before the footsteps faded away. Click – another door closed. The firing up of the hot water system preceded the pitter patter of the shower. Teri peeked out from the corner of her eyes and squinted at the faint glow from under the en suite bathroom door. As she laid waiting for the pitter patter to stop, estimating that it would be another seven or eight minutes, she rehearsed what she would say to him. *Why are you so late?* No, it was too aggressive. *How could you forget it was our day?* It was too accusing. *How was it?* It was too casual. She sighed, rolling over to her side. She gave up rehearsing any lines – she shouldn't have to. He was her husband, not His Majesty.

As her eyes struggled to remain open, the noise of the shower stopped. She waited for the bathroom door to open but as the seconds turned to minutes, Teri kept circling back to one thought: what was so important that he had to cancel their plans tonight? She shook her head. She couldn't wait any longer; she tore off the duvet and swung open the bathroom door.

"What are you doing?" Teri snapped, standing in the doorway.

Sam jolted in shock, his wet hair dangling over his eyes. "Don't worry. Go to sleep," he replied, running the tap over his work shirt.

"It's already two."

Sam lowered the shirt into the bathtub, trying to hide it

from view. "I just spilt something. Don't worry, I'll be in bed soon."

Teri puffed through her nose. "You never do the washing, and now you're hand washing?" She ripped the shirt from his hand to inspect it, but the bitter citrusy odour got the better of her. "What's that smell?"

"What's wrong with you?" Sam said, grabbing the shirt back from her and throwing it into the bathtub. He pushed past her out of the bathroom, deciding that he didn't want to be cornered.

Teri marched with him out to the lounge. "You didn't even message."

Sam stopped, unsure where he was escaping to. "You didn't have to wait up."

"No, I didn't," Teri said, turning the light on. "I wanted to."

Sam didn't know what to say. Seven heart-shaped helium balloons bobbed weakly around the dining table, having lost some of their buoyancy. Two balloons rolled around on the floor, deflated. He swatted the balloons away, revealing a chocolate forest cake – Amy's favourite – with two wedges missing, a partially burnt number 9 candle, and *Happy Anniversary!* piped onto it. Beside it was an envelope written in Amy's unsteady handwriting: *To Mummy and Daddy.*

10

Ahhh! The sound of satisfaction. An empty pint glass webbed with foam slammed next to the two others on a Delaney's Irish Pub coaster. Robert checked his messages again. "Don't forget. Tomatoes and beetroot." He checked the time and shook his glass in the air.

"Coming up," a voice boomed from behind the counter.

Robert savoured the few minutes he had left. It was his time to unwind after a hard day's work; his peaceful place before he opened the front door to who-knows-what and faced whatever challenges that Lewis, and by extension, Gayle had to face during the day. He inhaled his fourth pint and headed out to his car. Tomatoes and beetroot, he reminded himself.

Watching the Roselands Shopping Centre sign approach in the distance, Robert flipped his indicators on and slowed down to enter the car park. As he turned into the entrance, he swerved back into his lane and spun around in an illegal U-turn. There was something more urgent than tomatoes and beetroot, he remembered.

Arriving at the hotel, Robert approached the reception

desk. It was almost as long as the length of the small foyer. The Kings Hotel was part of a local three-and-a-half-star chain of middling accommodations, boasting sixty-three rooms and a short walk to the local street market.

"Hello, how can I help you?" smiled the receptionist.

"Is Mike Ire around?" Robert asked.

"One moment please." She tapped the keyboard, her acrylic nails loud against the plastic. "Who should I say is asking for him?"

"Just a mate."

"Right. Well, he's housekeeping at the moment. Do you want me to leave a message?"

"I can wait."

"His shift finishes at five."

Robert looked at his watch. Another thirty-six minutes. He weighed it up. Maybe he should come back another day. "Which floor is he on? I'll quickly pop up to see him."

"What did you say you were here for?"

"Uhh..." he started, not having thought that far ahead. "He forgot... his Epi. Pen. The pen thing you jab yourself with when you go into anaphylactic shock. Like, when you can't breathe." He nodded to himself.

"Right... well, unfortunately, we can't let people without bookings wander through the hotel for security purposes."

"It's important. For him."

"I understand, Sir. If you can pass me the pen, I'll make sure we'll get it to him."

"You can't call him or something?" Robert waved his hand at the phone on the counter. "It's life or death. For him."

"I'm sorry, Sir. For the security of our guests and staff, we can't let people without bookings—"

Robert nodded. Whatever she was going to say, he

already had his next line cued up but luckily for him, it wasn't required. The receptionist knew when to pick her battles. She abandoned her rehearsed line and spoke into the walkie talkie: "Mike Ire to reception please. Ire to reception." She smiled at Robert in a frozen rictus. "Won't be long."

Watching the time tick over to 4.46 pm on his phone, Robert jiggled his leg to dissipate the nervous energy. Gayle needed the tomatoes and beetroot for dinner soon and the last thing he wanted was another lecture from her if he was late.

As he walked over to the reception to enquire again, the ding of a crisp bell sounded. A man in a uniform three sizes too large, with wavy hair and sporting a few straggly hairs that provided a poor excuse for a moustache, emerged from the lift. Robert had almost forgotten what he looked like and, for no good reason, pictured him as a beefed-up tough guy with tattoos all over his body because, wasn't that what all bullies looked like? Instead, Mike looked more like the type of law-breaking guy who watched Netflix using a mate's subscription, or the guy who "accidentally" scanned the cheaper Pink Lady apples at the self-serve till instead of the more expensive avocadoes.

"Mike! How are ya?" Robert called out, smiling as an old friend, and shuffling towards him. He threw an arm around the younger man, ushering him back into the lift.

"What up? What up?" Mike replied, tripping backwards.

As the lift door closed, Robert rammed him into the corner and curled his fingers around his throat. "Thought I already told you last time—"

"Get off me!" Mike tussled with Robert, slipping out of the chokehold and managing to keep him at arm's length. "I swear you don't wanna mess with me." Mike squeezed his fists into tighter balls, cracking his bony knuckles.

Robert scoffed and wagged his finger in Mike's face. "You play games with Lewis one more time—"

Mike swatted Robert's fingers away from his face before catching his wrist and slammed him against the mirrored wall, shaking the lift. "You think I'm scared because he told his Daddy on me?" Mike scrunched Robert's shirt tighter and crunched him into the wall again. "Chill, it was a joke, okay? He's a bloody bore. I gotta entertain myself somehow."

Mike dug his elbow harder into Robert's chest as he pushed his forehead into Robert's. "Don't be coming here tryna be a hero."

Pinned against the wall, Robert shook Mike's forehead off his and twisted away. It was Robert's turn to slam Mike's skinny frame against the wall. "You think giving him a bull-shit award is funny?"

"I said it was a joke. Something wrong with your hearing, you old fart?" Mike taunted.

Robert pressed his elbow harder onto Mike's throat. "I'm supposed to be at home, sleeping on the sofa already. Instead, I have to say hello to a bloody imbecile."

"Can't... breathe..." Mike managed to choke out.

"You play games with Lewis one more time, and I'll make sure you can't breathe. For good."

"What's your prob, dude?" Mike strained, the vein near his eyes pulsing.

"You hear me?"

"You're not scaring nobody," Mike said, gasping for air.

"You hear me!" This time it wasn't a question.

The ding of the lift sounded again on the ninth floor. A

father and his teenage son dressed for the swimming pool exchanged glances.

Robert straightened Mike's collar and fixed his hair. "Just because we're housekeeping, doesn't mean we shouldn't look after ourselves." He beamed at the two strangers and mimed a breaststroke action. "Great day for it," Robert said before stepping out of the lift.

ROBERT CRANED HIS NECK INTO EACH ROOM. "I'M HOME," HE called out when he couldn't find Gayle. He shook his head as he turned on his heel, following the voice in the distance. "I went to the hotel..." he begun as he popped his head into the kitchen.

"Yeah, I called them straight away," Gayle was saying, her back towards the door. Robert listened in, trying to decipher his wife's conversation. "Told the managers they couldn't treat Lewis that way. Even wrote them a complaint. Yeah, I know... worst of all, the husband didn't even want to do anything."

Robert's curiosity turned to discomfort. He cleared his throat and raised his voice. "I'm home," he repeated. Gayle waved at him as she spun around to face him. "I said I went to the hotel after work..." he tried to continue but she pointed to the phone stuck to her ear in case it wasn't already obvious. He gave her a thumbs up and walked away.

A moment later, Gayle called out. "Did you get it? I texted twice."

"Yeah, the green one," he grunted nonsensically from the sofa in front of the TV that he had just turned on. His eyes closed and his head dropped to one side. As he drifted into his nap, a slight breath exhaled onto his face. He opened his eyes, jumping in his seat, startled to find Gayle's face pushing into his, her arm raised, ready to take a swipe at him.

Gayle scrunched her nose, tripping backwards as she flapped her arms in front of her, swatting the smell away. "Delaney's again?" She sighed, shaking her head. She folded her arms, scowling at him and puffing through her nostrils. "Did you get the tomatoes and beetroots?"

"I said, the green one," Robert replied as he nodded off.

11

Festooned with rainbow lighting, the Casper Plate was a local favourite, tucked away among rows of identical apartment blocks. Its modest but appetising menu of pizza and pasta were consistent winners but its claim to fame was its deep-fried chilli pig ears, which drew both the curious and adventurous alike.

"Tonight is a night of celebration, so no arguments. We can kill each other tomorrow," Robert joked.

"It's just a promotion," Sophia said. "I didn't want to make a big deal, but Dad wanted to celebrate it with your birthday." Her mother frowned; it wasn't in her husband's DNA to care for celebratory events. "Seriously!" Sophia protested.

Robert held up his glass of water. "Happy twenty-first again, darling," he said, pecking his wife on her lips.

Lewis cringed as he brushed the vicarious germs from his lips. "Yuck, yuck. Eewww."

Robert moved in to plant a kiss on Lewis, but his son closed his eyes and pulled away. "And Soph," Robert continued, "congratulations on your promotion. If you keep this up, your mother and I will be able to retire soon."

They raised their glasses, clinked and sipped their drinks. Lewis joined in with his orange juice, though the cold sweetness triggered his eyelids to flutter.

"All you need to do now is get married and settle down," Gayle said to Sophia.

"Marry," Lewis repeated. "Birds and bees." He burst into a knowing giggle.

Sophia rolled her eyes. "Mum. Please. You're not getting grandkids any time soon."

Lewis took another gulp of juice, the sugar rush exacerbating his head tics and face pulls. Robert confiscated his glass and set it aside. "Easy, Lewis." He turned to Sophia. "Who's the bloke you were seeing before?"

"I wasn't *seeing* him, Dad."

"The guy with the hair like he just woke up?"

"It's called style. Not that you would know."

"Is he the one who can get fifteen per cent membership discount at the club?"

"Which club?"

"Golf," Gayle interrupted. "A sport to ruin a good walk, I'd say."

"*You'd* say? I thought Mark Twain said it," Robert replied.

Gayle shrugged. "Didn't he die decades before the quote was actually used?"

"Anyway, why don't *you* marry him?" Sophia said to her father.

"Well, I might do." Robert turned to Gayle. "What's your discount?" But there was no response from her.

Sophia tracked her mother's gaze to another table, shooting a glance at Lewis, then back at her parents. If they weren't going to do something about it, she would. She uncrossed her legs, ready to rise from her seat.

"Let it go, Soph. It's not the time and place," Gayle said.

Robert nodded in agreement. "A night of celebrations, remember? No arguments."

Sophia's chest puffed with anger. She wasn't busting for a fight tonight, but the snarky laughter and the mocking face pulls from two twenty-somethings at the table nearby was enough to propel her to her feet.

"This is bullshit," she said. She turned to march over to the offending table, ready to give them a piece of her mind, but she bumped into a man in jeans and a chef's coat; a coat that had been lovingly stained by all the meals and ingredients over the years, turning it from white to a faded technicoloured canvas.

"That's one world-famous deep-fried chilli pig ears," the chef announced, setting the plate in the centre of the table as he blew a chef's kiss. "Bellissimo!"

"Chef Jordan, good to see you," Robert said, extending a hand to shake.

The chef shook his hand before shuffling a few steps to Lewis and ruffled his hair. "How's my favourite man?" He held out a fist, ready for a bump but was left hanging; only managing to elicit a shrug from Lewis in response. Jordan pulled back, speaking to the table. "The kitchen's pretty busy but I saw my favourite Marexis and I thought to myself, I haven't seen you guys in months. I just had to say hello!"

Gayle smiled. "I'm sure you say that to everyone."

"I would *never* do that," Jordan dropped his jaw in mock horror, "because I don't know any other family called Marexi!" He bellowed out a laugh, amused by his poor attempt at a joke.

"Excuse me," Sophia said.

"Come on, where are you going?" Jordan asked. "The joke wasn't that bad."

Sophia wrinkled her face enough to squeeze a semblance of a smile, and tried to walk past him, but he leant into her ear. "All you need to worry about is enjoying the pig ears." She looked over his shoulder; a waiter was escorting the two rowdy youngsters out as one of them shouted something about infringing on their god-given rights, and the other recorded the exchange on his phone, threatening to post their injustice on social media for all the world to see.

"The food's great. Give my compliments to the chef," Sophia replied, sitting down.

Jordan tapped his finger on his lips, struck by a thought, then pointed his finger at Sophia accusingly. "If I remember correctly, last time you said you were going to move out, but I didn't get no invitation to your housewarming. I thought we were friends. No discount for you tonight!" He flicked his head to the ceiling in jest.

Sophia smiled, not wanting to bring up the sensitive topic given the many arguments she had had with her parents about it. No arguments tonight, she reminded herself. "Soon."

As the night wore on, the conversations ranged from the latest work gossip to weekend plans and holiday schedules. Despite her low expectations, Sophia found the chance to let her hair down with her family a pleasant experience by the time they left the restaurant with full bellies; some more intoxicated than others.

Gayle was unsteady on her feet as she fished the car keys out of her bag and headed to the driver's side.

"Not in that state, you're not." Robert nudged her into

the passenger seat as he placed the leftover birthday Oreo cheesecake on the dashboard.

Lewis pointed at his mother. "Bloody idiot!"

"Enough," Robert said.

"Drink drive. You are bloody idiot!" Lewis squawked.

"In the car, now." Robert ushered Lewis into his seat and buckled him up. But Lewis fought back, bursting into a tantrum. "That's enough, Lewis!"

The younger Marexi didn't want to go home. Not yet. Lewis trembled at first, shaking in his seat. His breathing became short and sharp, shallower with each inhalation. His eyes flickered, rolling to the back of his head, revealing the white of his eyes. He slammed his body against the seat, and rocked back and forth, trying to rip off his seatbelt. "Red car. No. Mummy!" he called out, violently shaking his head, a bead of perspiration rolling down his face. He threw his arms up, trying to slither his way out of the car.

With Lewis' limbs lashing at his face, Robert pulled back from restraining him. "Breathe, Lewis. In through the nose and out through the mouth. That's right," Robert coaxed. He gently pinched Lewis' earlobes, and rubbed them, calming his son. "It's all right, mate. No more orange juice for you tonight."

AS HE APPROACHED THE TRAFFIC LIGHT, ROBERT ADJUSTED THE rear-view mirror, slapping his hand over his mouth to mute the groan of his gaping yawn. He swivelled around in his seat to check if he had disturbed them. *Phew.* They were still asleep. For the first time in a long time, the picture of his family together gave him a warm, visceral feeling. Except for the minor hiccup when buckling up Lewis, it wasn't often that the family spent quality time like this. He was already starting to think about their next outing when Gayle shifted in her seat.

"Rob, I need to tell you..." Gayle murmured in her semi-conscious state. She trailed off unintelligibly before giggling sheepishly. The laugh was infectious, especially because she wasn't in full control of what she was saying.

Robert leant over, straining to decipher what she was saying. He wanted to ask her to repeat it but didn't want to interrupt her rest. He stopped behind an old beat-up red pickup truck at an intersection and checked the clock on the dashboard. Five more minutes until home. Rain drizzled, blurring the headlight beams, as he switched on the windscreen wipers. When the traffic lights turned green, Robert followed the pickup turning left, slamming the brakes as the pickup stalled. He tapped the horn, conscious not to wake his family. A hand stuck out of the truck in front, waving apologetically.

"Come on," Robert grumbled. There was a splutter of the ignition as the other driver tried to restart the engine. It convulsed but it couldn't be brought to life. Robert looked at his rear-view mirror. Just as well there wasn't much traffic. He manoeuvred around the truck but didn't get far. He was blocked on the outside lane by shrubs and traffic bollards on the inside. Robert jiggled his leg as the truck tried to restart again, and again, and again. With his patience sufficiently worn, he stepped out of the car, slamming the door.

The noise stirred Lewis and he grew agitated in his seat. His breath became heavier. The whites of his eyes flashed fierce and frenzied. His face strained a deep red, his eyes clamped shut. His arms and legs stiffened and contorted in every direction, his body thrashing against the seat. "No, no, no..." he cried, urgently hitting Sophia's leg, each strike harder than the last.

"Stop it," Sophia said through tired eyes, slapping him away.

"Van, big van, car, red car," Lewis said, trying to rip off his seatbelt, then trying to unbuckle Sophia's.

"Yes, yes, big red van," Sophia said, dismissing him as she turned away to continue dozing.

"Mummy! Wakey wakey!" Lewis called out to his mother, but she was too drunk to hear his pleas. He lunged towards the front passenger seat but was snapped back by his seat belt.

Annoyed that he was now getting wet in the rain, Robert left Lewis to his tantrums and marched to the truck. "What's going on?" he asked the other driver.

"Sorry, mate. Looks like I ran out of juice," replied a man barely in his twenties. He tried the ignition again, but the pickup just couldn't be brought back to life, no matter how many profanities it was offered.

"You're blocking traffic." Robert motioned to the side. "Why don't we push—"

A loud desperate female scream cut through the otherwise peaceful night, followed by screeching tyres. The men whipped their necks in the direction of the sound – Robert's car. A camper van barrelled towards them, its brakes screeching as the wheels locked, tyres ferociously skidding and burning up against the asphalt, billowing plumes of smoke and a nauseating smell of scorched rubber. "Mum! Wake up! WAKE UP!" Sophia screamed, her voice breaking as she rocked the back of her mother's seat.

The screeching seemed to last forever. By comparison, the impact, when it came, was silent, instantly quelling the primal screams. The camper van's reinforced bull bar ploughed through both vehicles like a bowling ball desperate for a clean strike, crunching the front of Robert's car and clipping the tail of the red pickup truck. The brute force spun the truck around and flipped Robert's car twice before it settled on its side. It was crushed the way an empty can caves in when booted like a football. The roof was as flat as though it had been measured by a spirit level. The damaged tail of the truck was repairable, but Robert could already picture the insurance agent increasing the driver's insurance premium for the following year. The bull bar saved much of the camper van though it bore streaks along both its sides from slicing through the vehicles.

"GET OFF THE BLOODY ROAD!" A VOICE SHOUTED FROM A distance, rousing Sophia back to consciousness, her little finger twitching. The cold, wet asphalt pressed against her bones. She opened her eyes but the blinding headlights and rain spitting in her face forced her to close them again.

"My dinner's getting cold!" the driver shouted again, banging on his car horn.

"Shut your face! There's people dying here!" another person retorted, which invited more horns.

"You wanna have a go? No one's talking to you!" the first driver yelled.

The second driver screamed a reply, but the shouting and car horns blurred into the background. The only thing Sophia wanted to know was whether she was dead. She wriggled her fingers, then her toes. Nothing moved. Her body was as heavy as if the road was pinning her down, not letting her escape. One of her nightmares was to be paralysed, helplessly trapped in a body that only a few hours ago was fully abled. The helplessness – no, uselessness – the loss of independence, not to mention the pitied stares from well-intentioned strangers, would be infuriating.

She turned her head to the side, opening her eyes again. Bloodied ragdoll bodies, lacerated with cuts that peeled opened like scored sausages, strewed the intersection. Shattered glass, mangled metal, and tomatoes and beetroots littered the road. Blotches of red liquid washed away as the rain fell increasingly harder. Worst of all, a dozen or so spectators stood around the mess, unsure of what to do, while traffic banked behind them. Where were the flashing red-and-blue lights that the movies always depicted after an accident?

Sophia willed herself to wake up from the nightmare. She gasped for air, but the sweet metallic blood in her nostrils was another bad omen. She had never been able to smell in her dreams. She lifted her head and tried to ease herself up, feeling blood trickle down her forehead.

"Don't move. Please don't move," a woman said, her arms reaching out, trembling, but she retracted them again. "Sorry, I don't know what to... I don't know if you've broken anything so, I don't know... please don't move." She crouched, covering Sophia with her umbrella. "The ambulance is on the way."

The woman's ramblings didn't reach Sophia as she laid her head back on the ground, catching sight of Lewis who was more scared than injured. She continued to scan the chaos, finding Robert cradling Gayle in his arms. She wasn't sure whether she was imagining it, but their conversation cut through the mayhem.

"Hold me. Tighter," Gayle said to her husband.

Robert obeyed and pushed the sense of the inevitable

out of his mind even though her matted hair, drenched in blood, was unsettling.

"Don't, Gayle. I'm here, I'm here... don't..." he begged. When that didn't work, he changed tack. "Tell me what you were saying before..."

"Just a little bit longer," Gayle said.

"I got the tom... tomatoes... and beets... I didn't forget... and... and Lewis won't be... they won't bully him any more... I went over..." Robert rapidly explained, hoping that somehow the efforts he had gone to would bring her back. "Gayle!" The rise and fall of her chest grew shallower, more prolonged. The rain pounded what was left of the Oreo cheesecake, washing the *Happy 21st again* sign down the stormwater gutter. The downpour hid Robert's tears as he squeezed his wife closer, but no matter how long or how tight he held her, Gayle became still. Too still.

12

———

Sophia's eyes were closed, paralysed.

It was a dream. Surely, a bad dream.

Chaotic scenes of the crash tumbled through her mind.

She opened her tear-filled eyes.

She was no longer lying on the hard asphalt but the soft cushion of grass.

The wind picked up, flicking her hair across her face, interrupting her vision.

She was in a daze. Kilometres away.

13

———————

The Velcro on the fluorescent-orange safety vest hung on by millimetres before it gradually ripped apart, leaving the sides flapping around the protruding waist of the factory manager. He sucked in his oversized gut and pulled the sides together again, but the frayed Velcro had had its day. There were only so many times it could strain over the bulging tummy before it didn't want to stick together again. He checked the tags inside the vest: XXXL. He shook his head. They sure didn't make them like they used to.

Snapping his earmuffs over his curly mop of hair, he looked at his watch. 7.31 am. He took a deep breath, pushed open the office door and walked out to the factory yard past the fifteen-metre-long sign: *Tectonic Building Systems. Best and biggest supplier of wall and ceiling building systems since 1963.* He waddled his way onto the factory floor, clipboard in hand, and was hit by the roar of the forty-seven industrial machines crunching and shaping metal sheets, the rumble and beeps of forklifts whizzing by, and intermittent flashes of orange safety lights. As he looked out to the factory floor from the safety of the yellow-painted walkway – the Yellow Brick Road – he checked off the items on his list.

"Yo!" he yelled out to a passing forklift.

Benji fishtailed to a stop and glanced at his mirrors. "Shit!" he said to himself, reversing.

"How many times do I gotta tell ya?" Ming, the factory manager, asked.

Benji slapped a switch, activating a rotating orange beacon on top of the forklift, announcing to all the world that he was on the loose. "It was already on. I swear to God!"

Ming tapped the clipboard with his pen. "I swear to God, Benji, there ain't gonna be a next time!"

Benji stomped on the accelerator, skidding off. "You the man, Mingy!"

It had been a routine morning for Ming; he was panting, perspiring and taking three times longer than the recommended time to walk the floor. It was five to eight when he spotted a pair of dented, scuffed black steel-cap boots perched on the guardrail. He diverted from the Yellow Brick Road and crept up behind them, smacking his clipboard across Robert's shoulder.

"I wasn't sleeping," Robert shouted above the factory din, scrambling up from his nap. Decked out in the usual quartet of safety gear – high-visibility vest, ear plugs, safety glasses and gloves – his five o'clock shadow was more like a few days' stubble and the dark circles under his eyes gave away the little amount of sleep he had managed to steal over the last few weeks.

"I'm cool. You cool?" Ming shouted back.

"Yeah, just resting my eyeballs... eyelashes... lids. Eyelids. Wouldn't even bother wasting ink for a caution, if I were you."

"I know it's been tough for you... with, you know... your

missus and all. Just want ya to know, I didn't want to roster ya but you know how it is. Those Chinese orders keep coming in and I gotta have my best person on this beast." He patted the P45 machine.

"Yeah, nah, sure. I mean, no use moping at home, huh?"

"—when you can mope around here!" They both chuckled; Robert's more forced than Ming's.

"Listen," Robert said, "machine's been running non-stop twenty-four hours a day, six and half days a week. You need to get maintenance on this thing."

"It's already scheduled after the Chinese order."

"We used to tune it three times a week, now we're lucky if it's just once."

Ming placed his hand on Robert's shoulder, breaking it gently to him. "I guess things are tough for you at the moment, but I'll let you take care of your stuff at home, if you let me take care of stuff around here."

He smiled, patting Robert on the arm before marking the P45 machine satisfactory on his clipboard and waddled to the final leg of the floor inspection.

Robert perched his boots on the guardrail again, watching the beast churn out length after length of corner beads in an undulating, hypnotic rhythm. The exchange with Ming gave him pause. Why exactly was he at work so soon? He wished he was anywhere but at work, though he didn't want to stew at home. Besides, what would he do now that Gayle was gone? Shrieking metal snapped him out of his daydream. *Bloody hell.*

He punched the big red *Stop* button and looked up at the calendar hanging on the wall. A black outline, with 'Engineer' scrawled across it, encircled Thursday. That was three days away, and at that rate, he was annoyed that he might be rostered on the weekend despite wanting to keep himself busy. Robert disengaged the safety switch and released the sheet metal.

Entering through the barricades, he threaded his arm through the rollers. After a few laboured tugs at the obstruction, he wrenched the buckled sheet free and pulled himself up, sucking in a few deep puffs – he wasn't as fit as he thought. He kicked the rollers into alignment before feeding a clean sheet through the machine. Stepping out to the edge of the safety barricades, he slammed the gate, rattling it to make sure it was closed. With so much heavy equipment and moving parts, it was always better to be safe than sorry.

He thumped the big green *Start* button, stirring the machine back into action. He had barely finished cursing Ming for not scheduling maintenance sooner when the metal crunched again. He let out a disapproving grunt, glancing at the clock. Sixteen minutes to three-thirty. It was close to the end of his shift but not quite close enough to make it the afternoon shift's problem. Grumbling, he threaded his arm through the rollers again and tugged at the twisted metal to clear the jam.

Robert almost dislodged it on the fourth pull, reigniting the machine back to life. The only problem was his hand was stuck. He jammed the metal back to stop the rollers from inching forward, desperately trying to wriggle his fingers free, but the rollers kept creeping forward. *Shit!* Why was this happening? He had done it at least half a dozen times earlier in the day. Perhaps that was precisely why it wasn't working, having worn out a bearing, a spring, or tension belt. Doubt crept in. Had he activated the safety switch, or did he leave it unlocked? He wasn't sure anymore.

The rollers inched forward, crimping his fingernails. Thank goodness for the jammed metal, no matter how slight the resistance it provided.

"Help!" Robert screamed, hoping someone, anyone, could hear him above the rumble of the factory. Anchored by the machine, he couldn't even raise his hand high enough to draw attention to himself. All he could see were greasy rollers and if he couldn't see the factory from where he was, no one would be able to see *him*.

"HEY!" he screamed until it grated his throat, angling his cries towards the roof. He tried to yank his fingers out but only succeeded in almost dislocating his shoulder from the brute force and awkward angle. As the jammed metal gave way, Robert bargained with himself about the extent of injuries he might be able to live with. There was an article in the local paper about a food worker succumbing to hypothermia after being trapped in a walk-in freezer over the weekend. Her colleagues only found her on Monday morning frozen against the door as she tried desperately to operate the emergency release handle. Would he suffer a similar fate? Trapped in the belly of the beast for hours, days on end?

He didn't have to wonder for long. The crisp crunch of his fingers being flattened seemed louder than it was as the unforgiving block of metal crept forward. No matter how hard he tugged and twisted his hand, it was futile. All Robert could do was watch his fingers slowly disappear under the steel rollers in vain, millimetre by millimetre. He screamed in pain, panting, sweating. When would the rollers stop? It probably had enough torque to crush his whole body, not just his hand. Why wasn't he more insistent on maintenance sooner; he kicked himself. Stars swam in his vision as he fought to stay conscious.

"Help!" he strained again but it was barely audible. The combination of the pain and exhaustion of being cramped in an awkward position suffocated his cries. He closed his eyes, readying himself to rip his arm off his shoulder joint. He drew in two short breaths. One... two... thr—

The machine stopped. He opened his eyes but before he could make out what was happening, a voice boomed into his ear. "I got you, mate!" Ernie, the afternoon-shift operator, shouted above the noise.

Robert's head slumped as he closed his eyes again. Thank goodness sixteen minutes wasn't seventeen.

14

Amy gripped the edge of the kitchen bench as she peered into the sink. At six years old, she needed to be involved in everything, even the mundane chore of washing up. "Careful, it's slippery," Teri said, passing the plate to her daughter.

Starting from the centre, Amy slowly wiped the plate in a concentric motion, meticulously drying every drop before placing it into the rack. "All done."

"Good girl." Teri turned to the bin, but Amy already beat her to it, stomping on the foot pedal, flinging the bin lid open. "I hope you're this enthusiastic doing chores when you're older, Amy!" Teri emptied the bin and headed out of the kitchen with Amy following like a shadow. "Stay here," she instructed her daughter.

Amy curled her lips down and crossed her arms. "I can do it," she insisted.

"It's dark already, there are too many mozzies. I'll be right back." Teri escaped out the front door before Amy could register any more disappointment.

Tossing the refuse into the green recycling bin, Teri wheeled it to the kerb as she constantly waved her hand around her face and arms to swat the mosquitoes away. As she spun on her heels to run back to the house, a flashing light in the parked BMW caught her attention. She patted herself and felt her own mobile phone in her pocket. Sam must've left his in the car. However, as curious as she was, she didn't fancy getting eaten by those damn mosquitoes. She took three strides to the house before turning back to the car. What if it was an important call for Sam? Goodness knows he was always on his phone. She fished the keys from her pocket and grabbed his phone that was wedged between the driver seat and the middle console.

As she made her third attempt to get back into the house, a notification lit up the screen. She wondered then hesitated. It'd only be a quick look. It wouldn't kill anyone. She turned it on, which prompted for the password. *Damn it.* She hadn't thought that far. She tapped her fingers on the phone, then was struck with inspiration. She punched in Sam's birthday, but the phone vibrated and sounded an error message. She tried her own. Nope – it vibrated in disapproval again. She sighed before her eyes lit up. How could she have forgotten? She punched in Amy's birthday. *Finally.*

Teri darted her eyes around to locate WhatsApp. She scrolled down the list of chat messages from May, Henry, Sophia, as well as three other work colleagues whom she only vaguely recalled. Her eyes locked onto the first message. Careful not to leave a tell-tale sign of a read message by clicking on it, Teri turned the phone sideways to landscape, which previewed a little more of the message. "I'm on leave – you shouldn't be messaging. Like I said, I won't say anything if you..." was all she could read. The tone and the message itself didn't seem to be work-related. "I won't say anything if you..." what? The truncation was irritating.

Teri's finger itched to click on the message so she could view it in full, but she thought better of it and scrolled to the next message. Did Sam really have an appointment with his boss that was so important that he had to cancel their ninth wedding anniversary plans? Not that the plans were much – a stay-at-home celebration with Amy – unlike the first few, but still! Her thumb hovered over the message but she wavered again. What if there were work-related conversations that she shouldn't be reading? Not that she would say anything to anyone but what if Sam found out? Trust was the cornerstone of any relationship and although she wanted to trust, she also needed to verify.

"You okay?" Sam asked, emerging from the front door. "What's taking so long?"

Teri clutched Sam's phone against her chest, her blood flowing a little too quickly. She wiped her clammy palms onto her sleeves as she spun around. "You left your phone in the car," she said, holding it up as evidence.

"I thought I lost it." He walked over and took his phone off her.

She matched his stride back to the house, alternating between darting glances at him and back to the ground. Should she or shouldn't she, she wondered, before throwing caution to the wind. "Who else went with Henry?"

"What?" Sam looked up from his phone.

"Did anyone else go?"

"Just me." Teri stopped him in his tracks, folding her arms and pressing her lips together. He sighed, locking onto her eyes. "I told you, it was a pre-arranged business event that I couldn't get out of."

"Was it? You never came home and hand-washed your shirt at two in the morning. And you had work the next day." Teri quickly corrected herself. "*Later* that day."

"What are you getting at?"

"Did May go?" She studied his body language for the smallest of clues – every unconscious tick, averted glance, or stutter wasn't too small to avoid scrutiny.

"What?"

She didn't want to let him know that she had read some of the messages. The truncated message still irked her, but it was too late to retreat now. "She said she won't say anything if you... what?"

Sam rubbed his temples. "Again, I'm very sorry for missing our anniversary. I *will* make it up to you."

"You didn't answer the question."

He threw his arms in the air and took a few moments to compose himself. "Me and Henry were inspecting the venue for my retail conference—"

"I've never heard of a CEO inspecting the hotel himself. Don't you have teams to do that?"

"Can you just let me finish? We chose one of the most expensive hotel venues to reward our top performers and it's a secret because we want to *wow* them." He flicked out his fingers like a magician dazzling their audience. "I mean, without our top performers, I wouldn't be where I am." Teri opened her mouth to reply, but he cut her off. "And that's why May can't say anything. It's a secret."

Guilt crept in for questioning him. Teri tried the fill the silence with something, anything, to downplay her outburst but nothing came to mind. Trust was the cornerstone of any relationship, she reminded herself, as she felt the temperature rise given that *she* was the one questioning that trust. He had given her an explanation, but she couldn't pinpoint her unease. She turned away from him, slapping her arm, shooing a mosquito away. "It's late," she said, marching towards the house.

15

The peace was disturbed by ear-splitting blares from Sophia's phone alarm. Get up! NOW! It seemed to squawk. She stirred in her bed, managing to flick her bleary eyes open, just enough to make out the time: 6.03 am. She let her eyes shut again and buried her face into her pillow. Another two minutes wouldn't kill anyone.

Five minutes later, her eyes snapped open. She checked her phone: 6.34 am. *Great.* Work was the last thing on her mind. Maybe she should have taken some time off. However, as soon as she toyed with the idea, she expelled it. She had no time to succumb to touchy-feely problems like the rest of them. She wouldn't – no, couldn't – be one of *them*. There was still much to do for the Chairman's results announcement and Sam's conference. Plus, she couldn't jeopardise her promotion. That would only give her colleagues more ammunition to fire back at her. She couldn't give *them* the satisfaction.

After a quick shower, Sophia rushed into the lounge, still adjusting her blouse. As she scanned the room for her handbag, a silhouette slumped on the sofa startled her. Her father.

Robert was crumpled in his chair, his head flopped to the side at an acute angle. Who knew how long he had been in that position, but his neck would sure be painful when he woke. His left hand cradled his right on his lap, which bulged at twice the size with bandages that bloomed with patches of red at the fingertips.

Sophia searched for the remote control to turn off the early-morning news, but something stopped her. It didn't feel right. Her heart beat faster as it took a few seconds for her brain to clue her in. Robert wasn't moving. Even if he was deeply asleep, he was too still, too silent. Opened boxes of Zoloft and tramadol were discarded on the coffee table.

Unfamiliar with either prescription, Sophia wasn't sure how dangerous they were but any medication around a motionless body couldn't be a great omen. She watched for the expansion and contraction of his chest but couldn't make it out given his awkward position. Surely he was only sleeping – they only spoke a few hours ago. She brought her ear to his nose and mouth, feeling stupid as she did, and bracing for him to wake up and burst her eardrums at any second.

She held her breath to listen to his. She couldn't hear anything, couldn't even feel the waft of his breath. Her pulse beat faster as she brought her hand close to his mouth. A warm body was a living body, she reminded herself. She swallowed but her mouth was dry. Her pulse raced as she inched her hand closer. Was she ready to find out? As the panic set in, Robert snorted like a pig, his body shaking in his sleep. She jumped back, slapping her hand over her mouth to mute her squeal.

Satisfied he wasn't dead and embarrassed at her own

jumpiness, Sophia searched for the remote control again. In addition to the boxes of prescription medicine, the coffee table was littered with an assortment of outdated newspapers, magazines, advertisements, used cups and half a dozen unopened letters, some of which bore the logo of the Department of Human Services; one with *REMINDER* stamped in heavy red letters. She picked up an envelope, sliding her finger under the flap, threatening to tear it open but she was already late for work. It could wait. Where was the bloody remote?

Her eyes swept the room: nothing on the sofa, nothing on the bookshelf... nothing on the... *Aaarrrggghhh!* She spun back to Robert to check if he had moved but he was still undead on the sofa.

Deep creases scrunched her face when she recognised the figure lying underneath the dining table. "Get up!" she demanded, her heartbeat levelling out as she approached the pink yoga mat. Lewis clutched the basketball that his mother had used for her home exercise against his chest. "Hurry up!" She walked towards him but stopped, struck by the acrid smell. She ran through the possibilities of what it could be, starting with the most dangerous. Gas? No, it was more pungent and heavier. Was the refrigerator left open? She approached the fridge and pushed the door to make sure it was closed. It was.

She checked her phone again and returned to Lewis, throwing her arms in the air.

"I'm already late."

Lewis squeezed the basketball tighter against his chest, rocking it to comfort it like a baby. She paced back and forth, unable to get the words out.

"Why can't you just..." she started, her arms stiffening as she waved them aimlessly, threatening to turn violent against him. "I said, hurry..." she tried again but what was the point? She blew out a loud breath.

Lewis squashed his lips together in his hand, trying his best to suppress his hurt, his grief, his tears. He shielded his face in his arms, hiding it from his sister. Watching her brother whimper in pain, it didn't matter what the time was any longer. She crouched to the ground and laid next to him, blocking out that awful, pungent smell which was now stronger. She searched for the right words as his face contorted and his lips quivered, but what could she say to a person who probably hadn't grasped the concept of loss and death? Explaining that their mother had gone to heaven may be comforting for most, but would he expect her to return? Would it scare him if she explained that their mother had gone to sleep? Or, would he worry that he might not wake up too if he went to sleep?

She let out a sniffle; the memories of her mother gone too soon catching up with her. But she couldn't be weak in front of Lewis. If she wasn't strong for him, who else would be? He was as vulnerable as a baby in the womb, unaware of the outside world, protected by the ball he was curled up in. She rubbed his earlobe and gently stroked his protruding tummy as she pushed the stench of urine on his pyjamas out of her mind. After all, everyone had different coping mechanisms after the death of a loved one. A lump in Sophia's throat snuck up on her. "I miss Mummy too."

16

The walk to the station took longer than usual, each nudge and knock from other passengers in the train was extra irritating, and the commuters seemed louder than was ordinarily tolerable. It was like starting the day with batteries already drained and anything that needed to be done was a damn chore. Walking into Eastle's foyer, Sophia swiped her pass at the turnstile.

Whack! She walked straight into the barriers.

A security guard yelled something at her. "Miss, stand back," he repeated when she didn't respond. "Do you have a pass?"

Without wasting the slightest acknowledgement on the guard, she swapped her credit card for her staff pass, swiped herself through, and stormed into a vacant lift, relieved that she would have a few moments to herself. It was days like this that she needed to be alone, especially after Lewis set her schedule back an hour.

"Wait up, wait up," a distant voice called, followed by the scurry of footsteps before an arm speared through the closing lift doors. Sophia darted her eyes to the offender and rolled her eyes. "Cheers," the colleague said, thanking her erroneously. "How's it going?" he asked as the doors closed.

"Hi," Sophia replied, avoiding eye contact. Didn't he know that she had little patience for superficial conversations at the best of times? And this was Monday morning.

"Good weekend?"

"Mm-hmm." She fixed her gaze on the in-lift video, which espoused something about corporate social responsibility. Not that she cared much about it, but it gave her an excuse to zone him out. Wouldn't it be great if someone, somewhere, somehow addressed the awkward ride in the lift? The video could throw up trivia to keep people's attention, just long enough so they didn't have to speak to their fellow passengers. Who wouldn't want to know that 2.25 billion cups of coffee were consumed around the world every day? That pickled ginger served with sushi was to cleanse the palate between each dish instead of being an accompaniment? Or that Bruce Lee's Chinese name literally translated to 'Little Dragon'?

After eight seconds that seemed like an eternity, the lift arrived on Level 39. As soon as Sophia swiped her pass to enter the office, all eyes locked onto her, only averting when she walked past them. They must have already heard about her mother. Gossip sure travelled fast. Had she made the right decision to return to work so soon? She pushed it out of her mind. Personal stuff was personal, and she was at work.

With the gossip from her colleagues reducing to whispers and knowing glances around her, Sophia logged into her laptop but the jarring sound of *Access Denied* rejected her command. With facial recognition, touch ID, voice identification and other biometric authentication methods, why did her computer still require a password? *So* twentieth century.

Sophia re-entered the same password, but it threw up the same abrupt alarm. She drummed her fingers on the desk, incremented her password by one to *iforgot15* and smacked the *Enter* button, drawing surreptitious glances from her neighbouring colleagues. It was the last straw for her already short fuse, and the bloody password debacle wasn't helping either.

"Why don't you mind your own business?" Sophia snapped at the woman in Public Relations. For the three years she was on Level 39, she had only spoken with the woman once – when she needed the firm's house view on the sale of complex wealth management products to vulnerable customers. Despite sitting six and a half metres away from each other, they hadn't spoken since.

"You heard me!" Sophia drilled a stare into the Public Relations woman and her two colleagues who froze with wide eyes and guilt plastered on their faces. "Mind your own—" she started laying into them again.

A hand tapped Sophia's shoulder from behind. "Do you have a minute?"

SOPHIA STARED AT HIM, SILENT. SHE WASN'T ONE TO BE lectured at the best of times and she didn't feel like listening to a sermon this morning.

Sam sat on the edge of his chair and returned the stare. It was less of a glare than a look of curiosity. "How are you?" he asked.

"Good," Sophia replied curtly. There was a long silence.

If he wasn't going to say anything, why did he call her into his damn office?

"I guess you didn't get my texts." She drew an exaggerated sigh. How many ways did she have to say no? But something about him told her the texts weren't about drinks again. His approach was softer; he wasn't as eager. "Why don't you take more time off?" Sam continued.

"I'm fine."

"If you're worried about the conference, I'll get Chris and the guys from Investor Relations to take care of it."

"Said I'm fine. It'll keep me busy," Sophia replied, her voice straining. Her focus blurred; her eyes moistened as she crunched her teeth to hold herself together. It was the first time that anyone had shown any real sign of care for her wellbeing after her mother's passing. She continued to stare back at him, pretending that she hadn't dropped her guard. Her vulnerability even surprised her. Her eyes fluttered, trying to blink the tears away.

Sam pushed a box of tissues across the table before he stood up and walked to the door. He pulled the strings by the wall, closing the venetian blinds to prevent nosey busybodies from looking through the glass doors and intruding on her moment of weakness. "They don't need to see this," he said, walking back to his seat. "I know you just said you don't need the time off, but the offer is still there."

Sophia sniffed softly, still pretending the tissues were a redundant offer as if having feelings, let alone after her mother's death, was something to be ashamed of. Personal stuff was personal, and she was at work, she reminded herself.

Sam broke his gaze and leaned back in his chair. "Just so you know, HR's assessing my salary recommendation on your promotion."

"Thanks," Sophia said, stony-faced yet belying her excitement. It was the first piece of good news in a long time. She was finally getting the advancement that she deserved.

"We'll sort it out soon." Sam swung his chair around his desk, and placed his hand on her shoulder, gently squeezing it. Sophia tensed, startled by the contact. "I'm here if you need me," he continued, dropping his hand to stroke her back.

Sophia froze. Sam leant in and kissed the back of her neck. Her pulse raced and her head screamed for her to do something – anything – as her eyes darted around, calculating her next move, but came up blank. She strained to look at the door behind her from the corner of her eyes, trying to see if anyone was outside, but the blinds were conveniently closed. All her muscles ached when she realised how rigid she had become. "Is there anything else?" she asked.

"I just wanted to make sure you're okay." Sam rolled his chair closer as he brushed his lips from her neck up to her cheek, smothering his mouth onto her face.

She pulled away from him, disgusted by his opened mouth. "No, don't," she said, not wanting to create a scene. What happened to her usual assertiveness? She was not the type to be intimidated, yet the asymmetric power dynamic prevented her from being more forceful. Was it a coincidence that he had called her into his office at her weakest moment, exhausted from balancing the demands of work and family, and still navigating through the grief that she hadn't yet fully processed?

Sam held her face and turned it towards him, kissing her on the lips. "I know you're going through a tough time."

Sophia couldn't escape her confusion. What was stopping her from leaving? She pressed her lips together and tilted her head backwards, trying to escape his mouth. Her movements were slight. She didn't want to do anything to offend him and jeopardise her impending promotion. Sure, it shouldn't excuse his unwanted advances, but she hadn't worked so hard for nothing.

Sam slithered his hands to her thighs. "You don't need to be nervous."

Sophia squealed in shock, jolting to her feet. Kissing was one thing and she hated herself for letting him go that far and for her own paralysis, but this was crazy. How far did he think he could go, mid-morning in his office?

"Stop—" she started, pushing him away before the swinging door interrupted her.

Sam leapt off his seat, trying to string together any words he could think of. "So... uhhh... we'll need that by Thurs—"

"Everything okay here?" Henry cut him off. He furrowed his brows at Sam but directed his question to Sophia as he pushed his glasses up higher on his nose.

"Uhh..." Sophia hesitated. What could she say without burning bridges?

17

Robert gulped a mouthful of water and tipped his head back. He tossed the box of Zoloft away and looked around but there was no sign of the other box on the table that was still littered with sales advertisements and other junk mail. A stack of unopened letters overflowed a tissue box that doubled as a temporary in-tray. The problem was that *temporary* was fast becoming *permanent*.

He rubbed his frazzled beard, pondering where the box could be. He looked under the junk mail. Envelopes with bold red letters screamed at him. *Final Reminder! Urgent!* He dismissed them all. He'd get to them soon enough. For now, he needed the painkiller tramadol. He swivelled his head again, looking for it. It wasn't on his left or his right. He cocked his head up, then down. He shook his head. Was he already losing it? He picked up the box from his lap, popped two pills out of the blister pack and forced them down with some water.

Robert slowly unfurled the bandages on his right hand and grimaced. The fingernails on his middle three fingers were discoloured to a deep maroon-black and slightly flattened, resulting in a staircase effect compared to the uninjured portion of his fingers. He twitched his fingers to test their movement, but the splint did its job, preventing him from doing so. The doctors said he was lucky to have escaped permanent nerve or bone damage, and while it might take up to six months to return to work as a machine operator, he could be back sooner on light duties. Great... but what was the point of it, anyway? Work was the last thing on his mind. He and Gayle were supposed to retire in Vietnam or somewhere else cheap and comfortable. So much for that plan.

He heaved a heavy sigh. Was he ready for this? He had already put it off for long enough. He certainly didn't want his wife to think he was just tossing her out, but he needed to move on – for his own sanity. He wrapped the bandages back on his hand and peeled himself off the sofa that he had moulded into for the last three hours and gathered half a dozen flat cardboard boxes from the garage. He blew the thin film of dust off them, revealing the Tectonic Building Systems logo – one of the very few perks of working for a company with packaging material. He was only 'borrowing' them if anyone asked.

Robert collected Gayle's belongings from the bedside table – a small leather-strapped watch he had gifted her, her reading glasses, and a faded photo from a happier, more innocent time in which a younger Gayle was holding baby Lewis, whilst he held a not-much-older Sophia in front of a white weatherboard house where the overgrown lawn spilled onto the concrete kerb. With two babies to look after, who had time to mow the grass?

He gently wiped the glass in the frame, starting with the outline of Sophia. She had grown into a successful young woman, who, no doubt, would achieve many things that he could only dream of. He smiled – her drive must have come from her mother's side – though she also had the knack of saying hurtful things: "Sacrifices like when you walked out on us when I wasn't even two because you didn't want to deal with 'that retard boy'." Her criticism stung, especially when she had vocalised it during dinner. In front of Lewis. Who knew how much the boy had understood? It didn't matter. He was disappointed that Gayle had told Sophia about his so-called sacrifices, but was he even entitled to feel that way? It was too inconvenient a question. He moved on to cleaning the outline of Lewis.

The birth of his son should have been joyous, but he didn't expect that there would be... *complications*. "That retard boy" looped over in Robert's mind like an annoying ditty that wouldn't go away. He wasn't a saint. He was a normal bloke, with normal human feelings. He said and did things he didn't mean in the heat of the moment, like everyone else. He spent his life regretting his reaction to Lewis' birth. The more he tried to forget about it, the more he remembered how much it had strained his young marriage. He could have lived through the exhaustion of caring for two children, and even giving up golf, but the shame of having a child with 'special needs' – a politically correct way of saying that there was something not quite right about his son – was what drove him away.

So, when Lewis was seven months old, after a long drinking session, Robert came home and declared he had figured out the best solution: offer Lewis for adoption. It was a brilliant, win-win solution for both the biological and adopted parents. For him, it meant getting a break he needed whilst ensuring Lewis would be taken care of. For the adopted parents, the little boy would be the joy in their lives that they were looking for. "Win-win," he repeated to

Gayle at the time, but she wasn't having any of it. At first, she thought it was the alcohol talking, her anger turning to fury. He would never know the bond of having a living being inside his body for nine months. She could never abandon her baby! No, *their* precious little baby. Emotions were at breaking point and voices were strained hoarse.

"How could you even think of such a thing?" Gayle yelled through her tears.

"This wasn't the life I signed up for!" Why couldn't she see how perfect his solution was? He had jumped into his car and headed to the pub that he had just returned from, but as he approached the pub, he accelerated past it, driving aimlessly. He didn't want to spend a lifetime nursing a disabled kid. Looking after little Sophia was a handful already, and if he couldn't give baby Lewis away, he would leave the family himself.

Having made up his mind, he pulled up at his house and approached the front door, but it opened as he reached to unlock it. Gayle cradled baby Lewis, trying to feed the difficult eater. Their daughter clung tightly around her leg, looking down at her mother's feet. Robert and Gayle looked at each other in silence for a long time. Emotions ran higher with each passing moment. Both knew that whoever said the first word would break. He wondered how long they stood there. "Sorry," was all he could say.

A tear splashed onto the photo frame, drawing Robert back to the here and now. He sniffed, rubbing his nose on his sleeve as he hastily wiped the photo frame and place it a box marked *Fragile*. He needed to move on, not dwell on the past. He turned to the wardrobe.

Robert wasn't sure what he would find there but he may as well start with the most difficult area. Almost the entire space was occupied with Gayle's clothes. His were scrunched, creased and buried under any available space, save for two shirts and a pair of trousers. A wry smile cracked his tired, worn face – the sacrifices of marriage.

He sliced through a swathe of clothes in Gayle's wardrobe with his right hand, forgetting it was his injured side. He grunted in pain, trying to shake it off. He was more careful next time, using his other hand to remove her clothes, a handful at a time, hangers and all. He drew in a deep breath. He couldn't pinpoint the scent given the numerous perfumes that she had stashed away. He had never been a fan of the artificial smells, and it nauseated him whenever he had to walk through department stores where the perfumery section was 'conveniently' located at the entrance.

With Gayle's worldly belongings laid out before him, a torrent of memories flooded back: the moment he saw her at the local swimming pool, their awkward first kiss when he was so nervous he had planted his lips on her left nostril, and the joys of seeing both their kids come into the world. The edges of his mouth curled down, and a swell of emotion contorted his face, deepening his glabellar lines. He slapped his hand over his eyes, pushing the tears back in. Life was now just a collection of what his aging brain could remember. He wiped the corners of his eyes and steeled himself. It was time to let go or risk being trapped in a state of mourning. But he was in a quandary. What would he do with all her stuff? There were so many clothes, so many things... Should he store it away? Give it to charity? Would that be too cruel, too insensitive? He felt silly that he hadn't even thought that far.

As he reached into the wardrobe for more clothes, as if the act of *doing* would provide inspiration later, he brushed against something unusual. Flat, but not altogether solid, inconsistent with the jacket's fabric. A tag? An old receipt? It was too sturdy for either. He took it off the rail and felt for a pocket, but it had been meticulously hand-sewn shut.

Grabbing a knife, he sliced the pocket open without a care of preserving the garment. Curiosity got the better of him. Besides, even if the jacket went to charity, no one would want a dead woman's jacket, would they? And if they did, they wouldn't want it now with the lining ripped open anyway, he justified to himself.

Robert wriggled his good fingers inside the hidden pocket, slowly pulling out a crumpled note. He unfolded it, blowing a small puff of lint and loose paper fibres away, cautious not to tear the wafer-thin paper. The ink was smudged in places, the corners no longer neat and clean. Nose twitching, he held it away from him, distancing himself from the faint musty smell. It must have accidentally been through the wash a few times. He stared at the letter for a long moment, frozen in anticipation.

My sweetness, he read, *It's been 4 days since we saw or spoke to each other and I can't think of anything else. When we bumped hands reaching for the pepper at the same time, I wondered what it would feel like if it wasn't just a momentary touch.*

Robert's wide-eyed anticipation turned into a frown. The handwriting was carefully scripted though unfamiliar. It wasn't his or Gayle's. He didn't want to continue but knew that he had to.

I haven't felt that way in a long time, the letter continued. *It made me think of when I was a young bloke on my first date. If only you weren't with Robert...*

Wait, what?

He read the line again. *If only you weren't with Robert...*

He scoured the letter for something, anything, that

would prove it was all a mistake. The letter wasn't dated or addressed to anyone. He read it again. *My sweetness.* The thought of someone else referring to his Gayle as their sweetness made his stomach turn and dried his open mouth. His eyes bounced from one paragraph to the next, zigzagging as fast as they could down the page: *cherish our time together,* *be next to you,* and *our time at the tennis courts.* Tennis courts? Gayle never even liked the sport! He flicked down to the initials at the bottom of the page. Who the hell was 'PZ'? He probably knew about three or four people whose name started with P but none with Z as their surname. Was it a pseudonym?

Robert looked over to the shredded threads twisted around the knife; his heart heavy as a stone. His hand trembled then shook in anger. He scrunched the letter and launched it against the wall. How long had Gayle hidden this from him? How far did her relationship with PZ go? Was his marriage to her even real? Sure, he wasn't the perfect husband or father, and had been accused by his wife of being emotionally stingy but there was no doubt he loved her – at least, never in *his* mind. He shouldn't have started cleaning up. Ignorance would have been better. More questions whirled through his mind, but one was most pressing: who the fuck was PZ?

He sat up, casting his mind back to the night of the accident. She wanted to tell him something. Was this it? He felt helpless, cheated even, that Gayle was no longer around to answer his questions. How selfish going like that.

He stared at the ripped lining of the now-destroyed jacket, unable to focus. At first, the tears came slowly before his body shook as he sobbed. It was a far cry from his tough exterior, but life had a knack of kicking people when they're down. He pounded the wardrobe with his injured hand, bloodying his fingers with each strike. He let out an anguished cry. As the adrenaline wore off and the pain seeped in, the punches became slower and softer before they stopped. He clutched his damaged hand in his other. What the hell was he going to achieve by crippling his already wounded hand? What was the point of *anything*? So much for moving on with his life.

18

"Housekeeping!" a voice boomed. Lewis stood outside room 1011, pressing his forehead against the door as he listened for a response. Silence. He tapped the doorbell and announced in a loud voice again, "Housekeeping!" His voice had to come from his chest, he was told, not the throat. He had never understood what that meant. Sound was just sound and it all came out of the mouth, so all he had to do was to say it loud enough for people inside to hear him above the TV or whatever else they chose to do in the bedroom.

He counted to five on his fingers as the hotel procedure manual instructed, and again. When another five seconds had elapsed, he swiped his staff pass and walked in, pushing a trolley brimming with linen, towels, bathmats, toilet rolls and countless cleaning products. Following procedure, he walked through every room, poking his head in each, and called out, "Housekeeping" to announce his presence.

The door was closed when he arrived at the bathroom. His hand wavered over the handle, hesitant to open it. Although he wasn't sure why, this room was more peculiar than the others, not least given people showered in them while he needed to clean it. He had also never understood why this room sometimes bore the initials *WC*. It had something to do with it being a water closet, his mother once told him, but he had never seen water in a closet, nor did he see the need for water to be in one.

Lewis blinked hard, twice, his head twitching involuntarily. He steadied himself and pounded his knuckles again. "Housekeeping," he repeated loudly, and counted his fingers. He opened the door and ping-ponged his eyes around the room without moving his head. Satisfied the room was unoccupied, he turned back to get the hand caddy from the trolley but bumped into someone.

"I knocked, I promise," Lewis said automatically, staring at his feet. He was half apologetic and half hoping not to see a naked person like last time.

But it was only Mike, grinning and holding a piece of paper up to his chest. "Is this what you're looking for?"

Lewis looked up to meet Mike's eyes, and back down. He reached out for it but withdrew his hand, unsure. He looked at Mike again, who nodded and invited him to take the paper. "Best. Cus-tom-er. Ex-peer-rence. Cert-tif-cat..." Lewis read, looking back at Mike.

"Yeah, it's yours. You can keep it."

"Me?" Lewis tapped his chest, taking a moment for his smile to override his furrowed brows.

Mike snatched the paper from Lewis' fingers and threw it to the floor. "You can have this as well." He pulled Lewis into him, ripping his name badge off his hotel uniform, before arching him over the basin. "Not so tough without your Daddy, are you?" Despite his bigger frame, Lewis squealed incoherent guttural noises. "Who's gonna save you now?" Mike slapped his colleague over the head as he derisively mimicked his noises.

"I... I knocked," Lewis whimpered.

"That's why you're a retard."

"I prom... promise."

Mike hit him across the head again. "You don't even know what I'm talking about."

Lewis cowered and flinched each time his head came to blows. "Daddy... Dad-dy... said... said no hitting!"

"Duh-duh-duddy.. seh... seh... Can't even talk properly."

"I prom... promise... knock."

"Can't even count to five without your fingers. Retard!"

"No."

"What you gonna do?"

"No, no, no!" He pleaded Mike to stop.

"Or what? You gonna tell your Mummy? Oh wait, she's dead. Duh-ehh-dead!"

"No!" Lewis snapped. It was a line too far. He could tolerate the physical abuse even if he didn't know why he was being assaulted but bringing up his mother ignited a primal rage that even he knew was wrong. Lewis heaved Mike up by his uniform, though only succeeded in slipping the baggy shirt over his head, and rammed him against the wall. It was his turn to scrunch his aggressor by the collar.

Mike strained to counter Lewis. His bones almost popped out of his skin, his red face threatening to explode, but it was as futile as a child pushing an elephant.

Lewis shook him like a rag doll, eliciting a dull thud each time Mike's spine was driven into the wall. "No, no, no! Mummy said no hitting!" He mimicked the slaps over Mike's head as he begged for forgiveness. "He started... started it, Mummy. I'm a good bo... boy," he sobbed. Not wanting any more violence, Lewis let go of Mike's shirt and turned away, giving Mr Tough Guy a reprieve but the bully's head throbbed, leaving him crouched and leaning against the wall. Mike patted his head but didn't expect to see blood on his hand.

Lewis picked up the discarded certificate and flattened out the crumples. It was the first certificate he would have received from Kings Hotel and he didn't want to give it up but the cheap inkjet printing, smudging on contact with the wet floor tiles, gave him clues that it may not be all that legitimate.

"Bloody retard!" Mike cursed, eyes narrowing and nostrils flaring. He couldn't leave this unfinished. He punched the back of Lewis's head.

Lewis turned around; his eyes pushing out from their sockets in anger. He gritted his teeth as he lifted Mike by his uniform and crunched him against the wall again. He let out a roar, rattling his uvula, no longer using his throat to talk. "Mummy said no hitting!"

19

———

The emergency lights provided the only illumination, casting eerie shadows in the empty space. A lone figure cleaned the mess the office workers had left. He tugged on the hose to reach under the table, disconnecting the power cord from the wall socket. "Why do you do this?" He directed his question at the canister, throwing his arms up in frustration. As the vacuum cleaner whirred to a halt, the clicks of a keyboard became sharper in the silence. The cleaner spun around. "Home time, Soph. That's why the lights are off," he called out, looping the power cord around his arm.

The top of Sophia's head poked up from behind a monitor at the end of the room. "They still haven't given you an extension cord, Bobby?" she called back without looking up.

"They wouldn't even let me bring my own!"

"Yeah?"

"Don't you remember? Corporate Real Estate almost gave me a warning last time. Said they couldn't be responsible for any electrical hazards if I brought my own in because it wasn't tested by a certified electrician." He shook his head. "I'm a cleaner, not a nuclear scientist."

"I'll put in a good word for you. Now go home." Sophia said, still focussed on her monitor. She couldn't spare precious seconds engaging in banter. She was preoccupied with something far more important. She ran through the list on her notepad again: *Invite the CEO to open the conference –* check. *Receive PowerPoint presentations from all the different teams –* check. *Confirm external speaker –* check.

Ah! She tapped her pen on her book. Polo shirts. It was important for the team to be presented as a united front and what cheesier way to do that by slapping on corporate apparel – the tried and tested method. She bashed out an email: *Sam, I'm finalising details for your Excellence in Leadership Conference. What shirt size are you? Many thanks.* Not that he was obese, but no detail was too small to escape attention. She wanted to avoid last year's embarrassment where two members of his management team couldn't fit into their shirts. Sophia moved her mouse to the *Send* button but was she really offering 'many thanks'? The term was too liberally thrown around these days. How many thanks did she mean anyway? Besides, she couldn't only offer a little bit of thanks. She wondered whether a thanking scale could be used, like:

- *No thanks:* I don't appreciate what you've done or not done. (Read: I don't know why you haven't been sacked yet).
- *A little bit of thanks:* I'm giving you some thanks because you tried but it's still not good enough. (Read: You're lucky to still have a job).
- *Thanks:* You did what I asked for or provided what I need. (Read: You may stay in your job... for now).

- *Many thanks:* You did just that little bit more than required. (Read: I might keep you in the old Rolodex).
- *Most thanks:* You're tops! (Read: I might even have coffee with you).

She glanced at the time on her laptop. Did that muse just cost her two and a half minutes? So much for not bidding Bobby a proper goodnight to save a couple of milliseconds. She massaged her computer-strained eyes with enough grip to turn the tips of her fingers white. She deleted the reference to any thanks, abruptly cutting it off at, *What shirt size are you?* and sent the email. She didn't even leave the automated *Kind Regards* signature at the bottom – there was no room for those kinds of fake niceties, especially at this hour.

To her surprise, she received a reply almost immediately but not on email.

It depends who's asking (^_-) Sam messaged on WhatsApp.

Medium?

Still in office? Sam replied.

Yeah.

Though Sophia wished that she wasn't. She wished that HR would provide her the letter of offer for her new job soon so she could delegate the administrative drudgery to some other poor soul. Apparently, they were still benchmarking her proposed compensation against the market to ensure it was competitive. They didn't want to underpay her, they assured her, but she struggled to contain her cynicism. They were probably trying to find lower market comparisons so they wouldn't have to remunerate her as much.

U need a brk. Drinks? Sam texted.

Sophia contemplated the message for a moment, shaking her head. Drinks at this hour? On a Tuesday? He had to be kidding. She needed to set the record straight. She drafted a response, *About the other day, we should forget about it,* but it didn't feel right. It was more a suggestion than a request. She regretted that she hadn't been assertive enough when she was trapped in Sam's office and let him kiss her. No, damn it! She hadn't *let* him do anything. It was forced onto her. She'd had a stressful morning cleaning up Lewis' wet pyjamas and had had to contend with people bitching behind her back the moment she stepped into the office. Plus, she just wanted her bloody letter of offer. She should have told him all of that when he cornered her in his office, but better late than never. She deleted the text and sent a curt reply. *I don't drink.*

There's plenty of non-alcoholic options, Sam replied almost immediately.

His eagerness was off-putting, bordering on desperate. *S, M, L?* Sophia texted back, hoping that her prompt would bring the conversation back on track. She grew impatient as minutes whiled away without a reply. She closed the lid on her laptop and threw her notepad in her drawer. It had been a long day and if she didn't go home soon, she may as well camp in the office overnight. It would not only save on the time and cost of travelling, but the air-conditioning bill as well.

As she crouched under the table to clip off her heels, her phone buzzed. She rose, bumping her head on the table, letting out a painful groan as she rubbed the back of her head. She tapped her phone, clicking on a message as she slipped into her black ballet pumps. It felt like an eternity as the app displayed the spinning wait-a-moment wheel for a few seconds too long. She reflexed a shriek, bumping her head on the table again, when the message finally opened.

My size is LARGE, read the message.

Sophia's jaw dropped. She fumbled her phone as she repeatedly jabbed at the *Home* button to exit from the photo, wishing she could unsee the picture of the hairy beachgoer, dressed in a neon-green mankini that was just big enough to cover his modesty.

20

———

The Pearl Resort hall was an elegant art-deco venue that distilled the warmth of the early twentieth century into a room. Attendees, dressed in fresh-out-of-the-packet Eastle polo shirts, were seated at the fifteen round tables. Sam held court on the dais, microphone in hand.

"I want to thank Henry again for spending his time with us over the next few days," he said, turning to his boss next to him. "If you would like to say a few words?"

"Thanks, Sam," Henry began. "How's everyone feeling? I won't take long. This isn't the time for a long monologue." Scattered applause rippled through the room as he pushed up his glasses on his nose. "I want to congratulate all of you who have made it to this Excellence in Leadership Conference. Each of you have consistently demonstrated your excellence throughout the year, which has made a big difference to our customers and our firm. So, thank you and congratulations."

"Thank you, Henry," Sam said. "Without further ado, let the conference begin!"

The audience registered their approval with cheers and

applause as they knew the booze would now start to flow. Sam turned to his boss for a handshake, but Henry winked at him and tugged him in for a bear hug.

"This is great, Sam," Henry said into his ear to drown out the noise, his hand slipping down Sam's back, drawing scattered chuckles from the audience. "Looking forward to the next couple of days."

Sam tried to escape Henry's squeeze, but his boss wrenched him tighter into his chest. "Yeah, looking forward to it," he said, straining. The dread in his eyes belied his response.

A photographer and four ushers directed the audience to join Sam and Henry on stage for the obligatory team photograph, prompting the front of the room to be rushed in a chaotic yet coordinated mess. Ignoring the four steps, the more athletic leapt the half metre onto the stage whilst small cliques posed for their own photos and others busted out selfies with pouty lips, peace signs, and other Insta-worthy shots that they would later upload onto social media to show-pony their lives.

As the team corralled around the two bosses, Sam scanned the room. In the sea of people making their way forward, he picked Sophia out in an instant. It wasn't difficult to spot her threading in the opposite direction through the one-way traffic. Like losing a child in a crowd, he knew how she moved, her gait, her pace, even how her hair bounced as she walked. His dazzling smile dimmed half a watt as she headed for the exit. He forced his smile to reach his eyes as he had to live up to the excitement that he had just created.

"Lighten up, Sam," Henry said, cocking his eyebrows. "The fun's about to start!"

PLODDING DOWN THE CORRIDOR, SOPHIA READ THE MESSAGE on her phone: *need 2 update Exco on strategy on monday. pls see me. 311.* She checked the numbers on the doors as she passed them. 305... 307... 309...

Standing in front of 311, she raised her knuckles for longer than necessary. She huffed, summoning the energy she needed, before pounding two confident knocks, and waited. *Be firm this time.*

The door opened.

"I got your message," Sophia said.

"Come in." Sam rubbed his tired eyes as he motioned her inside, but she didn't move. There was something uncomfortable about entering her boss' private quarters. "All the meeting rooms are booked," he pre-empted.

She stepped into the room, standing by the doorway, studying it for anything untoward... like closed blinds. She wasn't going to be caught out this time, but everything was neat and tidy except for the messy table. A laptop was opened to a spreadsheet where there were more negative numbers than positive, plus a pie chart of Eastle's market share reducing compared to last year. Sophia closed the door behind her.

Sam walked back to the table. "I didn't see you at the team photo and lunch. Everything okay?"

"Listen, before we get into the paper..." She swivelled her eyes around the room. Anywhere was better than looking at him. She wanted – no, needed to – let him know that his touchy-feely hands at the café, the message of the green mankini, and especially the kiss in his office were all inappropriate and it had to stop but she didn't know how to broach the topic without blindsiding him. *Start with the minor transgression first.* "Your message of the green bikini or whatever—" She cleared throat, trying not to trail off.

Sam laughed, shaking his head. "Can you believe someone actually spent the time to photoshop me in that skimpy little thing?"

Sophia froze, taken aback by his cavalier attitude to something that gnawed at her from the moment she saw the photo. She flicked her eyes at him to check if he was really joking before a tinge of self-doubt seeped in. Was she the one overreacting? *No.* She stopped herself before more doubt could cloud her mind. She couldn't let him normalise his behaviour. "Sam, what happened in your offi... I'm not... I don't want... I mean, you have a wife and kid."

Sam took a moment to digest what she was getting at. He flashed his white teeth. "You looked like you needed some... uhh... support. It must have been difficult with your family situation... and... uhh..."

"Can you just... like... no is no, okay?" She walked past him and sat at the table.

"If I came across the wrong way, it won't happen again." She waited for his apology, but it never came; instead he planted a glass of red wine in front of her. "Everything's a little better with a drink," he said, taking a sip from a bottle of Perrier water.

She nudged it back towards him. "I'm fine, thanks." She wasn't there to socialise. She opened her laptop. "What does Exco want?"

"They weren't convinced that our numbers were realistic, so we need to relook at the credit card growth projections."

As he moved in for a seat, Sophia placed her notepad next to her, forcing him to sit opposite her. "They can't expect us to grow if they don't approve our budget requests."

"Let's model two scenarios," Sam deflected. "Growth with and without budgets approved."

Sophia tilted her chin towards the ceiling and exhaled. Not this useless exercise again but whatever, so long as she could leave as soon as possible.

It was late afternoon when she had finished making the final changes to the PowerPoint presentation – nothing like the last minute to be the most productive. "Sent," she announced, emailing the file. "There are two projections for each scenario. For Exco, use the projection that's phased for seasonality. That will explain why revenues fluctuate month on month. The other one has no phasing and is just for our reference." She looked up from her laptop when there was no response. "Did you get that?" but Sam continued typing on his phone. "Use the phased version," she repeated. "The annual number is the same under the two versions, but we'll hit our monthly targets this way."

"Yeah, yeah," Sam said, finishing his text message, and putting down his phone. "Phased version."

Sophia forced herself to blink instead of glare at him. She wasn't the one who wanted to spend her afternoon in front of a spreadsheet to remodel the credit card growth projections. She had better things to do. They were at a resort after all. "Are the numbers good or do you want to make more changes?"

"No, no. You've done a good job. Thanks."

"Let me know how it goes next week." She closed her laptop and grabbed her notepad from the seat beside her. As she stood up, Sam mirrored her, jumping to his feet.

"You sure you don't want a drink before you go?" he asked.

"I better get going," she replied, approaching the door. "Oh." She opened the door, holding the handle, about to leave. "I spoke with HR…" She turned around, startled that Sam was only an arm's length away but if Sophia was anything, she was persistent about her promotion. "About my salary, they said they're waiting for *your* approval."

Sam looked past her, flicking his eyes from side to side out to the corridor. "You know, my promotion. Job?" she continued.

Sam shrugged. "Yeah, yeah, sure."

She paused, unsure if he was listening. "Okay then."

As she started to head out, Sam slammed the door shut. He grabbed her head and stuck his tongue so deep into her mouth, she gagged. Sophia dropped her notepad and laptop, which smacked onto the tiled floor. He slithered his hands over her body, feeling every bit of skin he could. His wedding ring rolled over her as he pulled her dress up around her thighs. Unbuckling his belt, he thrust against her. She tried to scream but, with his mouth pressed against hers, she could only manage a muffled cry.

"Relax," he said in between his heavy breaths and moans. His urge was desperate like a person chugging the ocean after almost dying of thirst. His elbows pressed on her shoulders, digging into her collarbone, forcing her down. She grimaced; it hurt but no matter what, she would not buckle. Before she knew it, he reached for her underpants. "Don't be shy."

"Stop!" she shrieked. Her dress strap ripped, exposing her heaving chest, leaving her feeling more vulnerable. *Is this really happening? To me? My boss? My* married *boss?* She opened her mouth, trying to yell *Fire!* but nothing came out as if her vocal cords were cut. She twisted and turned with the clumsy coordination of a drunken toddler, writhing, contorting, and twisting – anything to escape his slippery tongue and wandering hands.

WHACK!

Her hand flew across his face. She had finally broken his grip.

With her heart rattling out of her chest, she whipped open the door, and ran, holding onto her dress to keep it from slipping off. She turned to make sure Sam wasn't following her, collided into a figure, and almost knocked the phone from her colleague's grip. Both women's eyes gravitated to the message on the phone: *Room 311. See you soon.*

Sophia looked at May, and back down at the message, wanting to tell her not to go there but May clasped the phone against her chest, hiding it from Sophia's view.

"Sorry, sorry," Sophia said as she ran down the hallway, taking another look over her shoulder.

Sophia's hands trembled as she panted for breath. She swiped her room pass but a red light flashed: *Sorry – try again.* She slapped the card onto the reader again, but still the same bloody red light. She steadied her quivering hand with her other, guiding the card over the reader until the light finally flashed green. Flinging the door open, almost ripping it off the hinge, she rushed inside the safety of her room. She collapsed against the door, her legs finally buckling as she slid to the floor.

Sophia trembled as she inhaled deep into her nose and blew out from her mouth, trying to regulate her short, shallow breaths. There are words where some letters are silent, like the *k* in *knock* or the *h* in *honest* but there are no silent sentences like, *I want to shove my tongue down your throat.* Nor should there be. Who was this monster who just tried to rape her? Would this have happened if she had been firmer in rejecting his earlier advances? Her stomach cramped. She wished she could have said or done something smart or made some sort of heroic stand about feminism like in the movies, but all her instincts had told her was to run. *Yes, running away was heroic.*

She controlled her breathing and closed her eyes. The thought of his wedding ring, and all that it was supposed to stand for, made her sick. Did it not mean anything to him? Did he simply forget to take it off? As much as she tried to suppress it, her stomach wasn't in an agreeable mood. She rushed to the bathroom and hung her head over the toilet bowl, retching. Her legs spaghettied awkwardly around her, but as sick as she felt, nothing came up.

Sophia splashed water on her face and stared into the mirror, collecting herself. She didn't like the pale, frightened, haggard woman reflecting back. How had she become like this? Where had the strong, independent woman disappeared to? She held out her hands but could not control the tremors. Water dripping off her face, she inhaled long, sharp breaths, as if the depth of each breath would replenish the strength that she had momentarily lost. She grabbed the toothpaste and squeezed an overflowing amount onto her toothbrush, most of it landing in the basin. She rigorously scrubbed her teeth until her gums were red and tender. She chased it with a swig of Cool Mint mouthwash, swilling and gargling the smarting liquid. She was on repeat, swilling and gargling, gargling and swilling, until she finished the remaining half a bottle, burning her mouth with the after-wash sting.

As the panic subsided, her terror turned into anger. She hurled the empty mouthwash bottle against the wall. "Fire, fire, fire!" she screamed, testing her damn vocal cords that had failed her in the moment. Where was her damn voice when she needed it most? *Fire* wasn't the SOS message she had needed to broadcast in his room, but apparently there was more chance of getting assistance using that instead of yelling *rape*. After all, no one wanted to be entangled in such a gross invasion of personal space that was a sexual assault. It was a sad reflection of society but now was not the time to debate the rights and wrongs of the universe.

She looked in the mirror again. *Damn it.* The thin shoulder straps on her dress were torn, and although she already knew, having held onto it as she ran out of Sam's room, the ripped and frayed threads hit home. It had been one of her favourite dresses too. A sleeveless, black and yellow floral number that flowed to the knees. Best of all, she had bought it online with next-day delivery at a seventeen per cent discount. Now, it had lost its lustre, but she wasn't going to be emotional about it. No, she wasn't like *them*. She let the dress fall, and stepped into the shower, soaking in the water. Grabbing the bath sponge, she scoured whatever filth Sam had contaminated her with. After a lengthy shower that environmentalists would have screamed murder about, she strode out of the bathroom.

21

In an age when everyone lacks time, and often the required cooking skills as well, the pre-packaged dinner had been providing the solution to empty stomachs since it was made popular post World War Two. Sophia watched the 'restaurant quality roasted beef meatballs and spaghetti designed to make you fuller for longer' dinner spin around in the microwave. But her mind was elsewhere. As much as she tried, she couldn't help but replay the incident over again. Why did she freeze? Did she lead him on? Should she tell anyone?

DING! The microwave snapped her out of her daze.

She reached to open it, but the internal light was still on, the turntable plate still spinning. *Hmm.* She pivoted to more mundane concerns: what was the IT helpdesk number to order a new laptop? What reasons should she give to justify a replacement? She let out a sigh. Why did everything need to be so complicated?

DING! She reached for the microwave again, but the timer still had forty-five seconds to go. She shook her head. Was she hallucinating? She took her phone out of her pocket. There were two unread messages – WhatsApp. From *him*. She clicked out of it. Anything would be better than dealing with him now. DING! She looked up. This time the turntable had ground to a halt and the timer was on zero.

THE SCRAPING ON PLATES, THE SOUND OF CHEWING AND THE gentle hum of the air conditioner were all amplified around the otherwise silent dining table. Lewis was glued to a YouTube video, imploring its viewers not to inject bleach into their bodies to combat viral infections. Yes, as a highly evolved human species, capable of flying to the moon and back, such warnings were still required.

Resting one hand under her chin, Sophia twirled the spaghetti with her other, winding it up until it was a knitted ball at the end of her fork. She thought she was hungry, but the WhatsApp messages were just another reminder of what she would rather forget.

"I said, are you okay?" Robert asked.

She hazarded a guess about the question that she had missed again. "Yeah, there were about 170 people there."

Lewis looked up at Sophia, then back to his phone before returning to her. Something wasn't quite right – her face was pale, her eyes were dimmer, almost sunken. He leaned over, wrapping his arms around her as he rested his head on her shoulder. "It's okay. Mummy always said everything will be okay."

She patted Lewis on the head. If only he knew. "Everything will be okay," Sophia repeated, if only to convince herself. Before she could feel sorry for herself, she turned to her father, changing the subject. "How was the talk with Lewis' manager?"

Robert looked up. His hair was uncombed, and he seemed to have worn the same clothes for the last three days. Sophia wasn't even sure when he last showered. "How come you're early?" he deflected. "I thought you said you'd have dinner at the... uhh... conference thing."

For a nanosecond, she contemplated telling him about what had happened, but she wasn't the most communicative person at the best of times – like father, like daughter. Perhaps her father already knew that something was wrong? It didn't matter. She didn't want to admit that her day had been shit or that she felt like shit. The mood around the table was gloomy enough without having to bore the world with her problems. Besides, her father must have his own problems to deal with.

"It's... they... I didn't need to be there. Anyway, he still has a job, right?"

"The manager didn't believe me when I said Lewis isn't usually violent. I guess seven stitches at the back of the other guy's head made it hard to convince him."

"So, has Lewis still got a job or not?"

"As long as he doesn't hit anyone again."

"Seven, huh?" she said, nodding.

Robert wagged his finger at Lewis. "No hitting. Promise?"

"Pushing is not hitting." Lewis smiled.

Sophia pondered it for a few seconds. How did he even know the distinction? She continued her conversation with her father. "What are you going to do with Mum's clothes?"

Robert shrugged. "Dunno."

"I googled what Zoloft is," Sophia continued. "You depressed?"

He paused, not bothering to look at her. "All good."

But Sophia wouldn't let him brush her off like that. She

could tell what he was thinking: why had she asked such a stupid question with everything that had happened lately. Of course, she realised that her mum, his wife, was not here anymore but he didn't need to be reckless with his medication. "So, why do you have a hundred mils?"

"I'm not the doc. It's what he gave me."

"Usual dose is only fifty." Sophia let it sink in for a bit as she waited for a reply, but the conversation was enveloped in silence. The clinks and scratches of the cutlery were amplified once again.

After a long moment, Robert met his daughter's gaze. "Burn them."

"What?"

"The clothes."

She slammed her cutlery onto the table, shaking her head, speechless. What was this? A competition of who could be more destitute? Of who could care less than the other? "Are you serious? No!"

"I'm kidding," Robert said, but his deadpan reply wasn't convincing.

"I'll drop them off at St Vinnies."

"You've got work tomorrow. I'll do it," Robert insisted.

"What happened to your wrists?" Sophia asked, changing the subject again. Robert glanced down, washing his hands over each other, trying to cover up the fresh long, horizontal cuts, but it was pointless. The wounds were on both wrists. Clear as day. He folded his arms, hiding his hands behind his elbow, which made her more suspicious.

"It's not deliberate, is it? Like, you're not going to... you know..."

Robert pulled back from his dinner, creasing his forehead. "Don't be stupid."

Lewis leaned over to his other side, wrapped his arms

around his father and rubbed his earlobes. "Everything will be okay."

Sophia swallowed, though she hadn't taken a bite; her throat felt raw. "I'm serious, Dad."

"What's wrong with you? Who would look after Lewis?" Robert replied.

22

Lewis shot the miniature basketball, sailing it to the other end of the bathtub. The ball bounced off the rim of the plastic hoop before dropping into the tub, disappearing under the bath bubbles despite the water level being only a few centimetres above his belly button. He sloshed his hand in the water. Where were they? He had at least four of them the last time he counted. He reached for the bright-green plastic flower sprinkler instead, scooping up the bathwater, filling it up. He lifted it above his head, but he had forgotten something. He dropped the sprinkler and put on his swimming goggles that dangled around his neck, pressing them firmly around his eyes. He couldn't be too careful.

As far as Lewis could remember, he loved to splash in the water but when it came to washing his hair, it was like lighting it on fire. He would shriek, opening and closing his mouth, gasping for air at the sensation of drowning. But as a big boy now, with the added precaution of goggles, he lifted the sprinkler and tipped the water over his head, blowing bubbles as the soapy water washed down his face. He squealed in excitement, jumping from his seated position.

There was something about bathwater that was different to normal water for Lewis; the slipperiness let him slither in the tub. He held his wrinkled-as-dried-prune hands to his face and smelled the fresh fragrance, almost getting soap in his nostrils. He brushed the bubbles off the tip of his nose and felt around him for the basketballs again. Finally! His fingers had found one. He picked it up, wiping the soap off the ball onto his chest. He covered his eye with one hand and turned his head to size up his target at the end of the tub again. With a flick of his wrist, he sent the basketball in the air, arching it perfectly into the hoop, hitting nothing but net.

"Yeah, yeah, yeah!" he called out as he slapped the water, splashing it around him. He blew air bubbles as he glided his lips across the surface of the water and along the length of his legs. He reached for the flower sprinkler – time for another wash. He glided his lips back across the surface until he was in an upright seated position again, singing a garbled version of the ABC nursery song. He had only got as far as *J* when he choked, coughing out water. His arms and legs flailed in the bathtub.

"Dad!" Sophia's muffled cry made its way through to the bathroom.

Incoherent, noisy and chaotic images flashed in Lewis' mind like light bulbs going off. He saw himself in his current surroundings: in the bathtub slipping and thrashing in the water, a silhouette of a figure hovering above the ground, Sophia's desperate scream, tears from his father who was eerily calm and silent. Then, an abrupt peacefulness. A breeze rolled over, gently rustling the blades of grass. The sound of nature was soothing and hypnotic.

"Dad! I'm busy!" Sophia yelled again, her cries forcing their way into the flashing visions in Lewis mind.

Water trickling into his lungs choked him back to the here and now as he coughed and gasped for air. His goggles snapped at the bridge of the nose, having flung them from his face and onto the floor.

The bathroom door boomed as it flew open, smashing against the doorstop. Robert plunged his arms into the bathtub, yanking at the plug. As the water slowly gurgled down the drain, he struggled to lift his limp, slippery son from the bath and wrapped a clean, soft towel around him. "Spit it out, Lewis, spit it."

Lewis panted, spitting out whatever he could. He bear-hugged his father with all his strength, convulsing as he choked up water. Robert rubbed the soap out of Lewis' eyes. "No, no," Lewis sobbed as he shook his head. It wasn't the soap.

Robert did the only thing he knew that would calm his son. He rubbed Lewis' earlobes, but that didn't help either.

Lewis hammered his father with the heels of his palms. He knew his blows were no longer pitter-patters like when he was younger, but he didn't know the strength of his own strikes as he pounded Robert's back to the bone.

His father twitched, letting out painful groans as each blow landed but he didn't let go. "You're okay now," he said to his son as they clung tightly to each other. "You're okay."

"Don't... ggg... go."

"I'm staying right here," Robert assured his son. "I'm not going anywhere."

23

———

The right side usually did the job... but not tonight. Maybe left would be better. *Turn.*

Sigh.

No. *Turn.* Maybe flat on her back.

Sophia had been repeating the cycle in bed for the past hour and a quarter. She was about to curse the blanket as she kicked it away, but she already knew that wasn't why she was sweating. Even as she tried to sleep, she still couldn't escape *him.* She couldn't rid the feeling of being violated, of being used, of being helpless. As much as she tried to forget it, she kept seeing his damn face close up; the face that had startled her as she tried to walk out of his hotel room. She didn't even want to think about what would have happened if she hadn't broken from his grip. Her throat dried every time her mind dared to meander there.

She flipped onto her side again and turned to more immediate issues: Should she tell anyone? Who could she confide in? She sat up, her restlessness getting too much, but that didn't satiate the discomfort either. She stood up and stretched her legs. Would people even believe her, anyway? Maybe she should call in sick for the next few days? She pushed the questions out of her mind.

As she padded to the bathroom, a beam of light emanated from under her father's bedroom door. The hands on the old-fashioned pendulum clock ticked over to 2.23 am. Was it that late already? Only four hours of sleep left before her alarm. That sick note increasingly looked more attractive... but no, she couldn't. She took much displeasure at those who feigned illness due to personal issues or plain incompetence. Yes, *those* people. She couldn't be one of *them*. Besides, it wasn't anything that a triple or quadruple shot of a Bianco Latte couldn't fix.

A dull thud hit the floor followed by a voice trying its best to muffle the cries of pain. Sophia jumped, her heart skipping a beat. She held her breath. She wanted to run back to her room and hold nature's call until morning under the sweaty blanket; instead she grabbed a broom and tiptoed towards her father's bedroom where the noise seemed to have come from. Shadows danced across the beam of light under the door. Her heart thumped harder. How many intruders were there? What if they were armed with knives or, even worse, guns? Her broomstick felt inadequate, but instinct stopped her from scurrying back to her room. She wanted to prove to herself that she was courageous, especially after what had happened at the conference. She tried to convince herself that she wasn't trying to overcompensate.

Sophia stood by the door and steeled herself, gripping the broom tighter. Her adrenaline rushed as she swung the door open. She raised the broom over her head, ready to smack the bejesus out of anything untoward. In the darkness she made out a silhouette floating above the floor. She gasped, fumbling with the broom, dropping it. It took her a few seconds – it felt even longer – to reach for the light switch, and a few more for her eyes to adjust to the sudden brightness. Like an out-of-focus camera finally locking onto a subject, the image before her became clear. Too clear. She let out a horrified shriek.

Her father hung from the light fitting by his neck. Beside him, the ceiling fan was hanging on by just an exposed wire – he had been too heavy to hang from there. "Dad! No!" she yelled.

She lifted him up by his legs, but he wasn't helping. He was eerily calm and silent.

Their eyes found each other; his belying the outward calmness. Usually brown, Robert's were hollow and colour-less, only having enough room for hurt and sorrow.

"No, no, no!" she screamed. "Get down, Dad. Get down," she pleaded. Her breathing was laboured, her body hard to control as her cries shook her. *This isn't happening!* As she held onto her father, an overwhelming sense of betrayal enveloped her. What could be so bad that he decided that hanging himself was the better option?

"Here. Stand!" She wrangled his feet onto her shoulders. His much heavier body weighing on her paltry frame was literally breaking her back, but she would not – no, could not – give up.

"Lewis! Help! Lewis!" Sophia screamed until her throat was hoarse; hoping, wishing that her brother heard and understood her. Her body trembled from the weight on her shoulders. She stretched her leg out to a chair, but her toes barely reached the backrest. Her throat was already dry, and despite the stabbing pain, she tried again. "FIRE!" she yelled as loudly as she could, and accidentally knocked the chair to the ground. "No! Dad! Please!" she begged. Where the hell was her stupid brother?

Robert crooked the edge of his mouth up at Sophia; a poor attempt at a smile. It was creepy and tragic. She couldn't hold him up for too much longer, but she wouldn't let go. *There will be a miracle. There has to be!*

"Don't... ggg... go," Lewis called out to his father, wandering into the room, half asleep.

Robert edged his neck to get a better view of his son.

"Hold him, lift him up!" Sophia screamed at her brother. But all Lewis could do was reach out his arms to his father, frozen. "Don't just... get the chair!" she ordered, but he could not process the chaos, the screams, his father floating above the ground.

Robert strained out a smile as a tear dropped before his eyes glassed over and his body became limp.

24

S ophia's world froze.

Her eyes filled with tears, her nose red, a stone stuck in her throat.

Her hair flickered across her vacant, still face, cushioned by the field of grass.

She drew away in an out-of-body experience, looking down at herself lying next to two tombstones.

The world froze unevenly. Her vigil lasted seconds. In the real world, five weeks had already passed.

She was in a daze. Kilometres away.

25

———

It was the twenty-fifth of the month, so dozens of managers filed into the boardroom. Some claimed their seat around the huge oval oak table, though careful to leave the chair at the head of the table vacant, whilst others relegated themselves along the wall. Everyone knew their place at the all-important monthly Executive Committee meeting.

A technician stood in front of the TV, pressing all sorts of buttons on the remote control with the speed and dexterity of a teenager switching his screen from an adult website to his homework when his parents walked into his room unannounced.

Henry entered the room, flanked by two women leaning into him as he finished his story.

"So, the doctor said, if it hurts when you stretch your back, don't stretch!" the CEO chuckled. The room fell silent, watching the boss, whilst the two women laughed a little too loudly and mechanically. As the women joined Henry at the head of the table, the technician approached the CEO. There was a fault with the audio connection.

Henry nudged his glasses higher on his nose, frowning. "How long has it been, Seb?"

"We couldn't get the budget approved."

"It's approved. Just get it done."

Not wanting to be the bearer of bad news for a moment longer than necessary, Seb turned the TV off and slipped out of the room as quickly as he could.

Sophia sunk into her chair. She wasn't looking forward to the pretentious performance that was usually part and parcel of high-level, firm-wide meetings, where most attendees paraded bite-sized headlines to an audience of one. She wasn't in the mood for that kind of pageantry, but work was work, and life must go on. She stared at the real-estate website on her laptop, lamenting that she would have already found her new place had it not been for all the... stuff... that happened lately. That plan had all but disappeared but at least fantasising about it kept her sane.

Forty minutes into the meeting, most people were wilting in their chairs, or replying to emails on their laptops, or both. Anything but focussed on the monotony that was Exco.

"We can't keep relying on favourable loan impairment charges to achieve our profit numbers. We need to focus on top-line revenue," Henry said to his team. He turned to Sam as he pushed his glasses up higher on his nose. "Okay, credit cards."

Sam adjusted himself in his seat, ready to recite his spiel. "We've made good progress since last month. We signed the partnership with Logey, so we can move this off the watch list."

"Are you sure?" Henry pressed. "Your revenues are still three hundred thousand behind target."

As strong as Sam projected himself to be in front of his

own team, no one wanted to look bad in front of the big boss. Sam was no exception. He searched for an answer but was never interested in the details. "Sophia, what's your plan to hit target?" he deflected.

She looked up from her laptop, her mouth agape, her eyes flickered to Henry then back to Sam. How could he put her on the spot in front of the entire Exco team like that? Whatever happened to *our* plan? She mulled over whether she should remind him about using the financial projections that were phased for seasonality. That would have taken into account the highs and lows of the holiday seasons and therefore would have had a better chance of achieving revenue targets each month. Instead, he had tabled the evenly phased projections. The one that she specifically told him was only for their reference. However, as much as she wanted to, she would not stoop to his level of politicking. She needed her job more than to be right.

"We have a number of initiatives... that will... as Sam mentioned before, we've signed the agreement with Logey, which will help close the gap. We will also make pricing changes—"

"So, you have initiatives. And you will provide a list to this forum after this meeting. For now, when will you hit your targets?" Henry turned to Sam, who opened his palms and deflected to Sophia again.

So much for being a supportive manager, she fumed. At a lost for an answer, blood drained from her limbs, and pins and needles prickled her legs.

"Okay," she said defiantly, meeting Sam's gaze. "We are not behind target. The phasing is wrong. I gave Sam a projection that accounted for seasonality but he—"

"Sophia, just stick to when we can achieve your target," Sam interrupted.

"When?" Henry said, nostrils flaring as he clenched his jaw and pushed his glasses up again.

As she tried to recall the details, the room seem to bore into her. Every eyeball was like the compound eyes of a housefly, made up of thousands of individual receptors, magnifying their vision on her. Her pulse quickened and her palms became sweaty. The pins and needles made everything ten times worse.

"Sorry," she said finally. "I've been away for a month. My father... he committed..." *No! Personal problems were personal!* "Let me get back to you," she said, vacantly looking at her laptop screen, wishing that she could disappear behind it. She blew a breath that she didn't know she was holding, ashamed that she had almost aired personal issues at work.

SOPHIA SLURPED UP THE REMAINING BITS OF SHIN RAMYUN instant noodles, complementing it with half a dozen slices of bread. It was more than she could stomach but someone had to finish the four discounted loaves she had bought in bulk before the imminent expiration date, and it wasn't going to be Lewis. Her mind continued to stew on the Executive Committee meeting. It had been a disaster; a headache she didn't need so soon after returning to work.

As much as she had expected more of herself, she was more disappointed that Sam had thrown her under the bus like that. Had her performance jeopardised her promotion? Had she already lost it after she struck him at the conference? Even if HR formalised her new job, could she continue to work with him? Her promotion should have been locked in long ago, though she worried about whether it would happen at all given that it had been months since

Sam first confirmed it. On the plus side, she had been restrained in confronting him about his unwanted advances, even to her detriment. Surely that counted for something. She dunked another slice of bread into the bowl, soaking it in the artificial-flavoured soup until it was soft enough that she could almost swallow it. It wasn't a chewing type of day.

The strain of not one, but two, deaths in the family and keeping up with all the details of Project Panda, *and* the day-to-day running of the business was proving too much. She hated to admit it, but she was only human. However, Sam was the one with approval rights, the power to offer her the promotion... or not. She poured the remnants of the instant soup into the sink.

"I had a hunch that you'd be here." Sam's familiar voice interrupted her peace and quiet.

She shifted away from him, continuing to pour the soup down the drain. He was the last person she wanted to see. "I'm finishing up. Do you need anything?"

"Quick question. How's the investor update presentation going?"

"Is the Chairman asking?"

He shrugged. "It'd be good to wrap it up soon."

Clearly, he hadn't read her email. "I dropped you a note before. It'll be ready in three weeks," Sophia replied.

"Hmm. Maybe I can ask Investor Relations to see if they can help speed things up."

She turned to him, sighing at the persistent questions, and wondered whether he had lost confidence in her after Exco. "Don't worry, it's ahead of schedule."

"Hmm," he repeated, his mind seeming to work over-time in a calculation that wasn't clear to her. "Anyway," he said, looking around to see if anyone else was around despite the empty staff kitchen. "I wanted to say... what I did at Exco was—"

"Wrong?" she interrupted, finishing his sentence.

"Well, what I was going to say was that, if you want to become a senior manager in my team, you'll need to be able to handle all sorts of questions being thrown at you."

Sophia's eyes grew bigger, forgetting to blink. Was he serious? Turning the tables on her? The plastic bowl snapped in her hand. "I told you to use the phased spreadsheet..." she started but it was clear that Sam had come to say what he wanted to say.

"I can't be soft on you in Exco. Imagine how that'll make *me* look." Realising he had revealed too much, he backpedalled, spitting out his alternative explanation as fast as he could. "What I meant was that it's my job to ensure you have the right development opportunities but it's ultimately up to you to seize them. Freezing up won't help."

"I need a break." Sophia said, ignoring what he had just said. It wasn't a request.

"Mm-hmm... how long?"

"Two... three... months." She tried to walk past him, but he blocked her by the shoulders. Really? Had he still not learned?

He retracted his arm, putting his hands in his pockets. "Take all the time you need." He smiled, but it didn't reach his eyes.

She had no intention of taking any more compassionate leave. It was a test and, true to form, he always had the right words. Never mind. It gave her extra time to better articulate what she really wanted to say.

"I didn't appreciate what you did at Exco and... and... at... the..." She couldn't bring herself to verbalise his assault. The suppression of the unresolved trauma stopped her as verbalising it would have made the assault more real. She hated the deep visceral feeling of being violated and betrayed. The noodle bowl shook in her hand as she tried to restrain herself.

Sam looked around again, making sure no one was around, wagging his finger at her before she could finish her sentence. "Careful what you say. You're not exactly irreplaceable. So, settle down." His demeanour hardened as his frown bore into her.

"Don't patronise me," she said, launching the bowl and cheap plastic spork in his direction. He ducked, escaping the projectiles, save a few spots of soup on his blue shirt. He should have counted himself lucky that she was considerate enough to empty the bowl before hurling it at him. So much for strategising how to delicately handle Sam and her promotion.

26

Not Sharky the Shark, Skippy the Kangaroo, or any of the dinosaur cushions. Lewis lay next to his favourite – Pillowy. The threadbare pillow was well-chewed at the edges; the familiar scent was as worn as the once red floral pattern.

"It's already ten. Go to sleep," Sophia said by the door.

Lewis shifted in his bed, curling up tighter to hide what he was doing but she already knew he was playing *Minecraft*, an adventure game where players created structures and contraptions from textured cubes whilst avoiding mobs and finding their own supplies and food. She held out her hand. "Give me your phone."

Lewis kept his focus on the game. "Five more."

"I already gave you five more minutes. Twice."

"Puu... pu-lease."

"Hurry up," she said, rubbing her tired eyes. "I need to sleep soon." It was shorthand for: she needed him to sleep so she could continue catching up on her work, but Lewis wouldn't have caught the details, nor did he need to.

"No!" He kicked his heels onto the mattress.

"I mean it. Now!"

He swung his head from side to side. "Not fair!"

"Why do we need to go through the same thing every night?" She tried to snatch his phone, but he twisted out of reach, accidentally hitting her forearm, but continued to play his game. "Ooooww!" she cried, retaliating with a thump on his back.

Lewis swung his arm aimlessly behind him as he wrapped his body to shield his phone. Despite being big enough to defend himself, violence was not the answer. "No, no, no!" he whined. He didn't want to lose his place in the game.

"Enough!" she yelled, struggling to reach around his body.

"Stop it, stoppp iiittt!" he grunted.

She poked him from the left, pushed from the right, peered over the top of him, and prodded at all different angles to expose the phone but he barely budged. Stuck, she lunged to the corner of the bed, grabbed Pillowy and held it aloft. "I'm going to put it in the wash if you don't give me the phone now!"

The pillow's musty smell provided Lewis a nostalgic comfort – a throwback to his childhood when he felt safe at Mrs Gianakos' day-care centre. The first time their mother made the mistake of washing Pillowy was a day of hell. Lewis threw a tantrum that would have sent a broken needle on a Richter scale off the charts. It had since been a long process of negotiation whenever it needed to be cleaned. The pro tip was to have a backup pillow on hand that was as close in pattern, shape, size and smell as the original.

"No!" Lewis snapped, looking up from his phone for the first time. It was a bridge too far. "Give it!"

Sophia held out her hand again. "Give me your phone."

He scrunched up his face. "Mummy! Mummy let me before."

"Quiet, Lewis!"

"Dad-dy."

"Just give me your phone!"

Lewis held out his phone, turning away from her. "Dad-dy!"

"They're dead, okay. Dead. Shut up already!" Even she was surprised by her blunt enunciation that drove home the harsh reality.

Lewis' lips quivered, his eyes squeezing closed as his nose wrinkled. "No, no, no!" he sobbed.

She snatched the phone out of his hand, "You're not getting it tomorrow," and stormed out.

Lewis buried his face into Sharky, letting out a roar of frustration as he bounced on his bed, flipping and flapping like a fish out of water.

SOPHIA RUBBED HER WEARY EYES. HER FACE WAS PUNCTUATED by heavy lines and shadows, a face of exhaustion and regret. Who knew that it was *this* much work looking after a semi-dependent person? Thank goodness Lewis was finally asleep. Never mind the physical exhaustion, the mental burden was just as paralysing. His condition affected those around him almost as much as himself. Worst of all, she couldn't stay late in the office to catch up on her work any longer.

Was this what having children was like? It didn't matter – it wasn't any excuse for not committing her all for the firm. She disliked *those* parents who arrived late to the office because they had to drop their kids off at day care, school or wherever they claimed, or left the office early because they had to attend their child's parent-teacher meeting. Her parents had never turned up to any of hers and she had turned out just fine, so what was their excuse? No, she couldn't become one of *those* people. It would just take a bit of determination and sacrifice and if that meant filling in an application from the Department of Human Services, so be it.

Sophia returned to her laptop, watching the cursor blink in the *Name* field. *Lewis Marexi*, she typed. Under *Reason for application*, she paused before typing again: *I am not equipped to adequately care for my brother. Not only does he need financial assistance but also someone who knows how to look after his special needs – both of which I cannot provide.*

Propping her hand under her chin, she re-read her inputs, pursing her lips. It wasn't compelling enough. It didn't have the *oomph* that was required to secure one of the limited places in the government's supervised care programme. She pecked at the backspace key, then held it down, zooming the cursor backwards, wiping out all her text. She drummed her fingers on the desk, channelling whatever inspiration she could in the dead of night. *Reason for application*, she mulled over again, then her fingers moved in a flurry: *Lewis is physically intimidating. He is bigger and stronger than me. The unpredictable nature of his autism frightens me. I fear for my safety, especially when he gets upset which can turn violent.*

She tapped her cheeks to wake herself up, clasped her hand over her mouth, and read the justification again. Was she really comfortable with what she had just typed? Not being close to Lewis was one thing, but it was another thing altogether to relinquish legal guardianship of her own flesh and blood, particularly someone so vulnerable. It was for the best, she nodded to herself, though she wasn't exactly sure who it would be better for. She pushed the inconvenient thought out of her mind. There was no need to complicate an already complicated situation.

She certified that she was making an accurate declaration and stared at the *Submit* button for so long that her focus blurred, but after spending the past half hour completing the form, it would be a waste not to submit it. As she pressed the button, there was a loud buzz – as if her computer was letting her know that it disagreed with her decision – sending her jumping in her chair. Her phone pinged with a message. She wasn't the only one up at this hour.

27

The silence compounded the already tense atmosphere. Sam dipped the tea bag into the cup three more times. His movements were slow but deliberate – a power move to show that he was in control. Sophia watched the performance with waning patience, wishing that he would get to the bloody point.

She avoided his eyes, focussing on his tea ceremony instead. The label on the tag wasn't a brand she recognised. It wasn't the average supermarket variety. It was more pretentious. Given the exotic characters, bordering on Oriental to Persian cuneiform, she surmised that it was probably imported green tea – delicately handpicked by a monk who had been meditating for the last five years in a remote mountain-side cave – promising nirvana when consumed. She suppressed a smile, which managed to crack her otherwise disinterested expression.

"Is there something you want to share?" Sam looked up from his teacup. "Okay, Sophia Marexi," he started formally, which confirmed to her that this meeting would be different. He glanced at his notes before continuing. "I apologise for the late message yesterday, but I wanted you to hear it directly from me. I spoke to HR about your pay increase. They weren't convinced that you warranted an above-average raise."

"Isn't it up to you?"

"It's within policy but I still need to provide justifica—"

"I thought the CEO already agreed?" she interrupted.

"Sophia, let me cut to the chase. We no longer require a programme director."

"What? Project Panda isn't even finished."

"Yes, you're right," Sam nodded.

Sophia shook her head, sitting taller in her seat. He always had a knack of manipulating people's words. "No, what I meant was that it's on track, but it's only scheduled to complete in three weeks."

"I've asked Investor Relations to pick it up. They will have it ready in two."

She stared vacantly at him, disbelieving what she was hearing. "No, I mean, it's scheduled to be done in three weeks." There was something about Investor Relations that kept ringing in her ears. She hadn't heard about them in a long time but there seemed to be constant mention of them lately. She filed through her memory. Didn't Sam mention them after the disastrous Exco when he pestered her about when the presentation would be ready? Was he already planning this then?

"I'd appreciate if you can give them a handover while we review the headcount for Senior Project Manager."

Sophia leant forward, hoping she had heard it wrong. "What?" Not getting the promotion to programme director was one thing but the last time she checked, Senior Project Manager was the title of her current role.

"It's just a routine review," he tried to reassure her.

Sophia knew there was no such thing as a routine review of headcounts. Sure, there were *strategic* reviews from time to time but not a routine process. It just wasn't done at Eastle.

"Is this about what happened at Exco or in the kitchen? Or..." she paused, contemplating whether it was a good idea to bring it up. "Or, what happened at the conference?"

"I want to thank you for your work on Project Panda," Sam said, speaking over her. "As you know, people are our most important asset, so we'll let you know the outcome of the routine review as soon as possible. Of course, we'll be taking into account how smooth the handover process is."

Sophia only caught snippets of what he said. Her confusion gave way to numbness and disbelief as his words sank in. Like being on the wrong side of punching gloves, the stacking of bad news knocked the wind out of her. Why the hell had she been working so hard all this time?

When she returned to her desk, Sophia stared at an Excel spreadsheet with an apparent infinite rows and columns of revenue projections against each credit card initiative. The cursor patiently blinked in the *Net Present Value* cell, waiting for her instructions to extrapolate the payback period over the next three years, but she left it hanging. It was far too complex a calculation given the questions and self-doubt consuming her. How had her world flipped so much? Only a few months ago, she had had plans to move out and start a new life – one without the burden and constraints of her family. And now, as if through some sort of conspiracy, she was without both her parents, no promotion, and her current job was being "reviewed" – whatever that meant. Worst of all, she was stuck with Lewis.

And Sam! He couldn't sack her, could he? He had already told her that she had the job. That had to count for something... right? The weight on her shoulders felt heavier; the brightness of everything around her seemed to dim.

Indistinct chatter washed over to her from colleagues. She had never understood the point of chit-chat, a time-waster which only got in the way of getting things done. If only they knew the turmoil she was in, but then again, she didn't want anyone to know. She couldn't give them the satisfaction of laughing in her face.

"Soph," a voice boomed in her ear. It seemed louder than it really was. She jumped in her seat, snapping back to reality. "You all right?" a colleague asked. "You've been staring at your screen for ages."

"Errr... yeah. Sure. Of course," Sophia stuttered.

Despite being surrounded by people all day, she was alone with her problems. Having never connected with anyone on a meaningful level, who could she pour out her soul to? She couldn't even fall back on her parents anymore. Usually a logical, rational person who could break down the root cause of an issue with laser focus, Sophia found herself in new territory. There was a lack of clarity, a fuzziness, a what-the-hell-should-I-do-now feeling that drained everything from her.

SHE SAT AT THE EDGE OF THE TABLE OPPOSITE A TALL, BALD, clean-shaven and bespectacled man. In a room that seated more than twenty, it was much too large for two. Although composed, Sophia was tense and more than a little anxious. It didn't help that Jimmy Thomas from HR had a reputation for being a no-nonsense kind of guy. Explaining her story to him made her feel vulnerable – a feeling that had once been unfamiliar to her. Wasn't 'vulnerable' simply a euphemism for 'weak'? If that wasn't enough to make her feel small and uncomfortable, the presence of a towering man and the oversized room sure did, but she was just grateful for the meeting at such short notice.

"I'm sure it has been difficult for you," Jimmy said after listening to her story for the past hour. His deep voice belied his physical stature. It was soft, warm and empathetic. "You've been courageous by getting in touch. The firm takes all allegations of sexual misconduct seriously," he continued, peering over his glasses which hung on the tip of his nose.

"What are the next steps?" Sophia asked. Reliving the incident had brought feelings of indignation and betrayal. The emotional and physical violation were also painful, but it would take a lot more to break her.

"Due to the seriousness of the allegations, I will personally look into this to make sure it is investigated thoroughly and that your privacy and confidentiality are respected. I can imagine this might be an unsettling time for you, so let's touch base again after I've had a chance to do some digging."

"Do you think I need to go to the police? You know, report it?"

Jimmy smiled. "That won't be necessary. This is an internal thing."

"I mean, to *officially* report it."

"This," Jimmy pointed to both of them, "is official. Anyway, it'll be quicker for the firm to sort it out. We have more resources. We'll leave them to catch the real bad guys."

She nodded. "Okay."

"If you need to take some time off, just let me know. I know things are a little awkward between you and your line manager at the moment. And before you ask, it'd be on full pay."

"Thank you, Jimmy. Thanks very much." At last, someone was listening. Not only that, Jimmy was in a position to do something about it, not some paper pusher who would need to go to their boss, who would, in turn, need to go to their boss to consider whether they should even look into the allegations. No – this was a HR department that took her allegations seriously.

28

The sun crept into the bedroom around the gaps in the curtains. A deep snore emanated from Sophia. EEEHH, EEEHH, EEEHH! The alarm squawked. As a device specifically designed to wake sleepy heads, it was great, though most people in their right minds would never want to be friends with it, especially at six in the morning.

The noise was usually enough to stir Sophia to life but no such luck today. She slept heavily, repaying her sleep debt that she had chronically accumulated over the countless early mornings and late nights. Lewis wandered in with sleepy eyes and messy hair. He nudged her. It was time to get up.

A harder nudge; she let out a grunt.

"Breakfast," he said.

Another grunt. She didn't want to move. She didn't want to make breakfast. In fact, she didn't want to do anything. She tugged the duvet over her head.

"Breakfast," Lewis repeated.

"Just wait!" She ripped off the cover, almost hitting him in the face, but lay starfished on the bed, eyes closed. *Okay, on the count of three. One, two... no, maybe ten?* After thirty seconds, she heaved herself up, rolled to the edge of her bed, almost thumping onto the floor, and waddled into the bathroom.

Standing under the shower, mixed emotions fogged her mind. She was anxious but couldn't craft any solutions. She was hungry but didn't have any appetite. She didn't want to fail but she couldn't accomplish anything. As she rinsed her hair, it felt thinner, her fingertips felt closer to her scalp, no longer cushioned by her thick forest of hair. She opened her palms – clumps of hair slithered down the drain. She ran her fingers through her hair again, this time gentler but no matter how delicate she was, her hair snapped easily. She tried to recall when her last period was, but with so much going on lately, she couldn't remember. When did she become *that* stressed to lose her hair and stop menstruating?

Freshly showered, she walked into the kitchen, readying herself for wet pyjamas, spilt milk, or whatever the latest drama was from Lewis. He sat at the dining table, silent, tugging his fingers, alternating from one hand to the other. The break in his morning routine disrupted him more than usual, though he tried his best to contain his anxiety.

"Breakfast," he said.

"Lewis, just shut—" Sophia blurted out before taking an aggravated breath. "Can't you see I'm doing it right now?" She dumped milk on the new-and-improved-chocolate-flavoured Cocoa Puffs that she had randomly picked up at the supermarket. The bowl was filled halfway when she stopped.

There were already two plates.

On each, two slices of toast were placed on the right, and one sunny-side-up egg on the left. Slices of grilled tomatoes sat at the top, and a knife and fork neatly flanked each side of the meals. Lewis continued to fidget with the exact positions of each ingredient to make it just how his mother had taught him.

"Breakfast," he said with a grin.

"Oh." Sophia softened. When did he learn how to fry an egg? "It looks great, Lewis."

He beamed. "Lewis. Great."

29

———

The conference room didn't feel any smaller than when she had last met Jimmy. Sophia was alone, waiting. To ease her anxiety, her mind drifted to mundane thoughts. Why out of all the meeting rooms the firm had, couldn't they meet in a more appropriately sized room? And the temperature – it was freezing! She checked her phone again to make sure the *Voice Memo* app was still recording. Although she was also going to make notes, what better proof was there to prevent the process denigrating into a he-said-she-said debacle?

A muffled sound, as if someone had accidentally pocket-dialled at the far end of the room, interrupted her train of thought. She arched her neck to check the conference phone. It wasn't left on from the previous meeting nor did it have any missed calls.

She fidgeted with her phone, trying to find the most strategic place. She planted it in the centre of the table, moved it to her left, then right, and finally flipped it over so the screen faced down. She couldn't risk it lighting up if she received a notification. It was better to be safe than invite unnecessary questions. In which case, should she be upfront with Jimmy about the recording to avoid questions later? She wanted to reciprocate the openness and transparency that he had shown her but recording their conversation may signal that she didn't trust him. In any case, she wanted – no, needed – to protect herself. Before she could make up her mind, the door opened, startling her. She plucked her phone from the table and jammed it into her jacket. Out of sight, out of mind.

"Apologies. My other meeting overran," Jimmy said, walking in and placing his notepad and envelopes on the table.

"Hi," Sophia said, trying to find a place for her hands, pretending she wasn't doing anything before he came in. "It's okay."

She folded her arms across her chest, but it was too confrontational. She relaxed them on her lap but that was too casual. She needed a middle ground. She rubbed her clammy palms on the side of her legs before clasping her hands over each other on the table like a contestant in a game show.

"How are you?" Jimmy tried with the small talk, sitting down.

"I'm... good... I guess."

"Have you taken any time off?"

"Not yet. I want to keep busy. You know, to keep my mind off things."

"I understand, it's not easy." He nodded. "Sophia, before we start, it's important that we both respect the confidentiality of this conversation. Do you have your phone with you?"

"Uh... yes." Her blood pressure rose.

"And any other recording device?"

It rose even higher. She flushed, taken aback by the start of the conversation. Jimmy's demeanour was different from last time. His leaning back in the chair, crossing his legs, knee-on-knee – it was all a little more assertive. Had he watched her before he came in? She surveyed the edges of the ceiling, but couldn't see any cameras from the corners of her eyes. In any case, it would be a gross breach of privacy for the firm to covertly record them. It didn't take long for the irony to hit her. There she was, questioning the firm's integrity when it was her who was recording. "No... no devices," she said, swallowing the lump in her throat.

Jimmy raised his eyebrows, waving his phone at her. "Would you mind?"

"Not at all." Her heart raced as she reached into her jacket. She fumbled with it a few times in the pocket, hoping that she held the power button long enough. She passed it to him, trying to relax her stiff arm. *Breathe, act normally.*

As Jimmy flipped the phone over, she was already formulating her response when he inevitably found out that she was recording them. She could feign illness, forcing their meeting to be postponed but the silliness of it would be as absurd as using the dog-ate-my-homework excuse.

"No battery?" he asked, looking at the black screen.

"Power button's on the side." Her leg stopped jiggling under the table, relieved that she had managed to turn it off. Like a ventriloquist, she exhaled a long breath – a full thirty seconds since her last – hoping he didn't notice her panic.

"We'll keep it that way." He placed the phone next to him. "As I've said previously, sexual harassment is a serious allegation. I've personally looked into this and spoken to a number of people, and we must have consequences when we find serious misconduct from our employees, no matter who they are."

Sophia nodded. A long silence. Did he expect her to show more of a reaction? She didn't know what else to say. "Thanks?" or "Please continue?" Punishing Sam would be great, but she had little expectation of that as it would be unrealistic for the firm to prosecute a senior executive given the lack of tangible evidence. She was just eager to find out when she could move on from all this mess.

"We have zero tolerance," Jimmy continued, "for fabrications designed to assassinate the character of one of our esteemed senior managers."

She nodded again. Yes, she agreed. "Wait, what?" She shook her head, making sure she had heard him correctly.

Jimmy sat up and uncrossed his legs. In this position, his jaw seemed more angular, his posture stiffer. Where did the warm, empathetic HR guy go? He slid an envelope across the table. Stamped *STRICTLY PRIVATE AND CONFIDENTIAL*, it was addressed to one *Ms Sophia Marexi*, and bore the firm's insignia – a circle resembling the yin and yang in red and white. She picked it up, searching him for the slightest of clues.

When she tore open the envelope, it was hard to miss the bold heading. It was enough to crush any spirit she had left. Not only did the letter have her full name, it also bore her employee identification number, role, department and line manager for good measure in case there was any confusion about to whom it was addressed. Her eyes zigzagged left to right, scanning the letter as fast as she could:

NOTICE OF TERMINATION

This letter is to inform you that your employment with Eastle Financial Group ("EFG") will terminate immediately upon you receiving this notice and no later than five working days from the date of this letter.

Your employment was terminated as you have failed to meet the agreed performance targets and did not live up to the firm's values and principles. Specifically, the following were observed:

1. Substandard performance: There have been continual delays in the delivery of Project Panda, and whilst some progress has been made, it was achieved through the diligence of others in the project working group. Further, you did not heed the continual feedback from senior management and others.

2. Unauthorised use of company assets: Analysis of printing queues showed that on 4 separate occasions, you printed 12 double-sided pages of non-work-related content. This is contrary to the proper use of company assets.

Any healthcare benefits will cease immediately, and you are required to return all company property, including your laptop, mobile phone and staff identification card before the end of the day.

Yours,

Human Resources.

Sophia scoffed. "You're joking, right? This is a joke." At least she hoped that it was. Her reaction was to elicit some response – anything – but Jimmy remained poker-faced. She clenched her jaw. If he wasn't going to say anything, she didn't know how to continue their discussion. Was he expecting her to simply accept the letter and be on her way? Words floated into her mind, but she couldn't string them together.

"Substandard?" she eventually spewed out. "Where's your evidence? Where's... where's my notice period? And ten pages? Really?"

"Twelve." Jimmy corrected her. "You're mistaken if you think stealing from the company is a trivial matter. Others have been dismissed for much less." He deepened his voice, so it resonated at a lower tone, and projected a more authoritative air – a subtle yet convenient intimidation tactic.

The room fell silent. It was only for a few seconds, but the stillness made it feel like minutes, and exaggerated all sounds: the minute shifts in the seat, the flipping of the pen in Jimmy's fingers... and the sound of the pocket-dialling at the far end of the room again. This time, it sounded like something brushed over a microphone. Sophia pushed the distraction out of her mind as she calculated her next steps. Should she retract her complaint to save her job or accept her fate and move on? The job market seemed to be fine for the moment, so getting another job should be straightforward, she hoped. However, the thought of establishing herself again in a new company, and the potential of not having any income during the transition period daunted her.

"Transfer me to a different department," she requested.

"We can't have a liar and a thief working for the firm."

"Transfer me and I won't go to EOC."

Jimmy let out a belly laugh. "Do you really want to fight this at the Equal Opportunity Commission? Do you know how many complaints, or should I say," – he mimed quotation marks – "'referrals', the government gets each year? Thousands. And, do you know how many of those end in a conviction? Hmm? Three out of every thousand. That's Zero. Point. Three. Per cent."

Sophia didn't know if the statistic were true, and even if it were, she pretended it didn't dishearten her. She forced a blink, trying to act normal as Jimmy continued.

"Do you know why it's so low? Because it ends up being 'he-said-she-said'. And *he* usually wins."

Sophia shrank in the vast, almost-empty conference room. The harsh reality of which side HR was batting for was starting to sink in. She fought a melting pot of emotions: shock, betrayal, disappointment, uncertainty... but above all, powerlessness. It was a strange, despised feeling of being steamrolled by a corporation that would not let one measly middle manager get in the way of its commitment to its shareholders. No! It wasn't about shareholders because that would have been about the broader good. This was about the indiscretions of one senior manager.

She looked at her phone next to Jimmy, wishing it were recording the injustice. Who would have believed that the tone had changed so much from their first meeting? Trapped and outmanoeuvred, she burned from the inside – the way coal pits simmered at first before igniting into tall flames. The hum of the air conditioner came into focus. Set at a balmy twenty-seven degrees Celsius, the cool breeze gave her goose bumps. She shivered, her voice wavered, but she persisted.

"I have a broad range of skills. You can put me in any department." She slid the termination notice back to Jimmy.

"You don't get it. Let me spell out the case to the EOC." He put on a lawyer's voice; dramatic, smooth and clear. "Dear Arbiter, it is highly unfortunate that we are here today as I am sure you are busy. Many would say Sophia Marexi is an ambitious young lady." He locked eyes on her as he recited his monologue with uncomfortable familiarity. "However, that ambition has led her astray as it has seen her do almost anything, let me repeat, almost anything to advance her career." He pointed his finger at her accusingly before continuing.

"This includes the attempted defamation of Samuel Abraham, a highly regarded executive at Eastle Financial Group, after he rightly rejected her sexual advances. For the record, Mr Abraham is happily married, saying nothing about the highly inappropriate nature of this – both personally and professionally. There is no evidence whatsoever for these baseless claims but as a sign of the firm's restraint and goodwill, we wish to avoid further litigation and seek your concurrence to dismiss Sophia Marexi for incompetence and unauthorised use of the firm's assets." He pressed his elbows onto the table, leaning forward to underline his point. "We can and will crush you. I'll personally guarantee it."

The message was crystal clear now. Sexual assault was as much about power as it was about sex. It was about the feeling of superiority, the wanton disregard of, and power over, the sexual assault survivor. The question was, why did Jimmy change? Was she that naïve to initially believe that he could have resolved this for her?

He flicked the Notice of Termination back at her. As he rose to leave, there was a tapping noise.

"Hello? Can you hear me?" a voice from the TV asked. They turned to the red light from the camera atop the blank screen. Sophia grabbed the remote control and switched it on. They were both confused by what they saw: a technician with his back towards the camera, repeatedly tapping his headset. The room he was in was a mess. Tools and toolkits were strewn across the table and floor, cables of all shapes and sizes snaked through, and a ladder was under a removed ceiling panel.

"Hello? Sophia?" Seb repeated into the microphone.

"Yes, hi. We hear you," Sophia said.

Seb spun around, swooping his face into the camera and

waved. "Can you hear me?" He couldn't believe it was finally working.

The counter at the bottom right of the screen continued to increment from 3:23:14.

"How long has this been on for?" Sophia asked.

Seb stretched his neck out to check the timer on the screen. "Three hours and twenty-something minutes, but it seems like you only just heard me. We've been testing all day."

"And what does that red dot mean? Next to the time."

"You mean the record button?" he rushed out of the room. "Donny! It worked! Where are you?"

Finally, a break. She fought the urge to say *many thanks* to him (Read: I might keep you in the old Rolodex) but *most thanks* would be more appropriate (Read: I might even have coffee with you. No – change that to *must*).

The colour drained from Jimmy's face. He lurched for the remote control in Sophia's hand, but she recoiled. She slid back the Notice of Termination letter but this time with more force. Jimmy took a moment to calculate, furious that the turn of events had compromised his position. He rifled through the other envelopes, flicking another across the table. This one had the same information: her name, employee identification number, role, department and line manager. The difference was the heading: *NON-DISCLO-SURE AGREEMENT (NDA)*. She was disgusted by the thought of the range of scenarios that the two other envelopes might cover.

She tore open the envelope. It offered $45,000 as settlement, though it had several conditions. In addition to the immediate termination of her employment, she must not reference, allude to, or disclose the settlement or any wrong-doing by Samuel Abraham against her to anyone, at any time, in any manner, or in any format whatsoever. If she did, she would be required to return the $45,000 settlement fee, sued for an amount the firm deemed appropriate based on its assessment of damages at the time as well as paying for the firm's legal fees. She would also have to turn over all evidence to the firm, whether written, printed or in audio form. If any evidence were to be made public, she would be legally obligated to denounce it as fraudulent and/or counterfeit. Further, to protect the NDA, she would not be availed a signed copy of the agreement. Instead, she may, at the discretion of the firm, view a copy of it in the presence of the firm's lawyers or appropriate representatives by submitting a written request. The firm would also have discretion over the time, duration and location of the viewing.

The deal was unfair, and by asking her to denounce any evidence should it appear in public instead of remarking blandly, *No comment*, the firm was asking – no, telling – her to lie. It sucked but she didn't have the time or resources to fight a big corporation like Eastle in arbitration or in court. The prudent approach would be to speak with a workplace employment lawyer before she agreed to anything, but with the toll this debacle had already taken, she just wanted to get on with her life; a life which was crumbling around her at a precipitous rate.

"A hundred thousand," she blurted out, trying to get a feel for where the boundaries were.

Jimmy looked away, unsure whether he should play the game. "Forty-seven."

"Eighty-five."

"Forty-eight. That's final." He cut her off before she could continue the game of verbal ping-pong.

She stared at the dotted line above her name. She was trading her integrity with pragmatism and would hate herself for signing the agreement but someone braver, more altruistic, could fight Eastle's institutionalised culture of sexual harassment. She would simply be glad to put this mess behind her, particularly when the original deal was dismissal without compensation. Besides, $48,000 should tide her and Lewis over for the next few months before she landed another job. She pressed the pen above the dotted line and squiggled away.

30

The train raced to the next station, rattling through a rough patch. Sophia's neck was crooked at an awkward angle as she rested her head against the window that rhythmically bounced against it. THUD! Her head smacked the glass, wrenching her from her sleep. She grimaced as she pulled herself upright, cracking her neck back to vertical. She did a stocktake of her belongings and cast an eye around her. *Phew.* Everything was still there. Plus, no weirdo was sitting next to her; just the ordinary sight of a wife explaining to her husband about how she got a great discount on two kilos of bananas, a father holding his sleeping toddler in one arm and checking his phone with his free hand, and a school-aged couple holding hands, debating the benefits of reducing carbs on a ketogenic diet. Why was everyone so happy? What was their problem, damn it?

The PA system crackled for a second before a voice came online. "The next stop..." was all Sophia made out. She strained her ears for the repeat announcement, but it was worse than the first. She looped her handbag over her shoulder, adjusted her hold on the cardboard box she was carrying and filed out of the train, down the steep flight of stairs from the platform and onto the street. The box, holding random contents from her ex-office, was surprisingly light after the work-related documents and other paraphernalia were discarded. There was a coffee mug, phone chargers and a couple of chewed-up charging cables. A few framed photos from previous conferences had also found their way into the box, along with silly photo-booth pictures, assorted stationery and a baby-sized red felt blanket which she had received as a Secret Santa gift one Christmas. Given the unhealthy amount of time she spent in the office, they might as well equip her with a blanket so she could sleep in the office, her colleagues joked.

Staring at her feet, Sophia weaved through the crowded main street, passing an endless row of mixed businesses, but the smell of bread from the bakeries, roasted coffee from the cafes, and the hustle and bustle of the supermarket soon faded into the distance. As she turned a corner, she almost kicked into a table set on the side of the pavement. She stopped, almost tipping over, and looked up. A diner signed their bill and waved it at the waiter inside the restaurant. She walked around the table, her thoughts turning back to her discussion with Jimmy. Had she compromised herself by signing the Non-Disclosure Agreement in the heat of the moment? Was it too late to have another conversation with him?

She turned into an intersection, cutting across to the roundabout in the middle of the road as she waited for a car to pass. When it did, she stepped forward to cross the other half of the road but tripped backwards. HONK! Another car whizzed by, the driver swatting his arms at her to get off the damn road. Sophia shrieked, almost dropping her box.

As her pulse settled, she glanced left to right, and back again, before crossing the road. She wanted to share her woes with somebody, but her life was almost all work and in leaving the firm, she had learned who her friends really were. She didn't have many. Only two people wished her well. Most avoided her for the fear of being guilty by association, and who could blame them, really? No one wanted to be seen with a liar and a thief even if she wasn't either of those things. Just as a person's stock rose with their increase in status and power, it was the opposite when they were out of favour. Any virtues they may have had would be gone for good. Their jokes, no matter how humorous, would all be stinkers, and any words they uttered were a waste of time. She could almost hear the analysts cry, *Sell, sell, sell!* as if she were a traded security.

She turned into her street, a quieter residential area with clouds of shadows hanging over the pavement from the tall, leafy trees. Sophia knew she wasn't the most loved person at the firm. She knew she could be mistaken for a female dog at times. She shrugged though no one was there to notice. When was the last time she had updated her CV? She didn't have too long to dwell on the question.

"Hey! Hey!" she yelled, struggling to run on the inclined pavement.

A neatly dressed man who had been peering into her lounge, stood down from his tiptoes and spun around. "Ah ha! You live here?"

Sophia eyed him suspiciously. "Who are you?"

"I take it you're not Robert Marexi. You must be Gayle?"

"No. Sophia. Her daughter. What are you—"

"Sophia? Matt." He extended his hand for a handshake but retracted it; she was holding the cardboard box. "You live here?"

Sophia rested the box on the ground, "Yeah," and planted one hand on her hip, already out of patience.

"Right, Sophia. You've got thirty days." He handed her an envelope with *Eviction Notice* written on it.

"What?" She clasped her arm by her side; the power dynamic had just shifted. "You can't—"

"Yes, we can." Matt opened his folder. "Here, here, and here... *and* here," he said, fanning through his A4 binder as he stabbed at copies of previous warning letters, most of which had *LAST WARNING* in bold red typeface. "And here." This time it was half a page of phone records made to Robert and Gayle.

"They've both passed away. Like, gone. Dead."

"So sorry for your loss." He tapped his heart. "Just doing my job."

"You don't understand. I didn't receive—"

"Rules are rules, darling."

"What am I going to do with Lewis? You have to give me more than thirty days."

"The landlord can actually evict you after two weeks." Matt walked past her.

"Hang on. You can't—"

He jumped into his company-sponsored Toyota Corolla that proudly displayed a *Because We Care* sign decaled across the side and drove off to his next appointment. "Have yourself a great day!"

Sophia's head spun. What the hell just happened?

31

Jimmy blew on his piping-hot Americano before taking a sip, wincing. "It's done." He puffed out his chest as he leant back into the cushioned seat. With an air of smugness, he spread his arm across the empty seat next to him. "You should've seen when I lowered my voice, you know that thing that I do…" Jimmy deepened his voice, "Like this…" before talking normally. "She almost started crying." He scrunched his face, quivering his lower lip in derision.

"Did she really?" Sam chuckled as he sat in the dining booth across from Jimmy. "What a princess," he said, shaking his head. "It's always the toughest ones that crumble fastest."

Jimmy tapped his fingers along to the Motown record playing on the coin-operated jukebox as he looked around Break Out – a retro café modelled on the 1950s American diner, complete with black-and-white chequered tiles and cheap polyester chairs.

"Why did you wait this long? You should've got rid of her long ago."

"It took time to get what I needed from her, if you know what I mean." Sam flashed a wink, smirking.

"Nice." Jimmy nodded approvingly.

"So, what's the exit narrative?"

Jimmy shrugged. "She couldn't cope with the pressure... it's regrettable... we thank her for her service, blah, blah, blah... the usual."

Sam lowered his hand, trying to hush Jimmy's loud voice. "And why are we going for an NDA and not a straight termination again?"

"What?" Jimmy stopped tapping to the music. He had heard the question. He just didn't like the interrogation.

"We spoke before about termination, not an NDA."

"It's... complicated. It's done now," Jimmy replied sheepishly. What else could he say? That he was outmanoeuvred? No! Imagine the shame that would bring on a twenty-seven-year HR veteran. "She can still talk even if we terminate her. It's best this way."

Sam motioned for the envelope. "Show me."

Jimmy slid it across the table.

Sam opened it and thumbed through the papers, zeroing in on the dotted line. He squinted and pressed his face closer before tossing it back. "The hell is this?"

Jimmy snatched the agreement with a frown, and mimicked Sam's actions: squinting at the page, pressing his face closer, angling the paper in all directions – hoping the light would make a difference. He looked up at Sam and back down, but no matter how many times he skewed his head at odd angles, the *FUCK YOU* signature stared right back at him.

32

The first day of unemployment was a strange feeling. It wasn't just the restlessness, the listlessness or the uncertainty. And while the additional sleep was welcomed, there was an unexplainable sense of hollowness, of being discarded, that made her feel used. Sophia had already raided her fridge more times than she could keep track of, and flicked through Netflix even more times, but even with the bombardment of shows, there was still nothing to watch.

She returned to her laptop, the screen crammed with employment and real estate websites. Her eyes stung as she strained to read in the dark, the bright colours of a myriad of internet browsers all vying for her attention. Sophia arched her back, stretching to the ceiling. There must be a way for the numbers to add up. She punched the buttons on the calculator again and reached for her notepad, but the page was already graffitied with scribbles, calculations and strikeouts. She flicked over the page, but there was more of the same.

Numbers were scrawled under the *Weekly Rent* column. At the top of the list was *$400* but it was crossed out, so was

$375, and $320, followed by a question mark. Other expenses were also struck through with the original amounts reducing by five, ten, twenty, and finally thirty-five per cent. The grocery budget seemed to be the hardest hit; it was not only good for the wallet, but also the bathroom scales, she tried to convince herself.

Sophia logged in to her bank account and checked her balance. $3,274.64 was probably enough to house and feed herself and Lewis for two months. Three months maximum. For many, that may have been enough of a buffer before finding another job but as a person who liked to be organised and always planned for the future, the thought of not having an income, even for the shortest time, unsettled her.

She had had grand plans of becoming head of the retail banking division within seven years, and CEO in under fifteen. She didn't want to make the same mistake as her parents and be blasé about her future, but no matter how many times she stubbornly repeated those mantras to herself, her vision was slipping from her grasp. She slumped back in her chair, deflated. Damn it, she was stronger than this. All she needed to do was google more employment and real estate websites. She pinned her neck to the side and in an abrupt twitch, cracked it. It was going to be a long night.

THE CLUSTER OF APARTMENTS WERE CRAMMED IN THE CUL-DE-sac, which nestled in a quiet neighbourhood. The red bricks were sturdy though a little dated, circa 1980s, but could have equally been 1970s. The narrow stairwell was dark and tiled in unsightly turquoise squares. It was so old that it could boomerang back into fashion.

"Sup! The name's Mohammed. You can call me Mo. I'll

be here if you have any questions," greeted the man from Golden Universe Realty. "Listen, if you wouldn't mind, Miss." He gestured to their shoes.

"It's fine." Sophia waved him off. "We'll leave them on."

"Sorry, I mean..." Mohammed pointed to the scattered collection of shoes in the hallway.

Oh. It was one of *those* houses. She flicked her shoes off and pushed them aside with the rest. "Lewis. Shoes."

He looked down at the floor.

"Take your shoes off," she whispered, coaxing her brother.

He pressed his chin into his chest. If he had been an ostrich, he would have buried his head into the ground. She pointed at his shoes, but he squealed and stomped his feet.

"Oh, that's different," Mohammed said, stepping back, holding up his hands in case whatever *it* was came closer.

"Lewis, you're not going to get germs," Sophia hushed into his ear.

Not wanting to be an innocent casualty in the domestic dispute, Mohammed remembered he had an urgent call to make. Not that Sophia cared. She reached for Lewis' shoes again, patting his ankle.

"Lift up your foot," she whispered, but he turned around. She reached for his other ankle but hesitated at the thought of the inevitable struggle and the scene that it would create. Instead, she led him by the wrist and out to the hallway.

"Keep your shoes on but wait here. I'll be ten minutes." She held up her fingers however there was no reaction – at least it wasn't a no – and re-entered the apartment.

The front door opened onto the living room, and if Sophia had to be picky, it was on the smaller side but liveable. She peered into the kitchen. Basic stove top – check.

Oven – check. So far, so good. Not that the kitchen mattered too much. It wasn't her favourite space anyway. The two bedrooms were untidy but not a deal breaker. The room that drew the most disagreeable reaction was the bathroom. It was dated like the rest of the apartment, and the whole block for that matter, with tiles that pre-dated great-grandma, and the leaking screw-type shower taps, and above all, the aqua-green bathtub was disgusting. She disliked everything about the apartment.

She circled back to Mohammed at the front door. "I'll take it if you can reduce the rent by $30 a week. Have you seen the bathroom?"

Mohammed scoffed. "Miss, listen. The market is lit right now. I have offers at $420. That's $30 above the asking."

"Uh huh." Sophia nodded as her eyes wandered to check on Lewis, and her brain ready to counter whatever he had to say.

"I can't stop you from putting $360 in your application but..." Mohammed nudged his head towards Lewis and raised a quizzical eyebrow. "You know what I mean?"

Sophia narrowed her eyes. "What do you mean?"

"Listen, I'm not saying what you're finking. I'm just saying, like," he tilted his head towards Lewis, and widened his eyes again, "you know what I mean?"

She stood a little taller, squaring up with Mohammed's eyes. "What the *hell* do you mean?" It was one thing for *her* to have unpleasant thoughts about her own brother, but it was another for a complete stranger to do the same. After all, Lewis didn't steal his childhood away from him.

"Chill, bruv. Miss. I said, Miss. Like, I can't stop you from putting into my hand an app at $360 but it's the lord of the land's decision, aiight?"

"You mean, the landlord's decision?"

He rolled his eyes. "Is what I just said."

She measured his words, still working out his intent. Of course, he would discourage her from submitting a lower asking price. Lower rent meant lower commission for him, but she wasn't going to fall for that. She pressed her application onto his clipboard and snapped the wire clip loudly. "We're ready to move in two weeks, Mo."

33

———

Sam shifted in the kid's chair again, pushing his knees up towards his chest. With a quarter of his bottom hanging off the seat, it was an uncomfortable position, but sitting with his daughter was the only way he could encourage her to eat faster.

"You have to chew like this," he said, chomping his mouth in demonstration.

Amy moved her jaw, giving him some hope, but once was enough. She held a spoonful of carrots and spinach to his mouth. "Come on, Daddy."

He shook his head and pressed his lips together. "No, that's for you." But she held the spoon resolutely in front of him. Sam couldn't help but shake his head at her audacity to negotiate what she would and would not eat. He relented, chomping on the spoonful of vegetables. "*You* have to eat the rest."

Amy smiled. "Good Daddy."

As soon as Sam finished chewing, Amy delivered another spoonful of vegetables in front of him. "Uh-uh," Sam countered. "This one's yours."

"It's too much!" she retorted as if it were her choice.

"You haven't finished," he said, dreading the thought of how long it would take before she cleared her plate. If he didn't monitor her eating, she could stretch dinner time out until she nodded to sleep in front of the iPad. He hated that he had to do it, but it was the least he could do to bond with his daughter, as his wife constantly lectured him. He reached for her iPad.

"If you're not going to eat, I'm going to turn it off." Amy twisted in her seat and stomped her feet. "You're not going to get your favourite chocolate-chip ice cream if you keep behaving like this." There was nothing like a bit of dessert blackmail.

Amy smacked her fork onto the table. "I'm full already."

"Do you want me to tell Mummy that you're not eating?" Sam didn't finish his sentence when his phone buzzed with a message. May had finally replied: *programme director role sounds interesting. can we talk in office instead?*

A smirk curled Sam's lips as he replied to the message: *You'll be working with senior stakeholders. Networking skills will be very important. I'll ask Angela to book us some time for drinks.*

"I said I'm finished!" Amy turned her plate upside down. "Ice cream, ice cream, ice cream!" She drummed her knife and fork on the table, spilling water from the plastic tumbler.

"Fffuu—" Sam started but restrained himself. "Who's going to clean this up now?"

He rushed to the kitchen as Amy cackled. It was always funnier when she didn't have to clean up. Sam fumbled in the unfamiliar surroundings of the kitchen, bobbing and jutting his head in all the corners and crevices. He flapped the pantry open, scanned it, slapped it closed, and repeated for the next four cupboards. He opened the drawers, but the tea towel was nowhere to be found. Without thinking, he swung the fridge open, but it wasn't there either. He spun around, scratching his head, double-checking to see if he had missed anywhere. He looked down at the counter – the tea towel was under his nose. He scuttled back to the dining table.

"Never EVER TOUCH—" Sam boomed, snatching his phone from Amy's hands, almost ripping the skin off her little fingers. She jumped in her seat, and her lower lip quivered as tears welled up. She clamped her mouth closed as tightly as she could, crossing her arms. All she wanted to do was play *Candy Crush*. He dropped onto the small chair and wiped her tears away. "That's Daddy's phone," he said, softening.

THERE WAS NO BETTER PICTURE OF A CLICHÉ THAN TERI showering Amy in the bathtub which overflowed with bath bubbles and a floating rubber duck called Mrs Waddles because "she looks like she waddles in the water." Instead of pouring two bottle caps of the Biggest Bubble Bath, Amy had thought it would be a better idea to use the whole bottle. Teri was displeased but she wasn't in the mood to argue with the queen of the household. Whatever it took to bathe Her Majesty.

"Are we done yet?" Teri asked for the third time in five minutes. She was eager to get out of the bathroom, having already spent half an hour watching her daughter play in the tub.

"More, Mummy."

"Longer, not more."

"No." Amy shook the bottle of the Biggest Bubble Bath to empty its contents, but nothing came out. "More!"

"Show me your hands." Teri held out both her palms, demonstrating.

Amy shook her head, waving the rubber duck in her mother's face. "Mrs Waddles said no!"

"Your hands will be all wrinkly, and if you stay longer, they'll be like that forever!"

"No, Mummy. You're making me hard!"

Teri froze with eyes wide open, forgetting to blink.

"Real hard!" Amy continued.

"Wha... Where did... Who taught you that?" Teri stammered.

The little girl giggled. "At dinner."

34

C lick. The browser switched to jobseekers.com. Click. Eastle Internet Banking. Click. realestate.com. Click. Microsoft Outlook.

Click, scroll, refresh. Refresh, click.

No matter how many times Sophia clicked or refreshed, she didn't like what she saw. It was the same damn jobs, the same damn rejections to her job applications, and the same damn properties that she couldn't afford. She even expanded her property search further from the city. First, it was twenty kilometres from the central business district, then twenty-five, thirty, and finally forty-five kilometres. She frowned at her own selection. Was she sure she wanted to live amongst the chavs and other undesirables?

Click. Internet banking. The decimal point in her savings account balance seemed to have shifted to the left too quickly, reducing the total amount at an alarming rate. She closed her eyes. *Breathe.* At least her credit card had a $45,000 limit. That would stave off homelessness for a few more months before she had the humiliating experience of queuing at the Department of Human Services to beg for the dole. So much for being done with living off government benefits. In the beginning, it was for Lewis' condition, and now, this. From the first time she had to practically beg for his benefits when she was an early teen, Sophia promised herself never to step foot in the offices of Human Services again if she could ever help it. She didn't want to be surrounded by no-hopers who leeched off the system. She was going to make something of herself. But, damn it, this shitty situation wasn't even her own doing. She hated the very thought of just getting the forms to fill in. There must be demand for an experienced, can-do banker.

She smacked the mouse, closing her internet banking browser without securely logging off. To hell with anyone who wanted to hack into her account. There wasn't much left to steal anyway. They could pay her credit card bill while they were at it.

Apart from the drop in her account balance and the loss of security, she couldn't rid the sense of embarrassment and shame. Her job defined her, it gave her a sense of purpose, a routine, and status – even if it was only in her mind. Her ego had taken a big blow. She didn't like the feeling of sinking into quicksand. Without gainful employment and the sense of achievement, she was all but invisible to society. Isolated, helpless, and with each rejected job application, an over-whelming failure. The only person she had now was Lewis, and that was as good as talking to a brick wall, except she didn't need to feed and care for the wall. If only the world knew how unjust her life was.

Before she could wallow in self-pity any longer, an email notification popped up. She locked onto it straight away, hoping it was a reply from one of her job applications. Instead, it was a reminder that eviction was on the twenty-fourth, eight days away. *Great.*

Click. Microsoft Word.

She returned to her CV and deleted most of the contents. She saved the file again, replacing *v8* with *v9*. Aside from her name in the headline and *Experienced leader and passionate customer advocate* in the subheading, the page was blank. On her first few edits when she applied for jobs, she only made tweaks and minor embellishments. However, the stream of rejections, or worse, silence, from recruitment agencies and hiring firms was disheartening and deafening. She had edited her CV so much that, with each iteration, the document ended up resembling previous versions.

Following up on her applications was also a soul-crushing experience. The empty promises from personal assistants or HR consultants to "find out the latest and let you know" or the emails that were read but not responded to, were difficult to accept. She had to start afresh. As she punched the first words into her new document, she grimaced and hunched over the keyboard, attacked by a pulsing headache. The hours of straining her eyes in front of the screen finally caught up with her. The harder she tried to ignore it, the worse it became.

Click. Computer off.

THE LAST TIME MUST HAVE BEEN AROUND UNIVERSITY. THESE days, she almost always stuck to the minimum: skin-cleanse, moisturise, light foundation and lip balm. Sophia didn't have time for the rigmarole of dolling her face every day, but today was no ordinary day. She turned her phone to selfie mode and powdered her face. She smacked her lips together to even out the pale-mauve lipstick. She wasn't even sure of the last time she had used this shade of Sumptuous Fling, but it was the first thing she found in the drawer.

As she took a bottle of mascara out of her bag, the bus smacked into a pothole, bouncing her off the seat. She propped back up onto her seat and pumped the mascara brush into the tube, then stopped. Didn't that make it clumpy and dry out faster? She whirled the brush in the tube instead and applied it along the length of her lashes. Shouldn't it be in a wriggly motion so there would be more volume at the roots? It had been so long since she had last used it. Whatever. She combed her lashes to clear out the lumps. Okay. Done. Finally. She checked herself on selfie mode again, twitching her head side to side, up and down. It was uncomfortable to be caked up like this but... whatever it took.

Her leg jiggled, slowly at first, then incessantly. She crossed her legs to control her nervousness and looked at the scrunched-up handwritten notes on her lap. Product Analyst. It was a much more junior role than those she had been applying for. On paper, she had all the experience and qualifications being asked for, but it didn't feel right. Not only was the pay much lower, she was still coming to terms to stooping so low for this job. It was more suited for a grad-uate straight from university, but beggars couldn't be choosers. After twenty-seven rejections, she was just grateful to be offered an interview. She ran over her notes again: Show confidence, not arrogance. Display competence yet be open to learn. Be firm in decision making, yet flexible to new ideas. She folded the paper, now worried that she may have over-prepared.

As the bus rumbled to a stop at the lights, Sophia looked out of the window. It seemed that life continued for *them*, even if it had stopped for her. Pedestrians zigzagged the streets, racing to wherever they needed to get to, and a person in a suit shook his head as he stepped over a ragged person kneeling besides three plastic bags holding his worldly possessions – his arm outstretched, ready to catch any coins bypassers wanted to get rid of. Just a few weeks ago, Sophia could have been the suit walking over the ragged man. Back then, the only difference between that homeless person and her was a job. Now that she was no longer employed, how long until she squatted next to him?

She rubbed her eyes to clear her thoughts, forgetting about the makeup she had just applied. Perhaps she was being too pessimistic. Maybe she should try something different altogether. As the saying went, if she wanted to earn a living, a job would suffice, and if she wanted to be rich, starting a business could be the way to go. However, if she wanted to be mega-rich, she should start a religion. She flicked her phone to selfie mode again and dabbed at the smudged eyeliner to even it out.

Faith had never been her strong point and with things on the employment front not looking good, she could start a business. Her plan was great except for one small detail. Every business needed start-up capital and any capital she had was dwindling fast. With the limited options weighing her down, she leant her heavy head against the window. Too bad she didn't know any computer programming or she could be the founder of the *next big thing*. She sighed. What the hell was she thinking? It might be easier to rob a bank. How much did a bank vault have, anyway? Half a million dollars? A million or three? After working in a bank for the past six and a half years, she didn't even know.

The bus rolled forward and roared into second gear. "Sorry, sorry! My stop." She dumped her makeup into her bag, jumping to her feet.

~

"Three things set me apart," Sophia said, sitting up straight, palms resting over each other on the table as she made eye contact with the two people opposite her. "One, leadership. I can direct and influence a range of stakeholders to get things done. Two, customer focus. I obsessively put the customer at the heart of everything we do. And three, my track record. I've delivered major initiatives against tight timeframes, often with limited resources." For this question, she didn't have to memorise her notes. She believed it.

"That's great," the neatly dressed middle-aged woman said as she jotted notes on her Ireal Insurance interview feedback form. "And tell me about a time when you've had to deal with conflict. How did you manage that?"

Sophia flicked a glance at the business cards in front of her, spying for the interviewer's name. "Sure, Leena. It'd depend on the type of conflict and who it is. If there are differences of opinion on a business case, for example, I would present facts and demonstrate how the initiative links to the firm's objectives."

A younger man leant in, whispering into Leena's ear as he pointed at the CV. Sophia tried to catch a glimpse of what he was highlighting but nobody liked a busybody.

"Thanks, Manu." Leena nodded; her expression cooled. She narrowed her eyes and pressed her lips together. "What about conflicts of a personal nature?"

"I get along with everyone. I'm a professional and treat everyone with the respect that I would expect from them."

"Hmm. Okay. Thanks." Leena tapped her notes to square them into alignment. "Manu, do you have anything else? Right. Well, Sophia, I think we have all the information we need for now. Thanks for coming."

"Yes. Thanks. Nice meeting you." Sophia exchanged handshakes as she glanced at her phone. It was only thirty-five minutes into their scheduled one-hour discussion. As Leena strode out, Manu scrambled to collect his notes and writing pad to follow her.

"Excuse me. Was it something I said?" Sophia asked.

Manu fixed his stare on the table. "No, no, nothing." He gathered his belongings and headed to the door, but a thought caught him before he made it out of the room. He swivelled side to side, as stiff as a board, searching for the words. Not finding what he was after, he reached out for a handshake. "Have a good day."

Sophia grabbed his hand, not to exchange pleasantries but to keep him from leaving. "You said something."

Manu tried to retract his arm, but her grip was firmer than he expected. "Thanks for coming." He shook her hand again, still avoiding eye contact. She squashed his hand harder, making him squeal like hot air forced out of a kettle. "Okay, okay, we knew you were from Eastle but didn't realise you were from the project office."

"I also have experience as a product analyst. I did it five years ago. I can do it with my eyes closed."

"Project office is under Sam? Samuel Abraham?"

"Yeah?"

"Well... uhh... he's—"

"What?" She squeezed his hand harder.

Manu squirmed, trying to hold in his cries of pain. "Uhh... we've got... I mean... he's..."

"You're not hiring me because of him?"

"Well... we can't... you... I didn't say that."

She threw his hand away in disgust. It all made sense

now. The countless rejections. All the, "I'll get back to you," but no follow up. How could she have been that stupid? She felt so used. She had already moved on, but clearly, he had not. Wasn't it enough to ruin her job at Eastle without ruining her career as well? Anger welled up inside her.

She stormed out of the office lift and onto the ground lobby, wiping her makeup off, furious that she had cheapened herself, thinking it would make an iota of difference. Her phone was already glued to her ear as she removed the visitor's pass around her neck, slapped it on the counter and strode out of the building, and waited... and waited... and waited for the other end of the line to pick up.

"You've called Sam Abraham. Leave your message," the voice message instructed.

"Call me," she said curtly after the beep before hanging up. But she wasn't done. She turned on WhatsApp. *Sacking me isn't enough for you?* she texted. She stared at her phone, fixed on the check marks. First, a grey check appeared next to the message (sent successfully), then another (delivered to the recipient's phone). She waited for the double ticks to turn blue (message seen). Seconds turn to minutes. A minute passed... two... then ten. Nothing.

---

ord Construct. A game where random letters had to be connected to form words of four or more letters. To conquer level 164, Teri was given the letters *A, R, E, A, I, F, F* to solve the crossword puzzle. It was a simple and addictive game, yet very frustrating. She reviewed what she had already: *fare, fair, fear, rife, fire, afire, riff, raff, aria, raffia.* Just one more. It had been a full nine minutes since she had solved her last word. She sighed, looking at Sam next to her in bed, earphones in, eyes glued to his phone. Together, but separate. That's how it was for the Abrahams lately.

She placed her phone on the bedside table, taking a break... then shrieked.

Sam brushed the back of his hand along her thigh under the blanket. "Hey, beautiful." He smiled.

Teri pulled away, surprised by his contact. "What was that?"

He leaned into her, dabbing kisses along her arm, making his way to her lips. "I can't say my own wife is beautiful?"

She flashed a coy smile and said, "Maybe," as she

surrendered to his smooches. She closed her eyes, but her nose twitched, scrunching up. She pushed him away.

"What?" Sam leant back into her to brush more kisses on her neck.

"Did you change colognes?" She dug her nose into his neck before pulling back again, frowning. It was a bitter, citrusy smell; not a cologne he had in his collection, but the smell was familiar.

"Shhh," he hushed, "talk later." He tried to kiss her on the lips, but her hands blocked him from getting closer.

With the frown still scrawled on her face, Teri tried to pinpoint the smell. "It's like that smell..."

"Okay! I forgot." He flipped onto his back. "Do we need to keep talking about it?" He stared at the ceiling, lamenting the missed opportunity of a romantic night.

"It's just... you never hand-washed anything before."

He turned away from her, "I already said sorry for our anniversary." He pushed his earphones back in to watch a rotund chiropractor on YouTube contort a victim-patient at disagreeable angles in order to obtain the loudest spinal cracks.

Teri reached for her phone on the bedside table before glancing back to him. She had been flipping back and forth since she first heard it. Since the mood was interrupted anyway, what difference would it make? She cleared her throat.

"Amy said something the other day," she finally said.

He grunted. He wasn't in a talking mood, especially after her rejection.

"Said it came from your phone," she continued. Sam winced as the chiropractor almost twisted the patient's neck off, letting out a ripple of crackles. "Sam!" Teri snapped, slapping his leg.

He tore his earphone out from his ear. "What?"

"Amy said, 'You're making me real hard,' when she was having a bath. She said it was from your phone."

"Where did she get that from?"

"I know!" Her eyes couldn't escape his phone. His constant texting and excited smirks were always a source of second thoughts. Those doubts could easily be quelled if she could just inspect – no, browse – his phone.

"She wasn't eating dinner, so I said she's making it real hard for me to give her ice cream if she didn't finish." He turned his back to her, still sulking at her rejection.

"She said you shouted at her and snatched the phone."

"Imagine if she sent an email to someone at work."

Hmmm. Teri wasn't sure how she felt any more. There was no hesitation in Sam's response. Did she misread the situation? Shouldn't she be relieved that there was no sexual innuendo? *You're making me hard. Real hard,* she repeated in her mind. She couldn't explain her unease when Amy blurted it out at bath time. It didn't exactly match his explanation, but perhaps the message was lost during her daughter's recollection?

Sam plugged his earphones back in. A couple of WhatsApp notifications appeared on his phone. He flicked away the message from Sophia, and went straight to Henry's, frowning when he saw it.

"What's going on at work?" Teri had to get it off her chest.

Sam didn't react to her as he rubbed his tired face, crafting a delicate response in his mind before replying to his boss: *Of course I want to but we already met Wednesday. Next Friday?* His thumb moved to the *Send* button, but he added a smiley face to the end of the message to soften the blow.

Teri tapped his back. "I said, what's going on with—"

Sam pulled out his earphones, sitting up in bed, cutting her off. "What's with all the questions? What's going on with *you*?"

"What are you talking about?"

Sam sat on the edge of the bed with his back to his wife. "You've been acting all weird lately. You're always on your phone, asking *me* all these questions. Sometimes I wonder if you're projecting, like you're trying to cover up something." He stormed off into the bathroom.

Teri looked around the room, lost. Projecting? Her? If anything, didn't he do just that? She tried to shake off his insinuation. She reached for her phone, opening *Word Construct*. She couldn't sleep now. She stared at it before striking inspiration, tapping the letters *A, F, F, A, I, R* into the game. Confetti and streamers spilled across her screen. Congratulations! She had made it to level 165.

36

___

Perspiration glistened on Sophia's face. She rolled onto her back again, revealing a damp outline. Like a Whoops-a-Daisy toy that snapped upright at the push of a button, she jolted up on her bed, disorientated. There was an intense burn in her heart, incinerating its core, draining her breath. Her body tingled with pins and needles and all her joints ached. She wiped the sweat from her forehead and commanded herself to snap out of it as if it were as simple as that. She pounded her chest, hoping the bruise would override the unfamiliar intense burning inside. It was futile. The incinerator burned bright and ferocious.

Night-time was the worst. In the still of darkness, there was nothing to distract her from all the negativity. Everyone else was asleep, the shops were closed, no buses or trains, and she couldn't go for a walk because, well, it was dark and likely dangerous. She reached for her phone. Still no missed calls or text messages from Sam. Her messages weren't even marked as read. She blew a breath out, tired of the conspiracy, and tired of the burden of caring for Lewis.

Uncomfortable on the damp sheets, she pulled the

blanket away and headed to the kitchen, downing a glass of water so quickly that she heaved to catch her breath as she slammed the glass back onto the worktop. She turned back towards her bedroom but instead of heading straight for the stairs, she circled around, wandering through the dark house. The night was peaceful – exactly the opposite to how she felt. Was she the only one suffering tonight?

Sophia walked past Lewis' bedroom and peered through the crack of the door. He looked so peaceful, like a mannequin, innocent in his sleep next to Pillowy. She could have mistaken him for a normal person; whatever *normal* meant. She wandered to her parents' bedroom, where the nocturnal light bounced off the dressing table mirror, casting pale shadows around the room. She must have forgotten to draw the curtains before she went to bed. She panned across the room from the doorway. Snippets of memories flashed back: "Congratulations on your promotion!" her father said. "Get married and settle down," her mother encouraged. Her eyes stuttered across to their bed, her mind seeing a sick little girl curled up under the blanket while her parents fussed over her.

Her gaze wandered up to the ceiling. As much as she tried, she could not avert her eyes from that damn spot. She took small steps into the room and, like a mosquito to light, she gravitated under the spot where her father had hanged himself. A shiver ran down her spine. She shook off her slippers, her feet damp on the carpet. She couldn't remember the last time her feet had sweated. She took in a long breath, almost smelling her own desperation on that fateful night. She pressed her sleeve under her nose, stifling the tears that were bubbling to burst out.

So many unanswered questions buzzed in her mind. Could she have done anything differently? Why didn't Lewis come sooner? If only she had known the signs of impending suicide. If only she had been stronger to lift him up. The more she thought about it, the more the bubbles of anguish, hurt and self-pity threatened to burst out. She crooked her elbow across her eyes, forcing the tears back. She hated to admit that she was human, like *those* people, but sometimes the toll was too much; except, sometimes was happening more frequently.

What's done is done.

She dragged a chair under the light fitting, scratching the floor. She tiptoed onto it as she lassoed the wiring around her neck. Wouldn't it be great to escape it all? It could be as easy as clicking her fingers. Another shiver ran down her spine. Her heart raced. *Ready?*

One Mississippi... A long moment passed before her next breath, almost hyperventilating.

Two Mississippis... She imagined the nothingness that would come after this worldly life. A life that had hardly been worth living lately. She was a failure without a way out. She couldn't find a place to rent because she was a failure. She couldn't get a job because she was a failure. Even if she found one, what was the point? Her sweaty hands gripped the cable around her neck. Her knuckles bulged, turning white.

Two-and-a-half... She was trapped. Trapped in a shitty job, in a shitty house, and worst of all, with her shitty brother. *Super.Cali.Fragi...* How long would it take to lose consciousness? Would it even hurt? *Listic.Expi.Alidocious...* She lifted her leg in front of her, ready to kick the chair away with her other. Her heart pounded so hard that the thumps found their way to her head.

Three!

She held her breath.

And... froze.

Her hands gripped the wiring so tight that it cut into her palms. As much as she wanted to end it all, it would be unfair to abandon Lewis, no matter how shitty he was. She knew first-hand how shitty it was when her father had so selfishly left them without even saying goodbye.

Sophia climbed down from the chair and lay on the floor, her adrenaline escaping. She let her head fall to the side in exhaustion, catching sight of something underneath the cupboard. Something white, small, but her eyes grew too heavy and shuttered to a close.

She was in a daze. Kilometres away. Her hair flickered across her face as she floated on a field of grass. Time froze. The outside world no longer existed. As the white thing floated into her vision, invading her daydream, her eyes snapped open. Curiosity got the better of her. She fished out the folded paper and read it in the dim light.

My dearest Soph and Lew,

Sorry. I know my words will never be enough. I hope one day you will find it in your heart to forgive me. I thought I had the strength after Mum's death. I had questions for her. I was too weak. It was too painful. Please forgive me.

Soph – Look after Lew. Please.

Sorry again and always.

Love forever. Dad.

Sophia pressed her knees to her chest, curling tighter into a ball. Like a failing dam that could no longer hold the pressure, her sobs burst out, spilling out the raw anguish and pain that she had robbed herself of expressing. What the hell was she supposed to do with that? If he couldn't handle life, how the hell was *she* supposed to? She would never forgive him. Never. Not ever. She shook with each cry, her jaws ached from trying to control her sobs, and the stone in her throat forced her to hiccup sharp breaths. Sophia pressed her palms onto her eyes, but the tears still found a way to leak through.

A head rested on her shoulder. "Mummy always said everything will be okay," Lewis said.

"I can't. I just can't anymore!" Sophia cried, burying her face in her arms. For a person who always had it together, she was ashamed to admit she couldn't cope, even if it was only in front of Lewis.

He lay next to her, wrapping his arm around his sister. "You can. *We* can."

For most of her life, Sophia had never felt close to her brother. She resented all the attention her parents gave him, deeming him a hindrance to her achieving greatness. She had always been ashamed of having a brother with *special needs*, but that disappeared in the moment. His arm around her was all she needed. There was no need for a long-winded Tony Robbins-styled speech. Sometimes, less was more.

37

———

May placed her flat white on the edge of the table, frowning. She slid her cup to the side, but her handbag already occupied the cramped space. She moved it to the other side but couldn't find room next to the mountainous Rainbow Decadent ice-cream dessert. Unsure, she pushed her cup to the only available space on the table, careful not to tip her coffee over.

"So unpractical," she said, looking at her drink under the arm of the antique Singer treadle sewing machine that partitioned her from the person sitting across from her.

"Why don't we sit over there?" Sam asked, pointing to the second-hand sofa under the *Cycle Up* sign, behind a bookshelf of disused books, as he swallowed a spoonful of the four-flavoured ice cream.

"It's fine," she said without checking behind her; she didn't intend to stay for long.

Sam rose to his feet, carrying the Rainbow Decadent ready for the transfer to the sofa. "It's a bigger table. It'd be comfier."

May remained heavy in her seat. She flashed a glance at the time on her wrist. "I've got a meeting at three."

There was a pause. Both didn't know how to continue the conversation given their last face-to-face encounter. She bounced her gaze around the room before settling on the vintage bicycles hanging on the walls. Even considering the rigid metal frames, thin iron-banded wheels, and the narrow hard-as-a-rock saddles, the basic design of bikes hadn't changed over the decades except, perhaps, for the penny-farthing with its absurd oversized front wheel and a saddle that must have sat at least a metre and a half from the ground.

"Everyone wonders the same thing."

"I wasn't wondering about anything in partic—"

"There's a mounting peg above the smaller wheel." Sam pointed at the penny-farthing. "So, to get on it, you have to roll the bike to get momentum when you're on the peg, so you don't fall off. If you don't break a bone doing that, you have to hang onto the handlebar and swing your butt up to the seat. Easy, huh?" He slid a spoon towards her. "This is almost as good as drinks." He shrugged as he dug into the ice-cream bowl again. "Almost."

But May wasn't there to socialise. "So, what happened to Sophia? I thought she already got the job."

She pulled in her handbag, balancing on the edge of the table, squashing it against the cast-iron sewing machine. "Thought maybe she didn't like something about the role that I should be aware of."

"You know I can't talk about someone else. Breach of privacy. Let's just say, she needed to find new opportunities outside the firm."

"Then, why me? A lot of people would want the role."

"This is a good role reversal. *I* need to explain why *you* should get the job!" He smiled, leaning forward. "You're already on the project team, so you know what we're trying to do. Plus, you wanted something challenging. Here's something challenging."

"Well." May fixed her eyes down at the table. She didn't want to come across as a nag, who was always focussed on one thing but if she were going to take up the role, it needed to be on the right terms. "What about the—"

"Don't worry, you'll be paid properly. Above market."

"I wasn't going to ask about that. I don't want to..." She sighed. "Sam, when I say no, it's a no." She pushed her handbag in from the edge of the table again.

"Like I said before, that's all in the past."

"Past?" She paused. How could he dismiss her so casually? She reached for her flat white under the arm of the sewing machine, took a sip and slid her handbag into its place. Set between her and Sam, it was an awkward place for her bag, but at least she didn't have to worry about it now.

"I'm conscious you have another meeting after this. Are you really going to let this opportunity slip by again?"

"Like I said, it depends on the terms..."

"Remember, what happened was consensual." He raised his eyebrows, nodding, trying to obtain her concurrence.

"Was it?" May looked away. She didn't need to partake in his not-so-subtle psychological games. She pushed her handbag towards the centre of the table as she made room for her cup.

Sam swallowed another scoop of ice cream, shivering. "I don't think this is the right place for this conversation."

"No, there's never a right place for what you did to me."

"Whoa, whoa, whoa!" He froze with his hands in the air. May couldn't tell whether he was trying to find the right words for his response or if a brain freeze had come over him from one too many scoops of ice cream. "Do you want the role or not?"

Her head dropped to her chest. If he didn't get what she was trying to get at, she would spell it out for him.

"Terms," she said curtly. "One, 'no' means 'no'. Two, the messages are not funny. Stop sending—"

"It was just a bit of tummy," Sam laughed. "And the pants didn't fit so I couldn't zip up the fly."

"You think this is all a joke?"

He leaned back into his seat, tossing his spoon into the Rainbow Decadent bowl, clanging it against the side. "Calm down, woman. You're forgetting that *I* set the terms."

May glanced at her watch again. She had learnt the hard way to schedule back-to-back time when meeting with Sam so there would be a face-saving reason to leave when she needed to – not that she needed an excuse today after the bridge that she was burning. She stood up and grabbed her handbag. "I got what I need." As she turned on her heels, marching past a bathtub full of soil planted with a variety of vegetables, she reached into her handbag and pressed *Stop* on her phone.

38

———

A haze shimmered off the concrete pavement, the heat potent enough to blister the soles of any foolish-brave barefoot walker. Sophia trudged with the resignation of a broken soldier. She pulled out her phone, still grated by Sam's sabotage of not only her job but also her career. The grey ticks next to her messages also irked her; he still hadn't read them.

She was almost there, or so Google Maps told her. In any event, it was easy enough to spot an open viewing. If the real estate agents standing outside the property didn't give it away, the plastic signs and feather banner flags did. She unfolded a note, scanning the details. She had viewed so many properties already that it was hard keeping track. For the gem at 115 Myrtle Road, inspection was at 11.30 am and it was only 11.07 am. In this white-hot rental market, deals were done minutes after viewing, and after missing out on the last nine properties, Sophia had learnt it was better to show up early. Price? POA – Price On Application. She just hoped that meant $300 per week or below.

"Sup! The name's Mohammed. You can call me Mo. I'll be here if you have any questions," greeted Mr Ismail.

"It's only me, Mo." By now, she was familiar with all the realtors since there were only a handful within the radius of her property search. "Friends look after friends... right?" She raised an eyebrow at him.

He gestured to her shoes. "Miss, if you wouldn't mind."

She turned back to look for her brother. Lewis was a good twenty-five metres away, sunbeat and flustered. His head was bowed, angled to the ground, as he stoop-walked with arms unnaturally still beside him. He stopped under a tree providing precious shade, cutting an awkward sight.

He craned his neck out for a better view and counted on his fingers. He was three houses away, instead of four – not far enough to be out of sight of the real estate agent. He dragged himself out of the shade and back into the stifling heat, stopping at the previous house where the naked sun roasted him.

"Lewis," Sophia yelled, waving her arms around. It wasn't a good idea to walk in the searing heat, but what was she to do on an ever-reducing bank balance?

"Lewis," she yelled again, breaking the peace of the quiet neighbourhood and sending a wandering cat scurrying for cover underneath a car. Again, it didn't reach him.

Instead, his arms trembled, his head snapped back, jerking erratically in all directions. Tremors shook him, causing his legs to spasm. As his knees were about to give in, his sister's voice boomed into his ear. "You better have some of this." She handed him a bottle of water, leading him by the wrist to the apartment.

At $285 per week, the property reflected the asking price. A greasy electric stove, caked with the cooking oils of every tenant from the last decade or longer, a small but passable lounge, and a single bedroom. Someone would have to sleep on the sofa but with four days until eviction, it wasn't the time to be picky. Not even the shower, with its hideous orange-brown rippled tempered glass, could turn her away. The strong odour, however, was just about enough. An organic, pungent, skunky smell; it was worse than cigarettes. Was that the smell of weed?

"You've got my details already," she said to Mohammed after her blistering view of the property. "$290 a week."

"Listen, Miss. Soph. I'm sorry—"

"Don't do this again, Mo. How much do you want? $295? $300?"

"Miss, listen. Market's hot at the moment. It's the best thing about a recession!"

What an insensitive prick. She understood what he meant. As the economy slowed, more people rented, instead of buying their own home. Given their job uncertainty, they didn't want to be tied down by a mortgage, and if she were a theoretical economist, she might have agreed with him, but the rising rent was affecting her real life, not some theoretical statistic in some academic economic model.

"How much?" She braced herself for a ridiculous number.

"A big three-two-five." He flashed his fingers as he said the numbers.

"$300 is my max." She held up her fingers. "Three. Please."

"You're having a laugh!"

"You don't understand. I *need* this."

"Listen, bruv. I'd love to help but we ain't no charity. I gotta put food on the table for me and the missus too."

She opened her purse, snatched out some notes and

pressed them into Mohammed's hand. "Here, that's $1,200 for the month's rent. Cash. Take it."

But he wouldn't. He slipped his hands behind his back. "Like, we ain't blind." Mohammed flicked his eyes over to Lewis. "I can't tell the lord of the land that the tenant's gonna be a uno female; I gotta write, 'plus a bruva from the same momma with special requirements,' you know I mean?" He punctuated *special requirements* with air apostrophes.

Sophia threw dagger eyes at him. "Yeah, I know what you mean." Her eyes were so sharp, Mo stepped back lest they jump out and shred him to bits. She crowded his face.

"You can suck it if you don't want both of us."

Her fury was less about the rejection of Lewis and more about his rebuff of her. She stormed out of the apartment, leaving her brother behind... but she didn't get far.

LEWIS TOOK A STEP CLOSER, BENDING HIS KNEES, ABOUT TO SIT but stood up again, scratching his head. He looked at her before sitting next to her. Sophia buried her face in her arms, under the same tree that had provided him respite. He shifted away from her; perhaps he was too close. He glanced over again but kept to himself. It wasn't his fault, he wanted to say. He didn't forget his sister telling him over and over that there was more luck securing an apartment as a single female than a tenant with an autistic brother, so when he overshot his mark earlier, he corrected himself as soon as he finger-counted. He was fine waiting for her in the sun. Honest.

He placed an arm around her as he looked the other way, not wanting her to see how bad he felt. "Sor... sorry."

"It's not you," she said without looking up.

He shifted away from her, giving her the space that she needed. He dug his nails into his forearms and pinched his hands to allay his guilt. He looked around and walked off, leaving her a hunched figure on the side of the road.

After a moment, Sophia looked up. It was too quiet. She looked to the right, no Lewis. Swivelled back – he wasn't at the house. She turned to the left. He was as still as a mannequin, back at the fourth house, wilting in the heat. She waved at him. "Come back!"

Lewis stood still. He wasn't going to move again, no matter how much he sweated. He stared at the ground, guilt preventing him from looking at her.

"Come on!" Sophia said as she approached him to drag him back into the shade.

But his legs wouldn't move. Instead, his pupils flicked over like the old-fashioned split-flap airport departure boards – slowly at first and without warning – the white of his eyes flashed. His hearing tunnelled, zeroing on his breathing which was much louder than usual. His body spasmed and convulsed. His legs finally gave way, collapsing and hitting his head. In his semi-conscious state, incoherent, noisy, chaotic images flashed in his mind: a scruffy man with long oily hair, the number nine flashed up along with a street sign, and a derelict white house perimetered by broken fencing.

"Lew!" he heard as he came to.

Sophia tapped his cheeks. "Shh..." she hushed, calming herself more than him as she rubbed his earlobes. "I told you not to—"

He opened his eyes and grimaced, feeling the back of his head. He was no longer on the searing pavement but on the lawn of someone's front garden. "Man," he said randomly.

"Sit," Sophia insisted.

"Bowl... pinch. Bowlpinch Road."

She touched the back of his head. "It's bleeding."

He was not interested. The knock to his head was nothing compared to the craters he made when he head-butted the plasterboard at home. He sprang to his feet, grabbing her by the wrist. He was on a mission.

THE FOUR-LANE TRAFFIC WAS NOISY WITH NEVER-ENDING tyres whizzing across the asphalt, tooting horns, and the occasional case of road rage for high crimes such as not indicating when merging into a lane. It didn't help that King George's Road was a major artery to the city. Sophia coughed into her hand and pinched her nose, trying to spew out the contaminants from her lungs whilst not inhaling more as a long black cloud of smoke billowed from a lorry's exhaust. Lewis grinned and giggled, bursting with excitement, still holding Sophia's wrist. "Come, Sis. Come."

"We have food at home," she said, conscious of their budget.

They stopped at a traffic light where a side turning branched off the highway. Lewis impatiently bashed the traffic button as he waited for the green pedestrian. Sophia looked at her tired feet and regretted not wearing something more comfortable than thin sandals. Lewis' shoes were no better: a sorry pair of white – formerly white – Dunlop Volley sneakers that were falling apart. She would clean them, but he didn't like the scent of newly washed things. Without warning, Lewis dropped her wrist and bolted across the road. She ran after him but the wall of vehicles barrelling down the road barricaded her. "Stop, Lewis!" she screamed but was drowned out by the traffic.

A delivery truck slammed on its brakes, skidding across the road. "What the—" the driver screamed. His profanity was cut off by his furious bashing of his horn, which encouraged more rage from other drivers as they swerved and whiplashed to a stop. Oblivious to the trail of destruction he had caused, Lewis ran towards a house, where a man with oily hair and clothes two sizes too big had just exited from. With a clipboard in one hand and a skinny brown paper bag in the other, it took a moment or three for him to lock the front door. He rewarded himself by taking a swig from the brown paper bag, stumbling down the steps. A twisted ankle was averted when he caught the railing at the last moment.

"Man!" Lewis pointed to the stranger.

Sophia ran across the road, waving apologetically to the angry motorists, and passed the Bowlpinch Road sign. *Hmmm.*

"Never do that again!" she scolded.

"Don't worry. It's just water," the man replied, slurring his words and unsteady on his feet.

Sophia recoiled, trying to escape the man's alcoholic breath. She squinted at his name badge: *Tony Jevtovic. CentraLand Realty.*

"Bowlpinch Road." Lewis pointed to the house as he guarded Tony from leaving. Not that the crumbling knee-high perimeter fence provided much of a hindrance.

She absorbed the property in front of her: the white paint on the weatherboard cladding was peeling off and was cracked in places. In most places. Well, in all places. Unattended greenery grew on the house, green moss emanated from behind the waterspouts and dandelions dotted the rain gutters – some had turned to fluffy seedheads to be blown off after making a wish. The garden was overgrown with knee-high weeds, and the concrete walkway, which snaked from the pavement to the front door, had almost disappeared under the overgrowth, save a few patches of grey concrete that peeked out the same way as a scalp beneath a comb-over. To the right, two lines of tyre prints emerging from the muddy crevice suggested it was a bog for vehicles on rainy days. The back garden, if she could call it that, was visible from the front gate. Given the property sat at an intersection, it was more of a side garden, offering as much privacy as a loo in a glass box. In real estate parlance, the house was a 'renovator's delight'.

"Let's go." She pulled Lewis along, already mulling over how she could make up the lost time they had wasted in finding this property. She should have been firmer with Lewis than to let him drag her all the way out here.

He brushed her away. "Hou—ouse."

"With a bit of tidying up and $230 per week, it could be your home too," Tony stammered.

"How much did you say?" she asked.

"Like I said, for $210 per week, it can be your home too."

Now he had her attention. "$210?"

"You drive a hard bargain, lady. I'll tell you what. $200 just for you. Sign now, move in today. She's been on the market for nine weeks." Tony swivelled his brown paper bag, stirring the last drops in the bottle. "I gotta get rid of her, if you know what I mean."

Sophia wasn't sure whether he meant the house or the bottle. Anyway, was it a genuine offer or would he regret it later? She wasn't the one plying him with alcohol, plus no one had forced him to bargain, and after being rejected for so many properties, she had long given up being picky. The issues that the other properties had – the leaking tap, the toilet that only half flushed, the swollen bathroom door that wouldn't close due to the humidity, the temperamental hot-water system and many more niggles – were all better than not having a roof over their heads. Sure, it was adjacent to a main road but that just meant she didn't need to set an alarm for the morning. At just $200 per week, when other properties were closer to $300, it was hard to beat. She snatched the clipboard sandwiched under Tony's armpit. "Two hundred?"

"Sign up, sign up!"

39

The dusty, stale and sour air assaulted her senses. The mouldy patches were like an awful blotch painting that no one had asked for. The black-grey-green stains of irregular shapes and sizes bloomed across the ceiling and walls, some growing on top of others, whilst tentacles radiated out of others like webs.

Sophia struggled to open the curtainless windows in the living room, a large black bin bag hanging off her arm – her temporary wardrobe. She looked around for an empty space. She didn't want to dump the bag on the flaky dull-red carpet, which kicked up dust and who-knew-what-else every time she stepped on it.

"Lewis!" Her call echoed across the empty space that was now home. A moment passed before heavy footsteps raced towards the front of the house, threatening to break the floorboards with each thud. She closed her eyes, praying it wouldn't give way as the creaks became louder.

Lewis swooped into the room with his arms extended sideways, leaving a cloud of dust in his wake. "Airplane... I'm... airplane."

She coughed, "Slowly, Lew, slowly," holding her breath and swatting the dust cloud away. As she carried her temporary wardrobe out, he shadowed her into the corridor, past the two bedrooms, to the back of the house and into the kitchen. Everything was in much the same state of disrepair. The only place she could rest her clothes was on the kitchen worktop, which was also covered in a thin layer of dust – well, she hoped it was only dust. She tried to open the window, but the wooden frames wouldn't budge. She tried again, yanking harder. This time, the window smacked the top of the frame, almost shattering the glass. Finally, some air but it wasn't much better. Being adjacent to a road as busy as King George's meant the air quality was probably as good as smoking a pack or two of cigarettes a day.

Everywhere she looked was bad news. She wanted to escape. Anywhere would be better than this dump. She needed to get out. Was this buyer's remorse? She spun around but couldn't find what she was looking for. She stepped towards a thin sheet of hardboard, no more than half a centimetre thick, and tentatively poked at it. At least it was reinforced with a Z-brace and fitted with a padlock. But, surely, it couldn't be the back door, their only defence from the outside world, could it? Did the padlock mean it could only be locked from the inside?

Lewis reached for the keys and tried to unlock the door but there was no need. The rusted metal latch helpfully fell off as soon as he touched it.

Sophia motioned him to the side. "Hang on." She nudged the door around the edges, careful not to punch a hole through the flimsy board. The worn brown packaging tape that sealed the bottom of the door almost disintegrated when she pushed the door open, revealing a small yard. Apart from the overgrown lawn and weeds that sprawled everywhere, there was also a random assortment of bushes. It was anyone's guess about what once had grown there as the only remnants were the bare branches, so brittle they made grandma's osteoporotic bones look strong and healthy.

Lewis flapped his arms, kicking his legs wildly, and let out a loud shriek. *Not another episode.* She suspended her cursing before it could escape her mouth as she stomped her feet and let out a sharp shrill. A colony of bull ants scurried into the kitchen, swarming up their legs. She yanked Lewis by the collar and double-backed into the kitchen. Rushing over to her bag of clothes on the kitchen bench, she grabbed a shirt and flicked, slapped and stomped on the invasion. She slammed the door closed and jammed the shirt in the gap under the door. Who would have thought the disintegrating brown tape had been serving a purpose? $200 per week? What a bargain. Did the previous tenants die from ant bites or respiratory illness from the polluting traffic?

WITH THEIR WORLDLY POSSESSIONS STREWN ACROSS THE house, Sophia rested on a box marked *Bedroom* in the hallway, checking her phone. The checkmarks next to the messages had turned blue. Sam had finally read them. She simmered with a dull rage as she strategised her next move.

She dialled his number, but there was no response. She re-dialled over and over but it diverted to voicemail each time. The monotonous drone of the dial tone was hypnotic, so she was caught off-guard when the ringing was cut short on the fourth call. He had hung up on her.

Pick up! she texted. She was in the middle of typing another text when her phone rang.

"I'm disappointed," Sam said. "You think I'm going to reply to your messages so you can take a screenshot of it? You think I don't know about your chats with Jimmy? Who do you think he works for?"

"I'll drop it all if you just stop."

Sam laughed. "Finding it a wee bit difficult to get a job, huh?"

"You win, okay? You win."

"This isn't about winning or losing."

"Then what do you want?" Her voice rose, already tired of his games.

"Just remember you did all this to yourself. I gave you *so* many chances."

She wanted to tell him to screw himself but the last time she had shown any bravado, it hadn't exactly worked out for her. "Just stop, and I'll drop it."

"You could've had it all. Now, look at you. Mummy and Daddy are dead, and you're stuck with... what did you say he was... 'that retard brother'?"

There was a long pause. Her restrained breath amplified down the phone line. "Like I said, I'll drop the case if—"

"You think *you've* got a case?"

"Sticking your tongue in my mouth, and... and... ripping my dress, and... holding me against my will wasn't good enough for you?"

"Don't pretend you didn't like it."

"You disgusting pig!" She hung up.

The call didn't go quite as she had planned. She despised being outplayed. Not only was waiting for his reply a waste of time, Sophia felt more abused. She had hoped that he had used the time to mull over his options, and as improbable as it was, deep down she had wished he would accede to her pleas, as the generous, empathetic Sam she had once known may have done. But now, she didn't recognise the monster that he had become.

40

———

Running west to east, the picturesque Parramatta River snaked through one of Sydney's busiest metropolitan areas. It had something for everyone: restaurants for those looking for a meal, cycle tracks and footpaths for the fitness-conscious or those who enjoyed the outdoors, water sports for the more adventurous, and the Riverside Theatre for a splash of cultural enrichment.

"You really didn't have to," Teri said, ambling along the riverbank. "We need a 'next time' so *I* can pay for lunch."

Sophia waved her off, pretending that their $65 lunch bill didn't worry her. "Don't be silly, Teri. Our catch up was long overdue."

"Well, it was very nice. Thank you."

Sophia forced a smile, wondering how she could raise the topic. Not that she didn't enjoy Teri's company but if she didn't bring it up soon, it would have been a wasted outing, not to mention a waste of the $65 that she could barely afford.

"I forgot to ask, how's Amy doing at school?" she enquired instead.

"She loves it." Teri beamed. "I was worried on her first day, but she was happier to play with the other kids than stay at home with boring old Mummy. I ended up crying instead of her!"

Sophia smiled, nodding. "It's a lottery, isn't it?"

"It's like that sometimes. What about you? Still busy at work?"

She looked over to Teri, checking to see if she really didn't know or if she was having her on. At least the conversation inched closer to what she had wanted to talk about. "Actually, I'm looking for another job."

"I thought you liked it at Eastle?"

"I do... did."

Teri turned to her friend. "Oh."

"Yeah." Sophia shrugged, nonchalant. "Looking for something new now."

"Still in banking?"

"Yeah, but, you know... Anyway, it's not been easy 'cause... Sam's been... his references aren't great... so, yeah..."

"Mmm..."

"It's not because of my work." Sophia quickly pre-empted the question that she felt was on the tip of Teri's tongue.

"Are you joining the half marathon?" Teri asked, changing the subject, not wishing to embarrass her more.

Sophia paused. With their lunch date almost over, she had put it off for long enough. She slowed her walk. "I don't know how to say this. Sam sacked me because I wouldn't..." she trailed off, unable to bring herself to say it. She didn't want to spoil their pleasant lunch, but she didn't know how else to put it. Just texting Teri to invite her out had taken twenty-three minutes and four drafts. Sophia swallowed, her throat dry. She changed tack.

"Would you mind speaking to him about the references? Please?"

"Because you wouldn't what?" Teri probed, peering through narrowed eyes.

"It doesn't matter, really." Sophia waved it off. "If you can speak to him about the references—"

"Because you wouldn't what?"

Sophia stopped, taking off her sunglasses and looked Teri in the eye. "Because I didn't have sex with him."

"What?" Teri's hand flew to her mouth.

"It was a couple of months ago. There's also been other—"

"Why didn't you say something then?"

"It's not that easy. He's the boss."

Teri paused, digesting the information whilst searching for the right words. Despite the rumble of a passing motorboat towing a screaming wakeboarder along the river, the women locked their focus on each other.

"What's not easy," Teri said finally, "is listening to you play the victim while you smear my husband. I know women like you. Everything's fine until it's not. You lost your job and now you want to bring Sam down too!"

"No, no, no..." was all that Sophia could say, taken aback by Teri's response. "I just want him to... I just want a job."

"In case you've forgotten," Teri raised her hand, flashing her wedding ring, "he's married."

Sophia rummaged through her handbag. Where was it? She always knew where it was when she didn't want it, but it had a knack of disappearing just when she needed it. Teri walked off but Sophia matched her pace, stride for stride. "Just give me a minute. I want to show—"

Teri stopped. "Think about what you're doing to his family. Think about what you're doing to *me*," she said, before storming off again.

Sophia watched her disappear into the distance. *Damn it*. She had hope Teri would provide some womanly empathy. She hadn't wanted to bring up Sam's transgressions. She had just wanted him to stop giving misleading character references. She had to make a living somehow. This was *his* fault, not hers. She sighed, reaching for her back pocket. There it was – her mobile phone – just when she didn't need it.

41

"One, two, three..." Lewis pointed to the mini disposable dehumidifiers that dotted the lounge room. "Four!" He held one up for a closer look. *Evaporate moisture and odour quickly,* the label read. He shook it, sloshing the water inside, and sniffed it. The stench of staleness and mould wafted up his nose, causing him to screw up his face.

"Not working," Lewis said.

Sophia shook her gloved hands. "No, no. It evaporates the yucky from the room and puts it in here," she said, tapping the plastic box, "not the other way around."

Lewis nodded. Now that he understood how it worked, he fanned the air into the dehumidifiers, helping it to trap the yucky inside the container.

"I don't think it works like that," she said, smiling, not that Lewis could tell under her mask. "Can you put one in every corner in all the rooms?" She pointed to the stack of disposable dehumidifiers that she had bought on special offer from the discount shop and walked back into the dilapidated bathroom.

Surrounded by bottle upon bottle of liquids, powders, sprays and granules, Sophia continued to scrub the dirt, grime and odours that were embedded onto every surface. It was back-breaking, joint-destroying and finger-cramping work to get every nook and cranny, but she didn't stop until it was all done.

She arched her back, taking stock of her hard work. Much better. The yellow walls were transformed to off-white. The shower screen was no longer coated in soap scum, and the black grout in between the tiles was scrubbed to light grey. It wasn't just for appearances; she couldn't bear the thought of the innumerable bacteria that must have plastered the walls and floors. Her eyes stopped at the toilet bowl. The water level was higher than usual. She had been dreading the moment but couldn't postpone it any longer. She stretched the gloves up to her elbows and held her breath.

Ready? Set? G-g-g... No.

She stopped. She couldn't see herself doing it. She took a few more calming breaths and steeled herself again.

Ready?

Go!

She plunged her arm into the toilet bowl, tickling her fingers around the S-bend to find the blockage as fast as she could. She tried not to picture all the... stuff... the previous tenants had flushed down the toilet as she pushed her arm deeper, cursing the local hardware store that was out of stock of plungers, augers or anything that she could use to avoid swimming in the flush water.

"Shit!" she shrieked, recoiling and ripping off her gloves. Her arm had dug too far, seeping water into her gloves. It sucked not having the right tools, or the money to pay someone to do it instead.

After thoroughly scrubbing her arm, she flushed the toilet again, staring at the rising water filling the bowl. Were all her efforts going to pay off? The water settled at the usual level before draining slowly. She pounded her fist on the toilet rim and missed, getting a good splash onto her face. *Great. Just great.* She rested against the clean wall, giving up. What a long way she had come. She would die if any of her ex-colleagues saw her now.

It had only been a few months ago that she was headed for a promotion and on her way to moving into her own apartment. Well, she had finally scored her own house, but this wasn't exactly what she had in mind. "Lew?" she called out, concerned that it was too quiet. "What are you doing?"

"What you doing?" Lewis parroted back, poking his head into the bathroom.

"You hungry?"

He grinned, disappearing as fast as he had appeared. Sophia rose to follow him but felt like Tin Man from *The Wizard of Oz* creaking back to life. Every joint hurt and she felt as though she had aged several decades. She held the walls as she made it to the doorway but was pushed back in as Lewis came running at her, armed with a roll of cling film.

"Put it back," she groaned, not in the mood for his antics. He pushed past her, unfazed, and unrolled the cling film, zigzagging it up, down, across and around the front of the toilet bowl, then back again, and some more; sealing it in a thick layer of air-tight plastic. It was all over before she knew it.

"I'm too tired, Lew—" She reached for the toilet but before she could peel the film off, he pushed the flush button, releasing water from the cistern and into the bowl.

"Stop!" she cried. She reached for it again as the water

crept to the rim. "You're going to flood us. I just cleaned it." She pushed him out of the room to escape the inevitable mess. "Move, move, move."

"Wa... wait." Lewis pointed to the toilet bowl as she dragged him away. With the air pressure trapped, the cling film inflated on top of the bowl like a balloon. He plonked his bottom onto the bulging plastic, popping the air pressure back into the toilet. As he stood up, water gurgled down the drain. An instant plunger.

Sophia looked at her brother with wide eyes, speechless. When she eventually found the words, what could she say except the obvious?

"You're a genius!"

"LUNCH," SHE ANNOUNCED, PUSHING THE PILE OF PHOTO albums out of the way to make room for the two bowls of instant Shin Ramyun noodles. It wasn't the fanciest of meals, but the friendliest on the purse.

"Better eat it before it absorbs all the water and gets chunky."

Lewis leafed through an album, poring over the mix of everyday shots and posed photographs. There was one where he was hugging his mother at the supermarket, another where the family posed at the swimming pool, another where Sophia had nodded off on the train, and more photos at various restaurants over the years. He traced each person's features, outlining their jaw, eyes, nose, and mouth, re-living the memories. He dug into the spicy noodles. "Hot, hot!" he said, poking his tongue out as he fanned his mouth with his hand.

"How did you know about the toilet thing?" Sophia asked.

He tapped his chest. "My work. From my work."

She stole a look at the albums. Why was she always unsmiling or disinterested in every photo? There was a sense of detachment, an incongruent vibe that separated her from her family, even in the one when they celebrated her then-imminent promotion at Casper Plate.

Lewis slurped up a ball of noodles, letting spots of chilli fly onto the protective screen of the album.

Sophia wiped it off with her sleeve. "Don't wreck it."

Curious, she took an album from the stack. This one was a little older with pictures of when they were six or seven. She grimaced at the questionable fashion that her parents had made them both wear. She shook her head in disapproval.

"Look at our hair."

"Our hair."

"Yuck?"

Lewis nodded at first before shaking his head. Sophia had a ponytail, complemented by a fringe cut straight above her eyes. For Lewis, it was the traditional bowl cut. Like almost every kid with an older sibling in their neighbourhood, he was not spared the hand-me-downs from his sister, and starred in a number of photos in effeminate apparel: a sweater with a unicorn, shirts with *Girls can do anything* and *Smile, sparkle and shine* splayed across them.

Having flicked to the end of the album, Sophia took another. Older than the previous two, these were from a bygone, happier time. In one photo, she cradled her baby brother in her arms on the sofa, softly kissing his forehead. Gayle's blurred hand made it into the corner of the picture as she rushed a protective hand in case little Sophia dropped her tiny brother. Lewis pointed to the photo, then to his chest.

"Lewis, Lewis," he told her in case she hadn't noticed.

"Yes, that's you."

Another showed the siblings as toddlers sitting on the ledge of a shop window with one arm wrapped around each other, enjoying their ice cream. Blue bubble-gum flavour was smeared across Lewis' mouth like a badly painted clown. Sophia was no better with her own strawberry-red lips. He pointed to the picture, grinning, "Ice cream," and traced his mouth to indicate the mess on his face.

"Mum and Dad used to take us whenever they had a bit of money."

"Because... your favourite," Lewis said, pointing at his sister.

Sophia pulled back from the album. Creases rippled her forehead as she cast her mind back to the time of the photo.

"No, we went there because of you."

Lewis shook his head. "No, no, no." He tapped his finger on her nose. "Because, your favourite."

Hmm. She looked at him. When did she become so jaded that she rewrote her own history? Funny how time distorted memories. She turned the page. In this photo, Sophia was in her primary school uniform, trying to piggy-back Lewis but failing terribly. Despite being only fifteen months younger, he was almost as big as her. She couldn't get a handle on his legs in the picture, which dangled to the side. He had wrapped his arms around her neck, holding on for dear life, and inadvertently strangling her.

"That was after school. I said I'd pick you up," Sophia reminisced.

"Too big. Lewis, too big."

"No, I was too small." She turned the page again,

revealing a torn and crumpled A5-sized drawing that was pieced together again. The stick figures were of a smiling family – mother, father, daughter and son – in a line, holding hands, in a garden where roses and flowers blossomed. In the background, smoke billowed from the chimney of a house with boxed windows. The top left was quartered by the yellow sun, its rays radiating out to the family, drawing out their smiles. At the bottom was Gayle's handwriting, *Everything will be okay.*

"Drawing," Lewis said, pleased that he knew the word. He slurped the last strands of instant noodles, once again peppering the album with dots of orange chilli sauce. He waited for her to scold him, but it didn't come. Sophia was still staring at the tears in the photo, which were all random, except for one that neatly sliced the son and daughter apart. The son's face was heavily scribbled out, the paper pressed in with anger. Was it that bad? How did their relationship deteriorate so badly? She already knew the answer.

No matter how much she had achieved, it had never been enough. She hadn't asked for elaborate or expensive gifts. In fact, she hadn't asked for any gifts. She had understood they didn't have money to splash around but was a simple, *Well done, keep up the good work,* too much to ask for? If her own family disregarded her, she would reciprocate and make it on her own. Selfish? Perhaps, but she preferred to call it *necessary.* But what did she have to show for all the hard work now? She slammed the album closed.

Lewis turned away, guilty about spotting the album with chilli sauce.

"Let's do something," she said, her eyes lighting up.

He scooped the bottom of his bowl, revealing coarse dots of the artificial flavouring. "Soup."

"Don't drink it. It's yucky," Sophia said but she couldn't

stop him from striding to the rubbish bin. He rifled through the trash, plucked out the chilli sachets and flaked the condiments into his bowl before adding hot water.

"Throw it in the sink or the ants will come in," Sophia continued.

But Lewis wasn't in a listening mood. As he approached the backdoor, Sophia jumped in front of him, but he side-stepped her and walked out to the backyard, tracing the trail from the door to the pavement before it disappeared into the unwieldy garden. Unsure of the exact location, he stomped his feet in a small radius and poured the hot chilli soup over the mound. A colony of ants scurried out of the hill, darting aimlessly. Before long, the insects slowed, then stopped.

Sophia was speechless. Again. First the toilet, now this? Was this also one of the advantages of housekeeping at Kings Hotel? It sure was more useful than what *she* had done at Eastle where all targets ultimately led to the firm squeezing clients for as much money as they could get away with.

Lewis grinned. "Let's do something."

42

"Ready?" Sophia looked over her shoulder.

"Go, go, go!" Lewis waved his arms, giddy.

"Three, two, one!" She pushed off and pedalled the bright-yellow tandem. It was one of the dockless, off-the-street hires that scattered the city – the bane of many as riders dumped them anywhere and everywhere, but for now, it provided enjoyment for the siblings. The harbour-side ride was beautiful, with joggers in the adjacent promenade, a mixture of families, children, and wannabe pro-cyclists, not to mention the sparkling harbour itself. Sophia struggled on the slight incline. A tinkling ding-a-ling sounded from behind before a child of eight in training wheels overtook them.

"Go, go, go!" Sophia called out but Lewis was enjoying his free ride too much. Fortunately for her quads, the slope reversed and as they glided down the other side, the cool crisp wind rushed into their faces.

Lewis screamed in excitement, lifting his hands from the handlebar before grabbing it again. The thrill of being free was exhilarating and he did it over and over. Even Sophia felt liberated but that didn't mean he had to ruin the moment and be careless.

"Don't, Lewis," she cautioned.

Riding past a coffee shop, Sophia slammed on the brakes, forgetting about the passenger behind her. The bike fishtailed and almost toppled them over.

"Sorry, sorry, sorry," she repeated, worried that she had frightened him and triggered one of his episodes.

"Again, again, again!" Lewis screamed, matching each apology.

Laughing at his apparent glee, she tried to turn the bike around, but it was stuck. At two-and-a-half metres, it was too long to perform a U-turn. She waved him off the bike, but it wasn't any easier as she wobbled and threatened to tumble over it at any moment. She would have had more luck performing the same manoeuvre in a caravan. She checked again for oncoming bikes, and, against her conscience, dumped – no, parked – the bike where it was, and walked with Lewis the remaining fifteen metres to the café.

"Was that fun?" Sophia asked, tall cappuccino in hand, as they sat at a small table.

"Mm-hmm. Fun," Lewis replied, in between downing an iced chocolate without the cream topping.

It had been weeks since she had enjoyed a cup of coffee, and who knew how long since she was out with her brother alone. She had been busy, she tried to convince herself, but it was disingenuous. Her unsympathetic antagonism didn't help, nor did her hostility which was ready to break out if he so much as breathed louder than usual.

"I'll be back," she said, excusing herself from the table. Not that Lewis minded. He was busy enjoying his treat.

It was either guilt or reminiscence of yesteryears, but

Sophia returned with two ice creams. She hesitated before splurging on them as café ice cream wasn't exactly value for money. They were at least twice as dear as the supermarket variety and without a job, it felt like five times the price, but what the hell. She handed him the blue bubble-gum flavour and kept the strawberry for herself.

"Ice cream. Happy, happy!" Lewis beamed.

"Lew." She motioned him to look up, handing him a serviette. A rogue piece of ice cream threatened to drip off his cone. He giggled and squawked before smothering the blue bubble gum over his lips until he looked like a clown with badly botoxed lips. Sophia's eyes widened in horror. What did she say about ruining the moment again? She closed her eyes and took a deep breath. *Relax.* As she opened them, Lewis poked his tongue out, pulling a face as he disorientated his eyes. Combined with his fish lips, it was too much. She burst out laughing, drawing glances from other diners. To hell with them. She smothered her ice cream over her mouth and onto his face, and it dripped from their nostrils and their chins. Their squeals and guffaws attracted more stares, which became glares, then daggers.

"Quick," she said, suppressing her laughter and pulling him out to leave. They wiped their faces and staggered out.

Walking back to the bicycle, Sophia turned her back to him and braced herself. "I can do it."

Lewis shook his head. Even he knew he was too heavy, no matter how determined she was.

"Come on," she offered again. This time, he didn't need further encouragement. He jumped onto her back, wrapping his legs around her waist and his arms around her neck, almost choking her. Crumbling under her brother's heavy frame, Sophia tilted forward so she could breathe and carry his weight, but it was too much. Her legs gave in and she tumbled onto the grass.

"You're too heavy!" she panted.

Lewis pulled her up from the ground and pointed to his back. "Piggyback."

"You can't," she teased.

"You can. We can!" As Sophia jumped up, he caught her on his back, carrying her back to the bike with the ease of a parent carrying a small child.

"I win," Lewis declared, punching his arms into the air.

THE LAWN WAS NEATLY MANICURED, THE LANDSCAPE TIDY AND beautiful. Old bunya pines, lemon-scented gums, and bull bays swayed in the breeze at Rookwood Cemetery; built in the 1860s and the largest necropolis in the southern hemisphere. Sophia walked the tandem bike over to two tombstones and parked it beside them. She grabbed Lewis' hand, holding it for a long time. She wasn't a believer in the solace of prayer but stood in silence to absorb the passing of her parents; to finally mourn them properly. Lewis stood beside her, silent.

They lay next to their parents' grave. She glanced at him as he watched the clouds float by. What was he thinking? Feeling? Who was he, *really*? Superman, Picasso or the man on the moon?

Lewis cackled. "Hi, Mummy! Hello, Daddy!" he yelled, pointing skywards.

"Hello," she said, playing along. It was cute that he had enough creativity to imagine their parents from the random patterns in the sky.

"How did you know about Bowlpinch Road?" she asked

out of the blue, not entirely sure where the question came from.

"I see it." He tapped his eyes in case she didn't know which part of the body was responsible for sight.

"You mean, you saw it before?"

"In my mind."

"With your eyes, you mean?"

"In my mind," he clarified.

She brushed it off, looking up at the clouds with him. Typical Lewis. It always took that extra effort to have a conversation with him. She squinted, trying to force the white puffs of cloud into facial features but as hard as she tried, she couldn't will them into the shape of her parents. Did Lewis have some kind of superpower? Did he really see them, or was it just his playfulness? She scanned the sky for other clouds, but they were all just random blobs too.

She puffed out a sigh, sending it upwards. It was the first time she had really had a chance to think about her parents since they died. Did that make her a bad person? She couldn't explain why she begrudged her mother. Perhaps it was easier to blame someone else if she didn't succeed. Gayle was an easier target because she had more emotions, or more that she would show anyway; always reacting to her daughter's fits and arguments, unlike her father, who brushed it off.

Guilt bubbled inside Sophia at the thought of how petty and selfish she had been. Why did people leave it too late to express their feelings? A tingle ran through her, rippling from her head to her toes. Her left, logical side of her brain disengaged. Was this the feeling of having emotions? Of being human? Of being one of *them*? Her eyes watered but she willed the tears back, refusing to blink so they wouldn't spill over. A breeze rolled over them, rustling the leaves above them until it picked up strength, flicking her hair across her face.

Lewis drummed his heels into the ground as he pointed to a pair of clouds.

"Love you, Mummy, love you, Daddy," he screamed, competing with the howls of the wind that was fast becoming a gale.

She reached for his hand, holding it tightly, preventing him from being blown away. It didn't matter if he was superman, Picasso or the man on the moon, she couldn't lose him too. As the clouds swept across the sky, Sophia wasn't sure if she was going crazy or if it was the caffeine or sugar rush from the café, but she could have sworn that a pair of clouds remained stationary.

"Love you," she said under her breath. It was only two words, but she couldn't remember when she had last said it to her parents.

As quickly as the wind came, tranquillity was restored. Her hair fell neatly around her face, the leaves on the trees oscillated to a standstill. Tears fell from the corners of Sophia's eyes. She hoped that they forgave her too.

43

———

The two-storey house was still and quiet, meticulously cleaned with not a single item out of place. Shoes were on the shoe rack, coats hung on the coat stand, and the vase replenished with blooming white and purple orchids. The peace didn't last long once the front door swung open. A school bag flew through the open door, hitting the wall in the hallway, and a maroon school sweater was thrown into the air, landing at the foot of the staircase. Amy barged in and marched to the fridge, helping herself to a packet of stringy cheese. She hid it under her shirt as she ran off, bent double, into the lounge.

A car door slammed shut, followed by footsteps into the hallway. Teri clicked the front door closed.

"Amy, change out of your uniform please. I'll give you the cheese stick thingy in a minute."

Teri headed upstairs to her bedroom, took off her blouse and reached for the sweater on the bed, catching sight of herself in the mirror. She scanned herself from head to toe, edging her torso towards the mirror as she reached her midsection. She grabbed the rolls of her belly, frowning at herself. Wouldn't it be great if she could lose a few kilos? She twisted round – her bum wasn't any better.

She stepped towards the mirror, crowding it with her face, and flashed a fake smile, scrutinising the lines. When did the crow's feet appear? She clasped her hands around her face and stretched it back, tilting her head at this and that angle, up and down.

"Character lines," she told herself firmly and headed back to her messy daughter while her phone chimed with WhatsApp messages. It wasn't what she needed right now. If Sophia didn't get the message before, she had nothing else to say. It chimed again, and again. How was she going to tell Sophia firmly but politely that she needed to back off? Wait, why did she need to be polite anyway? She wasn't the one making absurd allegations. She picked up her phone as she finalised the reply in her mind, eager to fire off her response, but she was sucked into reading the messages first.

I didn't want to bring it up, Sophia's text started. *I don't want anything from him but the references. It's not helping.*

Teri scrolled to the next message. At first, the photo of Sam and Sophia sitting behind a giant rainbow dessert was innocent enough; his brilliant smile juxtaposing against her neutral expression.

Horizontal creases etched across Teri's forehead when she pinched the screen to zoom in. Sam's hand was on Sophia's knee. Her mouth dried. In another photo, her husband was in a neon-green mankini, just big enough to cover his private parts. *I think my size is LARGE*, read the accompanying text.

Teri scrolled to the next message – a voice recording – and pressed *Play*.

"Don't pretend you didn't like it," Sam's recorded voice said. She played it again. It couldn't be. His cruel laugh chilled her bones and made her head light. *Don't pretend you didn't like it,* his voice repeated again and again in her mind. Teri threw the phone onto her bed, stumbling backwards as she distanced herself from it as far as she could, careening into the wardrobe. She looked up and caught the mirror again. All she saw was a fat, ugly woman reflecting back. Just as she thought. Yes, she *was* to blame for all this. If only she could lose a few kilos.

The door swung open. Amy barged in and turned out her palms. "Mummy! There's no more stringy cheese!" As she shook her head, remnants of cheese flew off the corners of her mouth.

44

———

he thin weatherboard walls provided next to no insulation. The portable heater was plugged in but not turned on. It was cheaper to wear socks, three layers of pants, and the thickest jacket she could find, even if it made her look like the Michelin Man. Sophia trawled through her emails, but the listings were all similar. Plus, she had already applied for most of the jobs and still hadn't heard a word in response. She flicked her browser to another page, pausing at the *Alert me for jobs relating to...* field. Was she sure she wanted to change her search criteria? Before she could feel sorry for herself, she bashed out 'administrative assistant' and hit *Enter*.

She amended her CV, changing her management leadership capabilities and focus on customer strategy to: *competence in providing administrative and clerical support including mailing, scanning, faxing and copying, managing calendars for senior executives, and maintaining office supplies for the department*. With each word she altered, Sophia felt Sam's reach continuing to humiliate her. Not that she had anything against administrative assistants. It just didn't reflect her skills and experience, not to mention her ambitions. Besides, how would she explain such a career move to prospective employers? It was a bitter pill to swallow but with her bank balance dropping fast, beggars couldn't be choosers.

She checked her phone again. Still no reply. She re-read her texts to Teri. Did she go too far? Her thumb hovered over the *Delete* button, but it was too late. The double blue ticks confirmed the messages had already been read.

A couple of unapologetic knocks rapped on the door. She perked up. Who could it be? They only moved in a few weeks ago and no one knew their address. Well, except for Tony Jevtovic, the estate agent. Did he have seller's remorse as much as she had buyer's regret? She approached the door, ready to tell him that it was too bad if he had regrets because she had already signed the agreement. It wasn't her who kept lowering the price.

Sophia opened the door to a man in a white short-sleeved shirt with a plain black tie, armed with a laptop bag slung across his body and a clipboard at the ready. He flashed a polite smile.

"Not interested," she said automatically, closing the door.

The man jammed in his foot before it closed. He grimaced from the impact, but the door bounced off his sturdy black leather shoes, one clearly more scuffed than the other.

"They teach you to use your right foot at church?" she asked sarcastically, looking at him through the gap as they both strengthened their tug of war against the door.

"Is Sophia Mar... Mar-ex-ee here?"

"We're not religious" – she glanced at his name tag – "Vernon Schimdt."

"Good for you."

"Mormon?"

He shook his head, "No, thanks," until he realised what she meant. He shook his head harder. "Oh, no. Department of Human Services." He held up his identification card, which hung around his neck. "You made an application regarding one, Lewis Mar-ex-ee."

She rolled her eyes skyward, filing through her memory. "Look, we've been busy. I'll submit his quarterly benefits form tomorrow. I'm sure it's in one of the boxes somewhere." She wasn't even sure when it was due.

"Great... that'll be for my Benefits colleagues. I'm here about the application for Lewis Mar-ex-ee's supervised care."

"Mah-rex-see," she corrected, and opened the door wider. She had all but forgotten the application. It felt like a lifetime ago.

"We've been trying to track you down. Sent you notices and even went to your old place in Campsie. Finally got this address from the rental bond guys at the Office of Fair Trading. You know, the place where you gotta deposit your six-week rent for this place?"

Sophia stared vacantly at him. Where were they when Lewis stretched her to breaking point? Where were they when she was desperately looking for a place? It would have been far easier to find a place for one person. Whatever. Better late than never.

Vernon waved his arm in front of her face. "Hello? Are you with me?"

"We don't need it anymore," she replied.

"Your application says," he read from his clipboard, "'I am not equipped to adequately care for my brother.'" He skipped down the form, "'Lewis is physically intimidating.

He is bigger and stronger than me. The unpredictable nature of his autism frightens me. I fear for my safety, especially when he gets upset which can turn violent.' That's your application, right?"

"I said, we don't need it anymore."

"The government has a responsibility to ensure your and Lewis' safety. You know how the media are these days. We'd be accused of negligence if we didn't do anything."

"We're good. Both of us."

"Have your circumstances changed? Is he on prescription medication?"

"There's no cure for what he's got."

"I mean, is he less violent?"

"He didn't... wasn't violent."

"Sorry? There *are* penalties for making a false application." He pointed at her signature below the paragraph in bold on the photocopied application form to underline his point. "You know that, right?"

Caught in her white lie, Sophia stammered. "He's... he's much better. Matter of fact, he only needs minimal supervision."

"Sounds like he doesn't need much care."

"Uh-huh."

"If your circumstances have changed since your application, you need to change or withdraw it. Do you wish to do so?"

"Mm-hmm."

"Which is it? Change or withdraw?"

"Yes."

"Withdraw?"

"Yes."

Vernon rolled his eyes. "Right then, we'll withdraw your fortnightly Carer's Allowance since you won't need it any—"

"What? No! Who said anything about Carer's Allowance?"

"You just said he only needs minimal supervision."

"Yeah, but... but that doesn't mean he doesn't need *any* care!"

He paused to ponder the point, tapping his pen on his chin. Maybe she was right. "That's an excellent point!" he said, before punching a *WITHDRAWN* stamp, scribbling + *withdraw allowance* onto the form and handing it to her. He checked his watch and turned on his heels, marching towards his car. Mission accomplished.

Sophia chased after him. "Wait. You can't—"

"Call the number in the top right corner if you've got any questions."

"I don't want to call a number. You're right here!"

"Ah! Of course." He turned back and rummaged through his laptop bag. He fished out another form and pressed it into her hands.

"How could I forget?" he said as he walked off. Sophia looked down at the papers. She could have sworn they both spoke the same language, so why the hell had he given her a customer satisfaction survey?

45

———

A popular 1990s sitcom played on the TV for the umpteenth time, but it was all a blur. Every now and then, there was an eruption of laughter – fake and canned to induce the audience to join in the *fun* when the punch line wasn't strong enough. It grated on her as it reflected how she viewed the world, particularly right now – fake and canned. Was this the insidious slide into depression? A malicious disease that stripped away all will and happiness? But Sophia was adamant that *she* was not depressed. That was for the weak, and she certainly was not weak. Depression was fake, made up by those who couldn't deal with real life. It was as easy as snapping out of it, she kept repeating to herself. The only problem was that she couldn't snap her fingers to save herself. She was already doing all she could to find a job. It wasn't her fault that the universe, or more accurately, Sam, was conspiring against her.

A warning message popped up on the TV. *Are you still watching?* Had she just wasted three hours of her life on the sofa? She checked her watch: 8.12 pm. She turned the TV off and flicked through the news on her phone. Despite the latest scandal hitting American politics, renewed political protests in South East Asia, and a global heatwave affecting major cities around the world, Sophia kept scrolling, nothing taking her fancy. She googled the symptoms of depression. Not that she had it, she reminded herself. She was just... curious. And it was better to be informed than ignorant.

Depression symptoms the first search result read, listing out the following:

- Trouble concentrating, remembering details and making decisions. *Check.*
- Fatigue. *Check.*
- Feelings of guilt, worthlessness and helplessness. *Check.*
- Pessimism and hopelessness. *Check.*
- Insomnia, early-morning wakefulness or sleeping too much. *Check.*
- Irritability. *Check.*
- Restlessness. *Check.*
- Loss of interest in things once pleasurable, including sex. *No sex life. Sam's assault didn't count.*

Just as she thought; she didn't have depression. Wasn't there a proverb saying something was true if repeated by three people? All she had to do now was find them. Would it count if Lewis told her that she wasn't depressed three times? Anyway, what would Google know?

She logged onto Facebook, something she hadn't done in a long time. *What's on your mind?* it invited her to share with the world. There was a lot, but nothing that she wanted to share. She scrolled through the posts. A friend beamed in the maternity ward as she cradled her newborn, another shared a link to a homicide, another propagated his holiday snaps in Greece, and a random advertisement about ramen. How did it know she ate ramen? Perhaps it wasn't random after all.

She flicked her Facebook feed back to the top, and it invited her again: *What's on your mind?* She paused. Was she ready? What the hell. *Click.*

It happened at a company conference. I was sexually assaulted, she began. After describing the abuse, and her futile efforts with the firm's HR department, Sophia ended her lengthy post with, *I can't even find a job now*. It was painful yet cathartic having to recall the incident. The words flowed easily, and she was lighter for having spilled it out in the open, even though she hadn't posted it yet. She re-read the message, sentence by sentence, word by word, careful not to disclose Sam's or the firm's details. Litigation was the last thing she wanted.

Her thumb hovered over the *Post* button. Would anyone even care about what she had to say? She wasn't the most social or frequent Facebook user, opting instead to be laser-focussed on her career. Before she could hesitate further, she pressed the button. It was now in the cyber ether. Too late for regrets.

Sophia had envisioned something significant, even monumental, would happen after she posted her message. She waited for responses... and waited some more. After thirty minutes glued to her phone and refreshing the page, no one replied. She wasn't sure what she was expecting but the world didn't exactly explode from the revelation. It didn't even care. Maybe they preferred an Insta-worthy picture of an overpriced avocado toast or even a photo of her eating ramen. Who knew what Generation Social Media wanted?

She diverted her attention to the TV. The images moved, the sound played, and the canned laughter didn't miss its beat, but the fog in her mind blurred it all out. Another half hour passed before she looked at her phone again. She tried to fight the urge to open Facebook to save the disappointment but couldn't help herself. As she refreshed the page, she made a deal with herself. If there were no responses, she would remove the post and get on with her life, like applying for jobs instead of indulging in her self-pity.

There was one like and one share. She wasn't sure what to make of the like. Was Herman Wong liking the harassment or her speaking out? Was he friend or foe? What a dumb reaction. He should have left a comment instead of giving it a thumbs-up. As she returned to the home screen, a notification from Messenger appeared; a friend request from Lenore Savoie. Sophia hardly used Facebook's chatting app. WhatsApp was more her thing. She was about to accept the invitation but couldn't recall who Lenore was. She cast her mind back, starting with work colleagues, university, high school, primary school, before going all the way back to kindergarten. There was no Lenore in her memory bank. She wasn't even sure if she knew anyone called Lenore in her life, and Lenore was the type of name she'd remember.

As a cautious social media user, Sophia wasn't going to be catfished into a scam. She wasn't looking for a whirlwind romance, to send money overseas, or to buy any visas. And she certainly wasn't going fall for any lottery scams (*please pay a small advance of only $750 and provide your home address and bank account to unlock your millions today!*). She was too smart for that. So, on a spontaneous hunch and against her intellectual rationale, she accepted Lenore Savoie as her Messenger friend. Three floating bubbles appeared immediately. Was she about to get catfished against her better judgment?

Hi, I'm a correspondent for local affairs at the Bankstown-Canterbury Standard. *Saw your post about workplace harassment. Can we talk?* Lenore messaged.

Ha. Ha. Funny. Sophia replied. It must be a slow news day for the *Standard* if they were contacting her.

We certainly don't treat workplace harassment as a joke, Lenore texted back.

Despite the correct response, Sophia hesitated to reply again, wary of getting into a ping-pong of texts for the next who-knows-how-long with who-knows-who. She tapped her thumb on her phone as she pondered her next move before flicking to the *Bankstown-Canterbury Standard's* website. She scanned the *About Us* page, scrolling down the list of smiling corporate headshots of the Editor-in-Chief, Co-Directors, Editorial Directors, Senior Reporters, columnists and other contributors. Her hunch was correct. There was no such Lenore Savoie.

Before she ended the text exchange, Sophia clicked the *Contact Us* page, which listed the options of how to get in touch with the newspaper: Mailing address, Street address, Phone/Fax/Email. She stopped at fax. The good old facsimile, telecopy, telefax – who in the world still had them? She dialled the phone number on screen.

"Good morning, you've called the *Bankstown-Canterbury Standard*, your trusted standard for local news and affairs. This is Melinda, how may I direct your enquiry?" said the voice on the phone.

"Yes, hi. Umm... can I ask a question?" Even Sophia couldn't believe her opening line.

"Go ahead, please."

"Do you have a... Lenore Savy... Savee..."

"Sav-o-ee?"

"Yes, Savoie. Does she work there?"

Melinda tapped her keyboard, already lining up the transfer. "She *is* in the office today. Would you like me to redirect your call?"

"No, that's fine. Thanks."

Sophia hung up. Did she really want to be involved in a local news article? Going public on Facebook was quite different to sharing her story with a journalist. Floating her story on social media was only a way of being heard. Was she ready for her trauma to be in mainstream media where people were quick to judge the veracity of a sexual assault allegation based on how *hot* the accuser was? If Lenore were a real journalist, she would want to squeeze out every little detail. The upside was limited but the downside, limitless. Apart from having to relive her ordeal for strangers, previous survivors were ignored, their reputations trashed, and accused of being liars or sluts, often both. So, on a spontaneous hunch and against her intellectual rationale, Sophia replied, "Sure. We can talk."

SET IN A RECTANGLE OF MULCH OVERLOOKING A VAST GREEN lawn, a colourful children's slide shimmered in the afternoon sun. Next to it, the rusted swing creaked as it swayed back and forth.

"Why didn't you take the money?" asked Lenore, a woman in her late twenties who could have been mistaken for a high school student.

"You mean the $48,000?" Sophia asked.

Lenore checked her notes again. "$45,000?"

Sophia scoffed. "That was before we made the deal." So much for her fantastic negotiation skills.

"It would've given you some breathing space. You know, with your job, your house."

Sophia opened her mouth to respond but closed it, changing her answer. "Do you know what a non-disclosure agreement is supposed to be for? Protecting commercial confidentiality. Not the guilty. I don't want to be some cost-of-doing-business expense that they can just write off. Do you know how dirty that feels?" She shook her head. "I'm not going to protect the guilty."

"Why don't you go to the police?"

Sophia let out derisive snort. She had asked herself the same question dozens of times. "And what? My word against theirs? Like he said, it's me against Eastle's lawyers. An army of them."

"Who's he?" Lenore pressed again.

Sam's name screamed in Sophia's head like an alarm that wouldn't turn off, but she held her tongue. Not because she wanted to protect him. She couldn't bring herself to say his damn name. There was a long silence.

"So, why now?" Lenore asked. "Why didn't you speak to anyone before?"

"It's not... you don't know what it's—" Sophia began. She blew out a long breath and composed herself. "You don't know what it's like. You feel trapped. When I look back at what happened, it's depressing. Yeah, it is. I admit it. I can still feel his wedding ring on me in the middle of the night. When I look forward, I'm... scared. When I stay where I am, I don't know. I just don't know what the hell I'm supposed to do." She looked skyward, trying to hide her red eyes. She took another deep breath and squarely faced Lenore. "You believe me, right?"

46

With double garages and even bigger double-storey houses, the smell of affluence hung in the air as Lenore exited her tiny hatchback and knocked on the door of number 17. A muted voice called from within, followed by hurried steps, before the door cracked open. A pair of brown eyes squinted at her.

"Uhh... yes?"

"Hi, does Sam Abraham live here?"

"You're talking to him."

"Lenore Savoie, Correspondent for Local Affairs, *Bankstown-Canterbury Standard*." She extended her hand, drawing him out to exchange a handshake.

Her youthful appearance took him by surprise. "Do your parents know you're out by yourself?"

But she wasn't going to be distracted from what she came for. "I want to speak to you about a story we're following."

"You haven't heard of a phone?"

"You didn't answer."

Sam took his phone out of his pocket. Four missed calls. "Unknown number," he said, shrugging.

"There have been allegations of sexual misconduct in the workplace..."

"If this is about Henry, it's got nothing to do with me. You should talk to him. I mean, I didn't want to do any of it."

"Sorry, didn't want to do what? With Henry?"

Sam wrinkled his brows. This wasn't exactly how he wanted to spend his Saturday morning. "What did you want again?"

"There have been allegations of sexual—"

"You got the wrong house." He turned to head back inside.

Lenore shadowed him, blocking his escape. Her ploy to get him out of the house by extending a handshake had worked. Now, she needed him to talk. "I just want to give you the opportunity to tell your side before we publish. What happened at the conference?"

Sam's nostrils flared but he kept his composure. "It was great," he started his shtick. "We recognised our top performers for their dedication and hard work."

"In your room."

"I don't have time for this." Sam stepped around her.

Lenore matched his step again, obstructing him. "Is it true that you sacked Sophia Marexi because she wouldn't have sex with you?"

"I never—" He blurted out before providing a more measured response. "It's unfortunate that Ms Marexi has resorted to casting false allegations," the mechanical corporate side kicked in, "but the fact of the matter is that she abused company property... printed thirty, fifty, maybe even a couple hundred double-sided pages for personal use. We can't have that. Imagine if every employee treated the firm's printers as their own. Never mind the cost of it all, think about how wasteful and unsustainable that would be for our one-and-only planet."

Lenore raised a quizzical eyebrow. "So, she was sacked because of your firm's sustainability commitments?"

"Look," he said, having enough. "She came to my room uninvited and begged for her job, which she wasn't doing very well in by the way. When I told her that we're a meritocratic firm, she jumped on me."

"Jumped?" she asked, resting her pen on her notepad, readying for the explanation.

He shrugged. "Seduced, sex, whatever you want to call it."

"How do you explain her bruises? And her dress. It was ripped."

"You're in media," he said sarcastically, "it shouldn't be news to you that people will do anything to get their five minutes of fame. Now—" Sam cleared his throat before sliding his corporate mask back in place "—it would not be appropriate of me to comment any further on the employment of any individual. *I* respect their privacy." He sidestepped her to head back inside.

Lenore hadn't travelled all the way to his house to leave empty-handed. She tapped the volume button to the loudest setting and pressed *Play*. "I'm disappointed," a scratchy, end-of-the-tunnel voice played from her phone. Sam stopped at the doorway, recognising his own voice, as the recording continued. "You think I'm going to reply to your messages so you can take a screenshot of it? You think I don't know about your chats with Jimmy? Who do you think he works for?"

Sam crunched his hand into a ball, popping a web of veins out on the back of his hand as he ground his teeth. "Bitch!" he seethed under his breath.

"Sorry?"

He turned around as she skipped the recording to another section. "Sticking your tongue in my mouth, and... and... ripping my dress, and... holding me against my will wasn't good enough for you?" Sophia said on the recording. At the time, Sophia felt strange listing the abuse like this, she explained, but it served a specific purpose. "Don't pretend you didn't like it," said the recorded Sam.

"Can I verify that's you?" Lenore asked.

Sam stared at her, calculating his response. He looked down at the voice memo playing on her phone, his fingers twitching to knock it out of her hand. Instead, he walked back into his house, slamming the door, but Lenore's barrage of questions didn't stop from outside.

"What did you mean when you said you didn't want anything to do with Henry?" She pounded the door again. "Sam? We'll be publishing this afternoon. I just want to give you the opportunity to..."

HEAD BOWED, SAM WALKED BACK INTO THE HOUSE, GAZING AT the floor, stewing. His eyes darted around, blinking excessively as if trying to summon an inspired thought for what he should do next. He didn't get far into the hallway when...

WHACK!

His head snapped to the right. He grimaced, holding his cheek. Caught off-guard, it seemed to have an extra sting to it.

Teri shook the pain out of her hand. Even she was surprised by the power of her pent-up anger.

"I knew it! I knew it all along but wanted to trust you!"

Her face was red, veins pulsed from her forehead, threatening to burst. Her eyes welled up, but she fought the tears, desperate not to crumble in front of him.

Sam held up his hands in surrender. "You don't believe it, do you?"

He slowly approached her, but Teri pushed him away.

"Disgruntled people will make allegations when they're sacked 'cause they can't do their job properly. It's sick but it's the unfortunate world we live in."

She held up both hands. "Stop."

"I don't even know where she got that audio from. Kids with their deep fakes these days can ruin anybody. They really ought to regulate it."

"Just stop!" She was sick of the lies, the spin, and all the times she hadn't confronted him earlier.

"Wait, you don't believe it, do you? Say for a second it was true, why is a journalist knocking on the door, and not the cops?"

"You want the police to drag you away? Is that what you want... for us? All the texting, locking your phone so I couldn't see it. The late nights! I knew deep down—" she tapped her chest "—but I was being strong for Amy."

"We'll get through this together."

"Together?" she repeated, not recognising the word as if it were a foreign language. She pulled out her phone and held up the picture of him in the neon-green mankini. "After this?" She ripped off her wedding ring, launching it at him. "Get out."

47

A small crowd gathered around the water dispenser, semi-crouched in a circle around a mobile phone, speaking in excited hushed tones. As footsteps clicked the tiles behind them, they straightened their backs and spoke aloud about something to do with the upcoming results announcements.

Henry Philipps, Eastle's CEO, glanced at them as he entered his office, which befitted the captain of a large financial firm, with its panoramic city views, luxurious furnishings and expensive vases. It was spacious, despite the eclectic collection of sculptures and artefacts, which included an African caricature lifting a snake that symbolised sustenance, a sculpture of a Chinese dragon to bring good fortune, and an ornately handcrafted Venetian carnival mask for a dash of fun.

He sat at his desk where his executive assistant had fanned a handful of newspapers, one on top of another, just the way he liked it. The headlines were similar for each paper: protests in an Asian nation threatened to topple its government, a cardinal resigning over sexual abuse claims, and the increasing geo-political tensions between the US and its adversaries. As he turned the page, another headline caught his attention: *Senior Eastle executive accused of sexual assault.*

He pushed his glasses up on his nose. Why hadn't he been given prior notification? What did he pay his Communications department for? He reached for the phone; it was answered in three short rings.

"Have you seen the papers?" He got straight to business.

"About?" Jimmy replied.

"Apparently, 'Senior Eastle executive accused of sexual assault.' Who are we talking about?"

"Hmm... take your pick."

Henry glided his finger over the phone to conference-in another person. He was pleased that he still remembered how to do it. Among other CEOs, this was a nifty party trick. His aging industry peers would have had to call their assistants to help them.

"Henry. Morning," Sam's voice rang out through the speaker.

"Why the hell am I reading that a Senior Eastle executive is accused of sexual assault?" Henry asked.

"You know how it is. Let somebody go and they'll throw mud at you."

"We all know this isn't like the others, but we'll take care of it... like the others," Jimmy added.

"We've had, what, half a dozen allegations before and you let this fall through four days before the Chairman's update? I don't want this hitting our share price," Henry snapped, slamming down the phone, nudging his glasses higher on his nose. Hand to chin, he paced back and forth before walking out of his office.

THE CROWD AT THE WATER DISPENSER WAS STILL IN THEIR semi-crouched position, transfixed on Sophia's Facebook post. For a group spending eight or more hours together, five days a week, gossip in any organisation was a near surety and Eastle was no different. It was the gossip that made the working day bearable.

"Who do you reckon it is?" asked Seb from IT.

"I dunno… I still find it hard to believe," said Amora from Digital Transformation. "I reckon it was *her* who was sleeping around. How do you think she got to where she was so fast?"

"That doesn't make sense. Why would she post a story like that so everyone can think she's a slut?" Caesar from Accounts Opening chipped in. "But she *did* spend a lot of time with Anthony before she got booted."

"Isn't he gay?" Seb replied.

"In Finance? No. It's Sam." May nodded, glancing away, unable to look them in the eye.

"He's married," Caesar replied. "Happily married, isn't he?"

"Did you see her get walked out by security?" May asked, changing the subject.

"How humiliating. I would've died!" Caesar replied.

"Wouldn't even let her touch her laptop… like a criminal," Amora continued.

The conversation fell silent as Henry strode towards a lift held open by the floor assistant.

"So, as I was saying, let's take it offline and circle back on the quick wins, and double our efforts to streamline our processes, and make the customer at the heart of everything we do," Amora said loudly, pretending to be the good corporate citizen that she wasn't by using as many corporate clichés she could think of.

48

It was patchy and thatched. More brown-yellow than green but at least the lawn was neatly trimmed and the weeds no longer so obvious. It was a far cry from when they had first moved in. Using the only mower they had – a corroded mechanical reel – they toiled for hours to turn the overgrown knee-high forest to a bed of lawn where they could now see their feet. However, the price wasn't pretty. Sophia developed blisters from the blunt shears left over from the previous tenants, and Lewis suffered scars and scratches on his arms and hands from wrestling with the brittle branches.

She picked up a shirt from the basket and reached up to the rotary washing line, so rusted that it was stuck at an uncomfortable tiptoe height. Unfortunately, the washing wasn't going to hang and dry itself. To her relief, her phone rang – any excuse to give her neck a break. Her heart sank when she saw the name on the screen. A broken neck would be less painful than a conversation with *him*. Her phone buzzed with messages as soon as it rang out.

We need to talk, Sam texted. A moment later, there was another, followed by another. *Call me.*

If sexual assault was more about power than sex, Sophia was determined to be in power this time. She antagonised him by reading the messages but not replying to them and returned to the neck-breaking work of hanging the laundry. Her phone buzzed with another text. This one commanded her attention. *Let's not do anything we'll regret later.*

The ringing wouldn't stop. She slid her phone into her pocket when another call came through, fighting to ignore it, but she needed to get it off her chest.

"Stop harassing me or I'm going to put a restraining order on you!" she yelled down the phone.

"Am I speaking to Ms Sophia Marexi?" asked the female voice on the other end of the line.

Oh. "Sorry. Who's this?"

"My name is Nikki Maduro. Legal counsel for Eastle."

"You got the wrong number. I don't work there anymore."

"Ms Marexi, I'm going to need you to pay attention because I'm only going to say this once."

Sophia shifted on the spot as if limbering up for the looming altercation. "Who's this again?" She pressed the phone into her ear.

"Nikki. Maduro. Legal. Counsel. Eastle. Financial. Group." She enunciated each syllable slowly in a not-so-subtle condescension.

"I. Don't. Work. There. Anymore." Sophia mirrored.

"This is not a joke. I'm going to need you to remove your Facebook post where you referenced the firm."

"You haven't even read it, have you? There's no reference to Eastle 'cause I didn't want to deal with..." Sophia restrained herself from cursing and searched for the right word, unsure of whether she was being recorded. "Lawyers," she said finally.

"I suggest you not be too cute. We have a whole department of... lawyers."

"Sorry, it stays up. Actually, no, I'm not sorry."

"I don't think you heard me. I am the legal counsel for the firm that you *used* to work for. You have until ten this morning to remove the Facebook post, otherwise Eastle *will* commence defamation proceedings against you without further notice."

There was something about being on the receiving end of legal mumbo jumbo before nine in the morning that rubbed Sophia the wrong way. "Is that a threat? Are you threatening me now?"

"I don't agree with your characterisation of our request and am instructing you to observe the 10 am timeframe."

"Instructing? It sure sounds like you're trying to bully and intimidate me. It's not my problem if you don't like the truth," Sophia said, igniting her feistiness that had been beaten down for so long.

"It's unfortunate that you feel that way, Ms Marexi. Eastle will now also seek your full reimbursement for all its legal costs pertaining to your false and defamatory allegation."

Sophia broke into a snide chuckle. "Good luck!" If only they knew the dire financial straits she was in. If they could find any money, they should let her know.

"I'm glad you find this amusing. It would be such a shame for you to lose custody of Lewis because you don't have the means to look after him... Your Honour."

The threat made Sophia's blood boil, blanking her mind. She stuttered as she scrambled for a good comeback but couldn't think of a single one.

"10 am. Today," the terse woman repeated before hanging up.

Sophia froze. The bravado that she just exhibited didn't match what she was feeling. She expected Eastle to protect itself at all cost, even if it meant steamrolling over her, but it was a low blow to drag Lewis into this. She was sceptical that they could conflate the two issues in legal proceedings, but what if they *could*? As Nikki said, they had a department of lawyers, probably with at least three law degrees each. Who was she to outmanoeuvre their legal eagles?

She abandoned the half-a-dozen random socks, four pieces of underwear and three shirts in the laundry basket and headed back inside. She had an urge to see her brother, but he was asleep, guarded by Sharky and Skippy, and clutching Pillowy. She needed to be with him because she'd be damned if Eastle got its hands on him. She squashed next to him and gently wrapped her arms around him, stirring him. Her mind meandered through random thoughts as she rubbed his earlobes. Who said autism needed to be cured? Would humans be guilty of halting its own evolution if they tried?

She combed her fingers through his hair and hushed him back to sleep. He couldn't be the sounding board that she needed, but it wasn't what she was looking for right now. She watched his belly expand and contract as her thoughts continued to wander. What if autism was a genetic development on the ever-growing continuum of evolution? What if our ancestors had broken off the first thumb that appeared, having determined that they were already satisfied with four fingers? How would humans open a jar of Vegemite today?

Despite the self-talk, or maybe because of it, she could not let her brother go, no matter the personal cost or how humiliating the experience would be. She couldn't win the

David-versus-Goliath battle against an army of highly paid lawyers. This wasn't a fairy tale, where miracles were gifted to those who needed them. It was real life. It was *her* life. She needed to move on. Even Vegemite came in tubes these days.

RESIGNED, SLUMPED ON THE SOFA, SOPHIA WATCHED THE TIME tick by: 9.53, 9.54, 9.55… As the clock ticked to 9.59, Sophia pressed *Delete* on her Facebook post. *Are you sure that you want to permanently remove this post from Facebook?* a message prompted. Great, just what she needed. A chance for hesitation. She hovered her thumb over *Cancel* for a long time. In the last seconds to the hour, she pressed the confirmation button. There! She did it. It sucked that Eastle didn't want to reach an agreement and it sucked harder for a corporate bully to silence a powerless victim, but it was time to move on, for Lewis' sake. She threw her phone down in disgust.

The tone of Nikki's request grated on her. *I am the legal counsel for the firm that you used to work for.* What was her point in emphasising 'used to work for'? As if the experience of being shamed in front of her team when she was walked out by security and being branded a slut who slept her way up the corporate ladder wasn't enough, the removal of her Facebook post was the insult that added to the injury.

You have until ten to remove that post, Nikki's voice repeated in Sophia's mind. It wasn't even a request. It was a demand, a power play, to show the firm would always be in charge.

As she mulled over what she would do next, a bolt of energy struck her. She grabbed her phone, tapping away furiously. After a thumb-aching six minutes, she flicked her phone across the sofa. She was done with it. She wasn't sure how Nikki *I'm-going-to-need-you-to-remove-your-Facebook-post Maduro* would react, but she was past the point of caring. After all, Nikki didn't say she couldn't post her story on other social media platforms, and Twitter was as good as any. Sophia steeled herself. Maybe she *was* playing it a little too cute but that was for some lawyer with their three law degrees to deal with.

49

———————

Corporate offices, it seemed, were similar no matter the firm. At the *Bankstown-Canterbury Standard*, rows of desks were set up like a high-school examination hall. Lenore sat in front of her laptop, two monitors and the morning's newspaper, all crammed onto a desk no wider than two arm-lengths. She sipped on her cappuccino, suffering from a bad case of Mondayitis. She scanned her emails, reading the ones highlighted in green (from her boss – it was always good to prioritise those), and deleted the spam proclaiming they were 'a sexy girl, looking for friends in your neighbourhood'. Helpfully, it also provided a link to a webpage. She bashed the *Delete* button, moving the spam emails to *Trash*. With all the anti-virus, anti-malware, anti-spyware, and anti-whatever-else, it seemed IT could do anything these days *except* filter those out.

Overshooting with the *Delete* button, Lenore suspended her finger in mid-air, almost deleting an email from another unknown sender. She pondered for a moment. Did she know a May Cupper? She didn't think she did but opened the email anyway.

Hi, I work at Eastle and saw your article today, it began. At least May wasn't proclaiming to be a sexy girl, looking for friends. *I'm also a survivor of sexual abuse*, she had written, and offered to reveal more, including an incident when she saw a colleague run out of a hotel room during a company conference. Lenore returned to her inbox. There were seven more emails from unknown senders, all asking for anonymity if they were to share their stories.

Lenore flicked back to May's email, scrolling down. As she reached for the phone to call the number at the bottom of the message, the phone flashed, alternating with the ringing. The number on the caller ID didn't display but, in the news business, with sources often opting for anonymity, that wasn't unusual.

She picked up the receiver. "Lenore Savoie. *Bankstown-Canterbury Standard*."

"Hi, I saw your article. Can we talk?" a female voice said at the other end of the line.

Lenore squashed the phone receiver against her shoulder as she brushed the newspaper off her desk, rummaging for a pen and pad. "Sure." It was going to be a busy morning, and looking at the already empty cup, she regretted not having bought that extra tall coffee.

50

"Housekeeping," grunted a voice from behind a door. A moment passed without an answer. "Housekeeping!" the voice announced again.

Lewis tapped his chest – that was where it should come from, not the throat. Not that he knew what that meant.

"Housekeeping!" the voice boomed one last time.

Lewis pressed his ear against the door, listening for signs of life, but didn't hear any. He tapped his card on the door reader. "Come," he said, pushing the housekeeping trolley in, eager to show Sophia around.

Having been rejected from the forty-seven office jobs that she had applied for, it was a sign from the universe to try something else. For roles that she had heard back from, she was either too qualified or not qualified enough, never the Goldilocks who was just right. If any good came from Lewis' scuffle with his now-former colleague, Mike, it was that the Kings Hotel had a vacancy for a housekeeper.

"Whooa!" Sophia said, scrunching her nose at the pungent smell.

The funky stench bordered on a gym sock after a good

workout or a baked beans fart that was held in for too long. Whatever it was, she couldn't pinpoint it. They scanned the room, but nothing was out of the ordinary. The room was spotless, chairs tucked away under the table, and remote controls all lined squarely on the coffee table. Sophia followed her nose like a Border Collie sniffing out illicit substances, neck outstretched, turning in this direction and that. She edged along the wall, zeroed in on a bin, and stepped on the pedal, flapping the lid open to reveal the stench inside. She staggered back, retching. The metal lid slammed back down.

"Yummy!" Lewis teased, mimicking and pointing at her as if to say she should have seen her reaction.

"I think it's vomit."

It was just the invitation Lewis needed. He lifted the lid. "Du... Duri-an," he said, zooming his face in for a closer look. There was also a sock and an opened empty can of beans.

"Close it."

"Yummy."

"It's not funny! Close it!" No wonder the fruit was banned on public transport and hotels in some countries. To make matters worse, this durian was rotting, intensifying the stench exponentially. Lewis squatted next to the bin and wafted the smell to his nose as he tried to contain his giggles.

"It's really not fun—" she continued but didn't finish.

Lewis froze and crashed to the floor, trembling, as his head jerked from side to side.

"I told you—" She stopped mid-sentence again. What was the use of a lecture now? She dragged the chair and coffee table away from him and threw pillows against the walls. He gasped, straining for oxygen like a fish out of water, and blinked hard before his eyes rolled to the back of his head. Sophia fumbled for her walkie-talkie. *Shit!* How to use one of these again? She randomly pushed buttons and twisted the two dials on top.

"Hello, hello?" she said into the walkie talkie, but only static and squeaks played back.

She raced out of the room to call someone but rushed back in. Wasn't it better to stay him in case he smashed into something? But she couldn't leave him without calling for help. Why was the walkie-talkie so damn complicated?

Her phone! Who should she call? She didn't even have the hotel number saved yet. The emergency number. Yes, triple zero. Her hand trembled as she punched in 0... 0...

Before she finished dialling, Lewis drew sharp breaths into his nose, tensed, and flopped to the floor. She approached him cautiously, her thumb still hovering over the last number on her phone.

"You okay? It's Soph." She pushed her face into his for a closer look. "Come on, Lew!" she urged.

Her hair tickled his face. He wasn't breathing. "Shit!" Her hand trembled as she punched the last zero on her phone.

"Police, Fire, Ambulance?" the emergency operator asked.

"Police. What? No, ambulance," Sophia said, her heart almost breaking through her rib cage.

"Connecting you now."

Lewis peeked through the corner of his eyes and zapped them closed so she wouldn't catch him, but he couldn't pull it off. He burst into a cackle.

Sophia slapped and punched him. "That's really not funny! Don't ever do that again!"

"Ambulance," another voice on the phone announced. "What is your emergency?"

"Can we get the police? We need to put this jokester in jail!" Sophia said, still calming her trembling hands as she evened out her breath.

51

———

At sixty-four, Vincent Cummins appeared every bit the banker's chairman, with hair neatly parted to one side, the obligatory white shirt and conservative red silk tie. He brushed his fingers along his bushy grey eyebrows that juxtaposed against his jet-black hair, pondering for a moment. He looked up from his computer, scanning his 173-square-metre office and out to the sweeping harbour views.

With the largest office on the executive floor, there was no doubt who was top dog at Eastle. Located in Sydney's central business district, and at a cost of $2,330 per square metre, his office was the size of a generous three-bedroom apartment. However, being at the apex of a financial institution wasn't about practicality. It was about status and power, like almost everything else in the firm.

As he reached for his phone, his sleeve slid from beneath his jacket, revealing a pair of wooden Wimbledon tennis racket cufflinks above the embroidered initials, VC. Before he could press his speed-dial, the receiver rang in his hand.

"You must have cameras in here, Eva. Can you get me Henry?"

"Already on the line," she replied, putting the expression, 'behind every powerful man is an even more powerful woman,' into action. Having worked together for the past thirteen years, she had a sixth sense of what the Chairman wanted and when. She patched the call through.

"Morning, Vincent."

"Henry." A pause. Vincent watched the share price of his firm slide even further on his Bloomberg terminal. Whilst the rest of the financial service industry wasn't having a great time either, Eastle's performance was worse. "Shares are down twelve points." He paused again to let the what-the-hell-are-you-going-to-do-about-it tone sink in.

"I wouldn't worry. Day-to-day fluctuations."

Vincent brushed his eyebrows with his fingers again. "That's just this morning. It's been 130 over the month."

"We're executing on our strategy and it will correct itself. Like I said, I wouldn't be too concerned—"

"It doesn't look good, especially when we have an earnings call with our investors in three days."

"Our focus is long term, not quarter on quarter... as you know, Vincent."

"It's not the strategy or execution." He read the headline on his Bloomberg terminal again. "I want the sexual assault story out of the press—"

"I don't know where they come up with that stuff."

"—before the earnings call." The Chairman hung up, leaving the flatline of the disconnected call droning in Henry's ear. Vincent didn't need any more excuses. What did he pay Henry the big bucks for?

∽

Walking into the firm's lobby, Sam was in a jovial mood, pleased that he was having lunch with Henry. Having good relations with the boss was always important for the general relationship and, more importantly, his salary and bonuses at year-end.

"It's quite warm," Henry said, already sweating in his tailored wool suit.

"It's a scorcher. Thirty-eight degrees or something," Sam replied as they walked out of the lobby and onto the street.

"And how's Mrs Abraham?"

"She's... uhhh... she's good. I think she's getting into this barista thing now. Who knows how long that's going to last?" He smiled.

Henry checked both sides before crossing the road. "And Amber... Audrey?"

"Amy," Sam corrected, a little unsure where the conversation was headed given Henry wasn't known for small talk. "She's great. Started second grade at the beginning of the year. Teri said she didn't even cry. Amy, that is. The wife was a mess!"

Henry stopped, leaving Sam to overshoot him.

"It's over there," he said to his boss, turning back, pointing to the restaurants up ahead that befitted a CEO and senior executive.

Henry pushed up his glasses and looked at the sign on the awning – just the place he was looking for. He walked into the Best Ever Sandwich Shop, a dimly lit eatery with a storefront no more than three metres wide. The shop assistant and customers, in faded and tired construction and maintenance gear, looked up, staring at both suits, sure that they had the wrong place.

"You can't book us. It's on the wall," the shop owner said, pointing to a frame hanging above the sandwich grill plugged into a power board that was overloaded with half a dozen too many plugs. The words *Certificate of Business Registration* were barely visible underneath the greasy glass. Henry held up his hands as he smiled weakly and headed for a table at the back.

A young punk with a long mullet, dressed in ripped jeans, shirt and trainers, dumped a faded black-and-white photocopied menu onto the table. "Yep?" he said, holding out a pen and tiny notepad, ready to scrawl down their order.

"We need a moment." Sam shook his head as if it wasn't obvious enough that they had just sat down.

"We have sandwiches. It's a sandwich shop. You want sandwiches, right?"

"Oh, okay," Sam stuttered. "Surprise us."

"We're a sandwich shop, not a magic store. If you want surprises—"

"Two steak sandwiches," Henry interjected.

"Drinks?"

"Let's see..." Sam started as he flipped over the photo-copied page.

"Water," Henry replied, pushing up his glasses.

"Bottles are over there." The waiter walked away, pointing to an assortment of faded soft-drink cans and water bottles that lined the countertop, caked with cooking grease.

Sam looked around, disgust plastered on his face. "There are other places we could go that are just a few—"

"The share price has taken a hammering lately."

"Yeah, looks like I'll need to hold onto my shares a bit longer," Sam snorted and reduced it to a smile before feigning concern when Henry didn't take the bait.

"We need to do something about it."

"Absolutely." Sam nodded longer than required, trying to get a feel for what his level of concern should be. "And we have a fantastic plan—"

"Legal and HR would normally have this conversation—"

"We will grow double digits this year and our—"

"But given our..." Henry gestured to both of them.

"—cost efficiency will improve by three points." Sam had recited the line so many times that his delivery was simultaneously fluid yet mechanical.

"Sam," Henry held up his hand to stop him. "I need to let you go."

"You what?"

"We can't have this sexual harassment thing hanging over us. The earnings call is in a couple of days."

"You're scapegoating me?"

"It's for the best."

Sam leaned back in his chair. "You're kidding me."

"I've agreed it with the Remuneration Committee already. We'll pay twelve months of your salary and you can cash in whatever shares and options you have. In exchange, you can't write about the firm or grant any interviews unless we agree, and even then, we'll need to vet it."

The two men stared at each other as if it were a game of chicken. Their eyes were calculating, their faces devoid of expression. There was a long pause.

"That was a good one," Sam said finally, breaking the tension. He wagged his finger at Henry as he broke out laughing, shaking his head. "You *almost* got me. Almost!"

Henry remained deadpan, only moving to push his glasses further up his nose. "You'll be comfortable enough on the payout until you sort yourself out."

Sam released his grip on the table and leaned across.

"You wouldn't have a clue how to run a retail business. I've heard you repeat verbatim to the Chairman what I say to you."

Henry looked away, waiting for Sam to finish before turning back to him and continuing. "HR will be in touch to work out the exit message with you. We want you to leave the firm with dignity."

"Don't give me this 'dignity' bullshit," Sam said a little too loudly, which invited surrounding customers to zero in on their conversation. He lowered his voice and pushed his face into Henry's. "You know what I know." Sam held up his phone. "You sack me, and the world will know about you too."

Henry remained poker-faced but his little finger quivered against the table. "It's nothing personal."

"After everything I did for you, *all* of it was personal!"

More eyes turned towards them, no longer hiding that they were eavesdropping. Henry pushed up his glasses again. "Don't be hysterical. It's not a good look. We'll sort out the paperwork over the next couple of days."

"Do it and see what happens. Don't think I won't—"

"Surprise," the waiter interrupted unenthusiastically, and dropped two steak sandwiches onto the table.

Sam stood up, restraining himself from flipping the table over. To hell with lunch. He didn't even want to be in this dingy place for the poor. He stormed out, bumping into tables as he edged his way through the narrow aisle. He felt ambushed by Henry's announcement but was more annoyed at himself for not picking up the clues earlier; the uncharacteristic small talk and the unusual selection of an oft-overlooked sandwich shop. How could he have missed them?

52

————

When Sam stepped out of his BMW, his hair was not its usual dapper self, and he wore several days' stubble. As he approached the place that he used to call home, he pressed his knuckle against the door, stopping short of rapping on it. He shouldn't have to knock at his own home. He tried to unlock the door, but the key wouldn't turn. He tried again, this time jiggling the key in the lock, but it still wouldn't budge. He stepped back. The lock cylinder was shinier than the rest of the panel. "Bloody hell," he cursed under his breath. Till death do us part, or till his wife of nine years changed the lock, more aptly.

He pressed the doorbell. A moment later, Amy opened the door. She looked back at her mother who was a few steps behind, unsure of whether to let him in. Sam picked her up, pecking her on the nose. "Hello, baby. Did you miss me? I missed you."

"What are you doing here?" Teri asked the uninvited guest.

Sam put his daughter down. "I called. I messaged," he

said to Teri. He motioned towards the lock. "You didn't have to do that."

"We're having breakfast."

"I have to at least get my clothes and stuff."

Teri was unmoved, still guarding the doorway. The gears in her mind seemed to turn heavily as she looked past him. Both were unsure of what to do.

"They sacked me," Sam admitted, filling in the silence. Teri flinched, caught off-guard. He had hoped that that would be his opportunity to manoeuvre the conversation in the direction he wanted but her response wasn't what he had in mind.

"You know where your stuff is," she said coldly, leading Amy away from him.

A week apart should have been long enough for her to soften, especially now that he was jobless. He even entertained the thought of returning home that day but with things going the way they were, it would take a small miracle, and didn't to push his luck.

Sam walked in, looking around, savouring the details. He walked past the mirror from Ikea that fitted perfectly in the hallway, the scented tealight candles they had bought in bulk three Christmases ago which they struggled to use up, the soft woven heart that they had won for Amy at the gaming arcade, and the scratches where their daughter had dragged chairs across the floor so she could reach the Tim Tams hidden behind the bookshelf.

Turning into their bedroom, he removed his work clothes from the wardrobe, emptied his underwear and sock drawers and squashed it all into a black bag. He used another for casual clothes and shoes. In all, it took no more than ten minutes. He didn't need much and regretted that the two people he needed most wouldn't be joining him.

His shoes tapped on the varnished floorboards – the same footsteps that he had traced countless times over the years – as he circled back to the front door. He lamented that it would be the last... at least for now. Memories of happier times with his wife crept into his mind: how she had made his heart beat that little bit faster the first time he spoke to her while waiting for his coffee at the local take-away, how lucky he had felt the first time they kissed, and how happily they held Amy for the first time. It all seemed so long ago. It shouldn't have ended this way, but sometimes *forever* had an expiry date.

He paused at the open door, turning back. "I love you. We can make this work."

"Don't. Please don't," Teri said through watery eyes, gritting her teeth.

He tried to hug her, saying, "I'm sorry, I'm so sorry," but she pushed him away and pulled out a form from her back pocket.

"No, no, no," he said, pushing it back. "We can get through this."

"Don't give me, 'we can get through this' now!" She tried to push the papers into his hands, but he hid them behind his back. She slapped the forms on his chest, but he wouldn't take them.

"Why didn't you think of me before?"

Sam backed up, finding himself on the other side of the front door. "You want some space. I get it."

"Why didn't you think of Amy?"

The little girl's lips trembled on hearing her name used in such a tone. Her face scrunched up, a precursor to the waterfalls that were about to burst through. It was too much for Sam. He couldn't bear the thought of his princess crying and retreated out to the lawn.

"Please..." he urged his wife, but Teri threw the divorce papers out after him. She slammed the door, rattling its frame and shaking the walls.

53

Eastle's so-called Terrific Trio – its Chairman, CEO and Finance Director – were huddled in the boardroom around the conference phone. Tomes of talking points, calculators, laptops and notepads were all at the ready. After months of preparation, the day had finally arrived.

An earnings call with investors and analysts was always a time of uncertainty, given that an influential observer could have a material impact on the firm's share price, especially when Eastle had already been on a steady decline in recent months.

"So, as you can see, we are investing in the right areas and have a solid plan to grow and improve our return on tangible equity to nine per cent over the period," Finance Director, Edmund Cheang, said to the conference speakerphone at the centre of the table.

"Thanks, Ed," Henry said. "So, Eastle is a well-funded business with strong capital prospects. We will continue to grow revenues and strengthen our competitive positioning. We are now open for questions."

The operator explained the procedure for asking questions ("press #6 and wait for your cue") before opening the line. "We are now ready to take the first call."

"Thanks. Deepak Sharma from Fund Investment Capital," the first caller introduced himself. "I have two questions if I may."

And so began forty-five minutes of questions and answers in which a myriad of esoteric acronyms such as NIM, JAWs, LCR, NSFR, CET1 and RoRWA were bandied about. With their aides scribbling notes for them to recite, the executives batted the questions away with bland statements about their optimism and confidence in its management team to turn the business around – anything to increase the firm's share price.

"No more questions, operator?" Chairman Vincent asked, not bothering to wait for a reply. "Well, thank you for being with us today. For those of you who have holidays coming up, have a great—"

"Hello? Can you hear me?" a voice said.

"Yes, go ahead," Vincent replied.

"Lenore Savoie. Correspondent for Local Affairs. *Bankstown-Canterbury Standard.*"

Vincent knitted his bushy eyebrows. It wasn't a financial name he recognised. He looked up at the PowerPoint presentation projected onto the whiteboard in front of them. An aide scrolled through the presentation as fast as she could to find the name as the Chairman turned to his briefing notes that were scarred with copious highlights. Not finding what he was after, he panned to his team but directed his response to the speakerphone.

"Pardon me. The what standard?"

"*Bankstown-Canterbury Standard.* We've been reporting local news that matters to the local community since 1972. And what matters is the elephant in the room."

Eyes darted around the conference room as the silence grew thicker. "Would you like to hear the operator's instructions again?" Henry asked. "We'd be happy to take questions in relation to the firm's results."

"Yeah, sure," Lenore said, brushing it off.

"What's your question?" Vincent chimed in.

"Does Eastle have a cultural issue relating to sexual harassment and abuse?"

"Right. Thanks for your question," Henry interrupted.

"Isn't that the reason why your share price has been declining?"

"That concludes the call today," Henry interjected. "Operator, you may end the call."

"It's not me you're trying to silence. It's all the women who have come forward—"

"Operator, you may—" Henry tried again.

"I'm—" Vincent interrupted, exchanging looks with Henry before correcting himself. "*We're* not aware of any allegations. Our staff are always welcomed to speak with their line managers or go to our Human Resources department if they have any grievances."

"With respect, Chairman, why would they go to their manager if they're the perpetrator, especially when HR works for management anyway?"

"I disagree with your characterisation about the integrity of the great people we have in this firm," Vincent blustered. "Putting that aside, we also have an anonymous and confidential employee hotline where staff can report their concerns without revealing their identity."

"How anonymous can it be if you need the caller's details to investigate the allegations?" Lenore countered. "Let's cut to the chase. I've been trying to reach your office, your CEO's office, your Public Relations team, your

Communications team – everyone and anyone – for comment on allegations about your firm's misogynist and sexual-abuse culture, but no one wants to know me. Should I lay out the allegations here for you?"

"Look, Lynette—" Henry interrupted, shooting an anxious glance at Vincent.

"Lenore."

"Look, *Lenore*, I understand that you are young and passionate, but there are proper procedures for the issues you're raising. We'd be happy to continue these discussions offline. Operator, please."

"Thank you, Mr Philipps," the operator announced in a robotic voice, "and to everyone for dialling in. This concludes today's call."

Vincent collected his briefing notes and headed out. Henry followed, shaking his head, trying to get his boss to share his disbelief. "We'll find out how she snuck onto the call."

"Our shares are down another two points," was all Vincent said as he walked out, gently closing the door behind him.

DESPITE THE 'ENERGISING COMFORT' THE GLOSSY advertisement had boasted about the petrol hybrid Mercedes-Benz C-Class with its leather trimmings and ergonomic seating, Henry was neither energised nor comforted on his way home.

"I've already spoken to Public Relations," he grumbled on the phone. "They'll issue a statement to refute the allegations and to send a warning to others that we'll take legal action for any defamation."

"I've asked Nikki to spearhead an internal investigation," Vincent said on the other line.

"A what?"

"Nikki will form a team—"

"With respect, Vincent, that's too many messages. It's not how we typically handle this. You can already see the headline, 'Eastle refutes allegations yet conducts internal investigation.' We can issue our standard statement as soon as we get your go ahead."

"There's only one message," Vincent said. "We're conducting an internal investigation."

Henry pushed his glasses up on his nose and massaged his temples. He expected the call to be a courtesy update, informing the Chairman of the usual plan but it was anything but. Why was there a need to deviate from previous practice and waste time on an internal investigation? It wasn't difficult for the firm to issue the standard press release to support its executives. They already had the templates covering a range of scenarios, including unfair dismissal, harassment, whistleblowing, and even persistent lateness to work. All they had to do was change the date on the documents. The more Henry thought about it, the more he took it as a personal slight. Who knew what an internal investigation would throw up? When did Vincent lose faith in him?

"Are you sure you want to drag the firm into a protracted and costly process?"

"Nikki will have a report in three weeks."

"I see." Henry's mind went into overdrive, formulating responses to dissuade his boss, however none sprang to mind. "It's a... uhh... good decision."

When the call ended, Henry replayed the conversation in his mind. There was something different about the Chairman's tone. He couldn't pinpoint it, but it was a headache he didn't need. He squashed his temples harder but even that didn't bring any relief. He flicked through his phone contacts before dialling again.

"Emmanuel, sorry for interrupting your evening, I know it's late."

"Not at all, Henry. You're not calling to cancel Saturday, are you?"

"No, no. I'm looking forward to beating you again at the weekend."

"A hacker like you? Not with that swing, you're not!"

Henry forced a chuckle, but golf wasn't what he was calling about. "Ahh... did you catch the call earlier?"

"The messages were clear enough but the sexual harassment thing – where did that come from? Our shares were two per cent down after that. We need to do a better job and get ahead of—"

"Yes, get ahead of the news cycle," Henry cut in. "Which is why I'm calling, actually. I was wondering... I mean... It would be good if an... uhhh... independent non-exec, like yourself, could... maybe issue a statement of... you know... support." For a smooth talker, it was an unusual display of hesitation.

"This is a collective Board issue as you would know, Henry. And yes, I will be raising it with them."

"Of course, by all means, speak with the rest of the Board. I'll see you on Saturday. I don't want to hear anything about your old back injury when I beat you." Henry forced out a laugh again before hanging up. He looked out the window, pensive. Even Emmanuel sounded different this time.

Henry's head thumped harder, his headache getting

worse as he dialled another number. "Jimmy," he said when the other person picked up.

"I wondered when you'd call."

"I spoke to Vincent." Henry said.

"Don't worry. It'll blow over in a few days. It always does."

"He said Nikki will conduct an internal investigation."

"What for?" Jimmy blurted. "I mean, sure. We'll just make sure it doesn't go out without our approval."

Henry pushed his glasses up, his voice wavering in anger. "I thought you said you fixed it!"

"I don't control who you get on the investor calls. Maybe you should have called Investor Relations instead."

"Remind me who's got a signed *Fuck You* NDA sitting on their desk, Jimmy? Not so smart, are you now, huh? You're going to sort this out. First thing you're going to do is call Sam and get him to delete the messages."

"IT can delete them."

"The messages on his *personal* phone."

"What?" Jimmy shook his head. "Henry, nothing's going to happen tonight. I'll talk to Comms and we'll issue a statement first thing tomorrow."

"You're not listening, Jimmy. The messages! And don't screw up this time or you can look forward to early retirement!" Henry hung up, staring at the messaging apps on his phone.

54

Mornings were usually the busiest time of day. Lenore glanced at the time on her laptop. Two hours and twenty-seven minutes until noon – that was when the paper went to print. She flicked through the scribbles on her notepad before reclining in her seat to check the headline on her laptop again. *Eastle's rampant sexual harassment culture* screamed across the screen. It was a departure from her usual stories, the most recent being the Let's Remove Graffiti community day, the extension of the Justice of the Peace hours from 4 pm to 4.30 pm at Roselands Shopping Centre, and the list of petrol stations with the cheapest prices during the week (Tuesdays). She jittered with adrenaline, galvanised by her call on Eastle's performance update. Her fingers blurred as she punched her way through another paragraph. Just when she least needed it, an unrecognised phone number rang through.

"Lenore Savoie," she answered, putting on her headset so she could continue typing.

"Richard Mance," the male voice on the other end of the line articulated clearly.

"This is the *Bankstown-Canterbury Standard*. How can I help?"

"You happy now?"

"And you are?" Lenore said, trying to pinpoint the familiar voice.

"I thought you reported factual news, not slander!"

As a journalist, Lenore knew better to let the subject talk. She tried to recall if there were any Richards or Dicks in her recent stories but came up empty. "And we are the most trusted source of local news since 1972," she said.

"What kind of person gets their kicks from destroying other people's lives?"

She stopped typing, piqued by the hint of desperation. "I've got time, if you can start from the beginning."

"Sam is a good man. He's a loving father, devoted husband and an exceptional corporate leader."

With the tone, pitch and cadence, the voice was a little coarser than she had remembered but surely it couldn't be. Why masquerade as someone else? As much as she wanted to ask, she bit her tongue. "We report the facts as we see them... *Richard.*"

"You destroyed him!" he screamed down the phone.

Lenore snapped her headset away from her ears, wincing.

"I don't know which liars you spoke to, but I demand an apology," the man continued.

"Apology for?" Lenore said as calmly as she could, not wanting to tip him over another edge.

"Don't play stupid with me! I didn't assault anyone. I'm a good husband and a good father."

If she had any doubts before, she didn't have any now. "Sam? Sam Abraham?"

There was a hesitation on the other end of the line.

"Hello?" she asked again. The only reply was a sniffle before the call abruptly ended. Lenore pulled off her headset with more questions than when she had put them on. What was the point of the call? Did he assume another identity because he was too ashamed to admit his wrongdoing? It was a new development that she wanted to include in her story, but it was speculation.

Just report the facts, she reminded herself. She glanced at the time again. Noon was fast approaching.

A CLOUD OF BREATH BLEW UP TO THE SKY. DESPITE THE freezing temperature, Sam stood on the ground-floor balcony of his rented one-room apartment. On his wicket, he could have chosen a larger space, but this would only be temporary, he told himself. No need to splash out. Whilst comfortable and well-furnished, the apartment didn't have any footprint of his former life with Teri or Amy. The modernity of it felt clinical and nondescript in the absence of family photos, the face masks that his wife stored in the fridge to keep them from drying, or the messy shoes that littered the hallway. He even missed strands of Amy's hair in the bathroom that were once his pet peeve.

He wiped the last of his sniffles on his sleeve and took another drag on his cigarette. A moment later, he clutched his chest, coughing out the first smoke he had inhaled since the birth of his daughter, almost seven years ago. He hated the feeling that gnawed at him. It was everything and nothing at the same time. It was Teri's dismissive look when he told her that he had lost his job. It was that journalist –

whatshername – who tricked him into talking. It was Henry taking him to that little sandwich shop to kick him out of the firm. He didn't want to degenerate down a spiteful route but a damn dingy sandwich shop? After all he had done for Henry? Bloody cheapskate! And how could he forget the bitch who had started all this in the first place?

Knocking Sophia down with adverse employment references had started as a bit of fun but he now realised he hadn't gone far enough. She had to retract all allegations of sexual harassment. No, of *any* wrongdoing. It was best not to be associated with the words 'sexual harassment' at all. She was supposed to accept the termination notice and disappear like the rest of them. Didn't she know how hard he had worked to become Head of Retail Banking? Wasting countless weekends with the bosses at the golf joint, or pretending to care about Henry's weekend, his wife, or however many bloody kids he had. He was entitled to enjoy the fruits of his labour. The more Sam thought about it, the more he paced around the balcony.

He took another puff of his cigarette, muffling his cough as he turned to his phone. Teri still hadn't replied despite his bombardment of messages. At first, his texts were long, pleading paragraphs (*We can work it out like we've done so many times before* and *Let's think of Amy*), but he had since given up trying to get through to her. *U there?* was his last message, sent forty minutes ago. Actually, thirty-eight minutes and twenty-three seconds ago, not that he was counting. He incessantly swiped his phone, hoping the screen would refresh but her last message was two weeks ago, reconfirming that she was seeking custody of Amy.

As he drew the last puff on his cigarette, he took out another from the half-empty packet – any excuse to delay facing the realities of the day.

So, is this it? u never gonna talk to me again? Sam typed on his phone, but as the twenty-three other messages were unread by her, he hesitated, and lit another cigarette. So much for nine years of marriage.

As he placed the phone on the table, it beeped with a message. *Finally.* He jumped with anticipation. Would she at least try to make their relationship work? Maybe she was reconsidering their marriage? At least there was some communication, and any communication meant there was some hope of restoring their lives together.

He fumbled his phone and read the message: *Sam, we need you to return your phone. Regards, Jimmy.*

Ugh. He didn't need a text from Jimmy. Who the hell writes *Regards* in a text anyway? *Already returned it*, he replied.

The other one.

iPhone's personal, not company.

Where are you? I can pick up it now.

What the hell's this?

Just doing what I'm told.

Sam took a deep puff of his cigarette, trying to contain his annoyance. *Henry put u up 2 this?* he texted. He was ready for a fight.

Let's make it easy for the both of us.

Ur not having it.

I can pick it up at your house in about an hour. Regards, Jimmy.

Sam froze, his frustration coming to a boil. How many ways could he say no? He should tell Jimmy to screw himself, but he was just a puppet in the grand scheme of things. It was obvious who was behind the demand. Besides, texts were forever evidence – once it was out in the ether, there was no taking it back. There were plenty of stories

about people getting caught out by inappropriate, embarrassing, or even incriminating texts. Sam wasn't going to be
one of them, so he replied, *I'll be home by 5.*

55

The neatly bound 138-page meeting pack sat on the table next to Henry, untouched. Emblazoned across the front page was *Monthly Risk Management Meeting*. And so continued the monotonous hamster-wheel of governance meetings that were a necessary evil of running a financial institution. Henry was surrounded by the C-suite of the organisation – a highly paid team tasked with identifying emerging risks so the firm could deliver on its revenue, cost and other strategic imperatives.

"So, what you see here is a nine per cent reduction in Unusual Activity Reports since we deployed machine learning to identify transactions that don't—" the Chief Risk Officer was explaining.

"We'll take it as read if it's in the meeting pack," Henry interrupted. He nudged his glasses higher and glanced at the time on the conference phone. "Anything else, Keane?"

"I was going to say, although we've made progress, the regulators expect—"

"Thanks, I'm sure it's also in the pack," Henry dismissed, prematurely concluding the meeting by fourteen minutes, to the puzzlement of the room. "If there's nothing else, happy Wednesday everyone."

Keane shot a barely disguised glare of disdain at Henry. Not that his boss noticed as he headed for the exit.

"Henry," the Chief Operations Officer called out as she followed him out of the room. "Are you good with the update to the Board I sent you last Thursday?"

He was oblivious to her question and the commotion of the room behind him as the attendees collected their belongings to leave the room as well. "Why not?" he said on the phone, walking out the room.

"Should be done by five today," Jimmy replied.

"ASAP or else we're both done."

Jimmy clenched his jaw, his grip tightening, almost crushing his phone. Talk about resenting doing the donkey work. "Sure," he replied diplomatically to nothing but the dial tone. He curved his hands around his face and peered into the window, looking for any movement. Except for Lego pieces and torn Uno cards scattered across the mat, there was no indication of life. He pounded the door again, pressed his ear against the glass and studied the house aimlessly.

He questioned his hunch about someone being home, despite the white Audi A4 parked in the driveway. He looked at his phone again. He had just spoken with Henry and already placed another five calls to Sam. He wanted to message the CEO about the delay again, but he already knew his boss didn't want any ifs, buts, or an empty hand without a phone. Jimmy was about to dial Sam for the sixth time when faint footsteps approached from within.

"Hello?" he called out, banging on the door. Moments later, the door opened, leaving his knuckles hanging mid-air.

"Yes?" Teri said with a scowl.

"Oh... Is Sam around?"

"And you are?"

"Jimmy," was the reply, but it elicited a blank response. "HR. Human Resources. Eastle."

"Was he sacked?"

"Well, I wouldn't... sacked is a strong... let's just say there was a mutual agreement that it was the right time for him to pursue other interests."

"You don't need to give me..." Teri rolled her eyes. "He's not here."

"When will he be back?"

"He won't be."

"He said he'd be here." Jimmy looked at his watch, unsure if Sam had said that or if it just rolled off his tongue.

"I said, he won't be." Teri waved the back of her hand in Jimmy's face.

It took a moment for him to take in the faded horizontal line on her wedding finger. "Oh. Okay," he stammered, trying to find the appropriate response. The door slammed in his face. *That* was why he hated dealing with family members. With an employee, he could be as tough and rough as he wanted, hiding behind real or imagined company policies. With family, it was different. It was unpredictable. He couldn't play the same power game with someone who wasn't bound by the firm.

Jimmy retreated to his car, giving up. He drummed his fingers on the steering wheel, pulling away from the kerb, unsure of where he was going as he weighed how best to let Henry know there would be a delay in getting Sam's phone.

He thumped the steering wheel as he gritted his teeth, releasing the resentment of being tasked to do the boss' dirty work. What did he expect from HR? He raged to tell Henry where to stick his request but his cushy nine-to-six job, or more like eleven-to-four with a two-hour lunch in between, sponsored housing, free tuition for his four teenage children, and his Premier Family Health Care package somehow provided sufficient reasons for him to bite his tongue. He kicked himself for his erroneous handling of Sophia's termination. Not that he would admit that too loudly. In all the times he had delivered the envelopes, it had never gone so badly. *That dumb bitch.*

A mechanical voice broke his concentration. "In fif-ty me-tres, take ex-it two through the round-about." He slid his eyes to the GPS. How the hell would it know where he should go if he didn't even know himself? Ignoring the instruction, he turned left at the roundabout.

"Re-cal-cul-ating route. At the next junc-tion, per-form a U-turn," the GPS announced.

"Quiet," he yelled at the inanimate object.

"Per-form a U-turn," the GPS repeated.

"Shut up." Jimmy pecked at the power button, but it repeated its instructions like a broken record. "Per-form a U-turn."

He ripped the device off the windscreen and threw it against the passenger door. "Re-cal-cul-ating route. In the next two kilo-me-tres, drive straight..."

"Shut up already!" He punched the GPS again and again and... he stopped. His eyes lit up, a thought striking him. It couldn't be that simple, could it? He reached for his phone, swiping through multiple screens impatiently. He clicked on the *Calculatr* icon, but it wasn't arithmetic he was after. A surveillance-camera logo flashed across the screen underneath Eastle's red-and-white yin and yang logo. "Ah ha!" His fingers tingled with anticipation.

How could he forget about the firm's multi-layered security that they applied to all corporate and personal phones for the privilege of accessing work emails, in case it was lost or stolen. After all, it was his own team that had drafted Clause 23, Section A, Sub-Point iii on Page 33 of its forty-six-page *Remote Working Terms and Conditions*, requiring all employees to duly read and sign as part of their conditions of employment. Of course, all employees duly signed it, but it was questionable as to how many actually read it.

He pressed the magnifying-glass icon and in the *Enter phone number* field, keyed in Sam's number. The map of Australia zoomed in on New South Wales, down to Sydney, then the blue dot pulsed at an unfamiliar suburb. He pinched the screen, zooming in and out. Was there something wrong with the app? Did he really need to go to Wiley Park – a multicultural working-class suburb with an eclectic mix of nationalities, and some thirty-five kilometres from the city? Where the hell *was* Wiley Park, anyway?

After following the directions on his phone for twenty-five minutes in the unfamiliar neighbourhood, Jimmy had second thoughts about how great his plan was. The number of abandoned shops and *For Sale* or *For Rent* signs outnumbered those that were still trading. The graffitied shutters on the shop fronts didn't comfort him much either.

Stopping at the lights, he watched the pedestrians crossing the road: two tradesmen with lengthy beards, one carrying a two-litre bottle of Coca-Cola, an Asian man in combats and sandals holding a small plastic bag, a trio of rowdy high schoolers still in their uniforms, dribbling their basketball and mock-shooting at an imaginary ring, and a person in a hijab pushing a baby in a stroller. As an Imam emerged from behind the line of high schoolers, Jimmy elbowed the side of the door, locking it. He wasn't prejudiced, he said to himself. He was just cautious.

After everyone had crossed the road, he let out a sigh of relief. No one had bothered him, not even a glance in his direction. Now, if only he could work out why *Calculatr* indicated that Sam was in this godforsaken dump. The best he could do was to turn his phone off and back on again – the sure-fire IT hack – but when it came back online, the pin still pulsed at the same address on Bowlpinch Road.

56

The lorry driver cursed and blared his horn as a hatchback cut into his lane, snapping a dazed Sam back to reality. He leaned back in his car that was parked at a junction, tired and vacant, watching the traffic whizzing by. In just under a month, he seemed to have aged half a decade. His wrinkles were more obvious, his hair more bedraggled and greyer than usual. He rubbed his face in his palms, massaging it back to life and let out a yawn big enough to swallow a tennis ball. Was he at the right place? He had been waiting for an hour and a half.

Sam rummaged through his bag, tossing out his sunglasses, newspaper, notepad and a sheaf of loose pages onto the passenger seat. Scanning the email printouts, his eyes skipped through the niceties from the HR Operations team leader wishing his family well and asking if he'd had a good weekend, and jumped to the middle of the text: ... *the forwarding address for the superannuation statements is...* He strained his eyes to match the number on the letterbox and the street sign. He seemed to be at the right place, so why was it taking so long?

He ruffled his hair and slid further down in the driver's seat. He wasn't going anywhere until he finished what he had to do. He picked up the newspaper: *Eastle's rampant sexual harassment culture.* He wanted to read it, but didn't, at the same time. Would the article name him? How would he be portrayed? Although he had been quoted in the press before, it was usually in the context of product launches or marketing events, not as a sexual predator. He tried to push the article out of his mind but the more he did, the more curiosity bit at him. He relented. The first paragraph didn't make for good reading: the firm had no other choice but to find new leadership to accelerate the execution of its strategy.

He tossed the newspaper onto the backseat. The insinuation of incompetence was a well-worn tactic that he knew all too well, but never once did he think the sword would be turned on him. He was Samuel Abraham for goodness' sake – the intelligent, charismatic and, let's not forget, good-looking, executive. He let out a heavy sigh and reached for his phone. Teri still hadn't replied. He swiped through his photos and selected the *Recently Deleted* folder. He browsed the blurred images taken at the conference with his team, a screenshot of a bank transfer, and a shot of the kitchen bin that was skewed at an angle – Amy, the cheeky bugger. What he wouldn't give now to let her play with his once-forbidden phone.

He scrolled through the next set of photos, unsure, not if, but, by how much, he hated himself. How silly was it to risk it all for this? He looked at the selfie of him and Henry shirtless at a beach, another where his boss cradled his head as they faced each other with only centimetres between them, and a screenshot of the text he had sent to his boss when Teri pressed him about what was happening at work. *Of course I want to*, the message read, *but we already met Wednesday. Next Friday?*

Hesitant, he played a grainy voyeuristic video. In the dimly lit hotel room, a notepad branded, *Excellence in Leadership Conference*, could just be made out. Bed sheets stirred in the background, synchronising with the moans and groans of two people sharing an intimate moment.

"Wait, wait," a voice said.

"What?" Sam said.

"I'm not comfortable with that thing." A shadow rose from the sheets and made his way to the dressing table, revealing a hairy mid-section. His hand groped around for the phone in the dark. "How do you turn this thing off?"

"Just leave it," Sam replied from the bed, scrunching up his nose as he tossed the nearby jacket onto the floor. He had never been a fan of the man's bitter citrusy smell.

The shadow pushed his face closer to look for the off button and nudged his glasses up on his nose. "Found it." The screen blacked out.

The here-and-now Sam looked out the window, rubbing the back of his neck as he pondered his next move. He clicked on the video. Would he like to permanently delete or recover it, the phone asked. He held his thumb over the options. He wasn't born yesterday. It wasn't the company emails that Henry was worried about. He couldn't have cared less about that. Henry would have a better chance of keeping his job if there weren't pesky things called evidence. In the absence of these damn things, it would just be a contest of credibility – a he-said-she-said ping pong match, where those in power usually had the final word, and that suited Henry just fine.

As Sam let his thumb fall onto the *Recover* button, his phone rang. He willed it to be Teri but the caller ID disappointed him. He should stop expecting her call; stop being needy and get over his sorry self.

The ringing droned in his ear, but it was best not to provide any clues that he was near his phone. He waited, as it rang again. Jimmy must have been desperate but there was no point speaking to him. It would all be resolved soon anyway – one way or another. When it rang a third time, Sam snapped his thumb on the *X* button, hanging up on the call. If Jimmy didn't get the message the first two times, he should have got it by now. The only problem was that the call was from Teri.

"Shit!" He called back immediately. The engaged signal was the last thing he wanted to hear. "Come on!" he urged. He called a second time, but the engaged tone persisted. He bashed his phone on the dashboard, cracking the screen. He needed a new phone anyway. He hunched over, bumping his head onto the steering wheel. A noise found its way through his self-pity. Was it a text message? He interrogated his phone through the splinters on the screen.

Where r u? the first text from Teri read. *HR guy came...* but the second message was obscured by the cracks. He tapped his phone, hoping the screen would react in some way. It was broken but still working.

I'm fine. how r u? he started. Should he ask about her and Amy first? He deleted the text and started over. *how r u? how's Amy? Hope ur both doing well.* He stopped again. The last sentence sounded like he was a stranger. Should he tell her how good it was to hear from her and much he missed them instead? Would it be too much in one text? His head dropped to his chest. When did texting become so difficult?

He threw his head back against the headrest, resting his eyes. When he opened them again, two silhouettes approached in the distance. He inched his neck forward, squinting to get a better look.

57

Barbeque sauce oozed out, dripping down Lewis' forearm and off his elbow. "I told you... not... throw... aluminium foil away," Sophia called out above the noise of the four-lane King George's highway, and in between hearty mouthfuls of her own chicken-tikka kebab.

Lewis took another bite, gushing out more sauce. "Ung-ghh!" He sounded in playful defiance, smacking his lips together for dramatic exaggeration. His cheeks ballooned to their limit as sauce continued to stream out from the tail of the kebab and onto his Kings Hotel uniform. They were both famished after their twelve-hour shifts. Not that Sophia hadn't done her fair share of hard labour in the past but being on her feet for twelve hours as opposed to sitting in an office chair all day was a different game altogether.

"You... gonna... chook," she said, still struggling with her own mouthful, spitting out lettuce.

"Chook!" Lewis squawked, making fun of his sister.

"Choke!" she corrected, swallowing noisily.

"Chook!" He mocked again, wrapping his hand around his neck and pretended to choke.

Sophia frowned at him before giving in to his infectious laugh and coughing up more food, which made them laugh harder. In her previous life, she wouldn't have found the funny side. After all, someone had to soak, rinse and wash the sauce out of his uniform, and it wasn't going to be him. Maybe this thing about living in the present had some legs. She tried to remember the last time she had enjoyed the lighter moments. Was it when Sam had tried to encourage her when she was stressed with Project Panda, saying that she had two hands, one named Cape, the other one Able, and together they were: Capable! No, even then she forced out a polite ha-ha because the joke was so lame. Or was it the time when—

"Arrrggtt!" Lewis bit his tongue and gurgled, eyes rolling to the back of his head. His blinking fluttered before his eyes clamped tight. He rocked back and forth as his arm trembled, reaching for his neck.

"Stop it. I told you it's not funny," Sophia lectured. His face pulls were on repeat like a broken robot looping through the same motions.

"Seriously, I mean it!" she yelled at him, but he was cocooned from the outside world.

His anguished whimpers frightened her. "No, Lewis," she panicked. Not again. What was she thinking about enjoying the lighter moments? There *was* a reason for being disciplined and focussed, she reminded herself.

She pulled him down, bending him forward, and slapped his back as hard as she could to dislodge whatever was choking him. It would have been better, though, if she hadn't slapped him with the kebab still in her hand as the rainbow of ingredients splattered over his shirt and spewed into the air. So much for saving on the extra load of washing.

As quickly as it came, it was gone. She recognised the pattern: the eye roll, the lightning speed of the episode and his anxiety in the aftermath. It wasn't just another seizure.

"You saw something."

"People fighting... blue car... crash..." Lewis said, bumping his fists together. He paused, looking at her, fear in his eyes.

"What?"

"Car crash." He pointed at his sister.

"Crash into me?" She shook her head. Don't be silly.

Sophia reached for the traffic-light button but was yanked back. Lewis grabbed her wrist, preventing her from dashing across the road despite the gap in traffic. After what he had seen, it was too dangerous.

"Nothing's going to happen," she assured him. When the green pedestrian lit up, he gripped her wrist tighter, swivelling his head from side to side, assessing the traffic – who knew when the brakes on the cars would stop working, especially the blue ones. As a drizzle started, Sophia fought the urge to walk faster; it was best not to upset an already agitated Lewis.

"Home," she said, sweeping her arms in a ta-da motion after crossing the road. They had made it back safely just as she had said they would.

"Go inside first." She tugged her arm away from his grip, but he still had it locked. "Got to collect the clothes," she said.

Lewis walked with her. "Let's go."

"No." She pushed him towards the front door. "I'll be two minutes."

Sophia shuffled to the side garden, stopping at the clothes line. As she tilted her neck skyward to tug at the clothes, the rain became heavier – the type of change that would make her switch her windscreen wipers from slow to medium. She tugged at the clothes harder, snapping the pegs off the line, hurrying to get out of the rain. She squinted, scanning the line for more. She couldn't really see in the poor light, but it looked like she had collected them all. She raced along the side of the house, using the little protection the awning provided against the rain as she hunched over an armful of clothes clutched to her chest.

Halfway to the front door, she jolted in fright, skidding to a stop like a car about to slam into the back of a truck, almost slipping on the wet concrete. She moved around the figure. "Lewis! It's raining. Go inside!"

"Was this what you meant when you said you wanted to move out of your parents' house?" Sam mocked.

Sophia froze, her heart beating out of her chest. "Get off my property!"

"You happy now?"

She wondered how he had found her but what did that matter? He was already here. "What do you want?"

"You're going to apologise. First to me, then Teri, then—" He threw the newspaper at her. "You're going to retract all your bullshit!"

She caught a fleeting glance at the headline; something about the culture at Eastle. "You better leave or the cops are going to be here soon," she threatened, stepping around him, out of the protection of the slim awning, and onto the muddy lawn in the heavier rain – the type which would make her switch her windscreen wipers from medium to fast.

"Cops? You weren't so tough at the conference." Sam

grabbed her arm, yanking her toward him, spilling a sweater, sock and a pair of underpants from her grasp. "When did you start wearing knickers?"

There was only one way she could dignify that with a response. She spat in his face.

"You like it rough?" He slammed her against the side of the house, cracking the old weatherboard, and choked her. "I can do rough! You've cost me everything. My wife, my kid, my job. You're not going to cost me my reputation. You're going to call the paper and tell her you got it all wrong. You understand?"

Sophia's eyes bulged as his grip on her neck tightened. Was this how a nothing-to-lose desperado becomes reckless or even criminal? "Go fffuu…" she tried, but she couldn't get the words out. Her chest gasped for air as she squirmed under his weight.

"Do it now!"

She struggled to break his grip and twitched in surrender. Whatever game Sam was playing had become too dangerous. A simple call to the newspaper wasn't worth her life. He relaxed his grip around her neck. Her chest heaved as she gulped precious air into her lungs. She opened her mouth to agree to his demand. "Leeewww!" she strained.

Sam raised his arm and backslapped her across the face, snapping her head to the side. He let out a demented laugh and painted her cheeks with his tongue. "That retard isn't going to save you."

Fury burned inside Sophia as blood trickled from her nose. She tried to knee his groin but every time she lifted her leg, she almost blacked out.

"Uh-uh-uh." Sam shook his head as he gripped her neck tighter. "I even gave you a chance when I didn't have to," he seethed.

A tear edged to the corner of her eyes as if the last drop of her life force were being squeezed out. How the hell had it come to this? How did she fail at the one thing she had promised her brother just a few minutes ago – to arrive home safely? Who would look after him now? Would he understand that she had tried to change... for him... for her... for them?

The rain soaked her hair and ran off the tip of her nose. She willed herself to wake up from the nightmare. It had to be a dream but the smell of metallic blood in her nose was awful – awful enough to let her know she wasn't dreaming. Sam's lips moved as if he were talking but she didn't catch a word. Suffocation tunnelled her vision. Was this it? The end? Of her? Her soul cried out at the injustice. Everything faded to darkness.

THWACK!

The blur of a frying pan thumped Sam to the ground. It was a mis-hit, sliding off the side of his head, but near enough was good enough in this case. Sam withered into a ball, grabbing his head.

"No. No! NO!" Lewis gasped for air, holding his neck, flinging his head from side to side, vicariously trying to relieve Sophia's asphyxiation. He patted her cheeks. "Wa... wake... up," he begged. "Mummy said no hitting. I'm a good boy. No hitting. I'm a good boy!" Lewis alternated as he cried. His incoherent wails sounded more like the grunts of a walrus than a person begging for forgiveness. His blinks became more pronounced as he flailed his arms.

～

As Sam stirred back to life, he wasn't sure whether he was hallucinating. Was Lewis really cradling Sophia in his arms, rubbing her earlobe in the torrential rain? He locked his stare onto Lewis as he found his feet. Lewis mirrored Sam's step, gripping the frying pan with white knuckles. They remained frozen, both reluctant to make the first move.

"Sam!" a voice yelled from behind. It was a welcome break to the impasse.

High-beam lights flooded him as he turned around. "Who's that?" Sam called out, shielding his eyes from blindness.

"I need the phone." The headlights switched off. Jimmy approached from his car that was parked across the muddied lawn.

"You can't be serious!" Sam said.

Jimmy turned to Lewis but directed his yells to Sam. "That's none of my business. I just need your phone. *Henry* needs your phone."

"You used *Calculatr* to track me?"

"Where is it?"

Sam didn't know what to make of it. If Sophia was incredulous about his tracking her down, he was almost in denial to find Jimmy on his tail. He broke out in a maniacal laugh.

"Have it!" he shouted, hurling his phone at Jimmy, barely missing his head. "You haven't heard of Cloud backup?"

Jimmy rushed to save the phone from the rain, testing the power button under his hunched body. He trudged back to his car that was fast becoming trapped in the bog.

"Or making copies of the photos, you stupid idiot. No wonder you're in HR!" Sam's insults continued.

Jimmy stopped in his tracks, turned back and let a right cross loose on Sam's chin. "Better than being a rapist!" he shouted above the pounding rain and the noise of the four-lane highway.

Sam stumbled backwards and hit the side of the house, landing close to Lewis, who waved the frying pan around, squealing hysterically. He nudged his sister to wake up, but she remained still. Too still. Lewis hyperventilated, his lips trembling, teeth clattering as he crouched over her, protecting her from the bad men.

But Sam was more focussed on the idiot who didn't know what Cloud technology was. He charged at Jimmy, flattening him into the mud and knocking the phone out of his grip. Sam jumped on top of him, raining blows onto Jimmy's head. "Say it again!" he taunted.

Pinned down, Jimmy sank into the mud as he rolled his chin into his chest, using his arms to shield his head from Sam's hard knuckles. Veins popped out of Jimmy's head in places where veins shouldn't be as he clawed at Sam's eyes, huffing and puffing his way out of Sam's hold, who collapsed to the ground, letting out an anguished scream.

Sensing his chance to get the upper hand, Jimmy kicked Sam in the stomach, flipping him onto his back. "Better than being a rapist!" he repeated. He pulled Sam to his feet, "You think you're better than me?" He clenched his fist, winding up, before knocking Sam's jaw out with everything he had. Jimmy dropped onto the lawn that had long become mud. His chest rose high and fell deeply as he tried to catch his breath in the pouring rain.

Sam staggered to his feet, disorientated. With arms outstretched, his wobbly legs tried to find their bearings. He stepped onto the road and into the path of a blue Holden Commodore; its horn screamed as the car barrelled towards him.

"No, shit, no!" the driver screamed, waving her arms at

him. Sam turned towards the noise, trying to move out of harm's way but the pain from the multiple blows to his head was too much. He didn't even know which direction was left or right.

"Get out! Move!" the driver screamed as she bashed the horn.

The car's headlights grew bigger as they shone onto Sam; the screech of the wheels locking became louder as the car careened towards him. Sam closed his eyes, lifting his arms to shield his face, and braced for the inevitable impact. He waited and waited but the inevitable had a different plan. Lewis grabbed the back of Sam's shirt and threw him back onto the lawn, landing him on top of Jimmy.

The blue Commodore fishtailed before ploughing into Lewis. He buckled over the bonnet and smashed his head against the windscreen like someone sledgehammering a watermelon. The car mounted the traffic island and crunched into the traffic light, whiplashing to a stop. Lewis slid off the bonnet and onto the cold, wet asphalt. Through the cracked and bloodied windscreen, the driver crumpled the deflated air bag from her view, trembling and distraught. There was a stillness after the calamity: a woman slumped against the house, two men covered in mud, and a burly younger man who had just bounced off her windscreen. As she rested her head on the steering wheel, her high-pitched scream transformed into the sirens of emergency vehicles.

58

Like light bulbs going off, random scenes flashed around: Sophia's poor attempts at piggybacking her brother who had grown much too big for her smaller frame, little Sophia adoring her baby brother in her arms, and a crumpled and torn page put back whole – no longer torn, no longer crumpled – to reveal a stick figure drawing of a mother, father, daughter and son holding hands in their garden where roses and flowers bloomed. The scribbles that dented the son's face disappeared. In their place was a beaming smile.

Sophia's motionless body lay beside her parents' tombstones. Her face was free from tension. Her eyes were closed. Her hair no longer flickered across her face. There were many things that she regretted. Not fending Sam off sooner, letting the institutional juggernaut push her around, the arrogance with which she had treated her work colleagues, the blame she had placed on her parents for her life and, most of all, the disdain she had for Lewis for being what she felt was the handbrake on her life. The good news was that she didn't have to worry about any of that any longer.

A soft breeze rolled across her face, gently lapping at her hair. In the distance, a repetitive drone called out her name. Initially faint, it grew louder as it approached.

"Sophia!" Lewis called out. He tapped her cheeks. She didn't move. It was her time to rest. She was kilometres away. At peace now. At last. The breeze picked up, rippling her hair.

"Come on, Sophia. Wake up!" Lewis impatiently tugged at her arm, pulling her up.

The corner of her mouth turned up, breaking into a smile before she could no longer suppress her laugh. She jumped to her feet, giggling, chasing him to the tandem bike. It wasn't easy to run with his arm in a sling, she could tell, but it didn't matter. He was bulletproof, wearing his favourite jigsaw puzzle shirt.

She threw the *Bankstown-Canterbury Standard* back into the bicycle basket. The headline lifted a weight off her shoulders: *Eastle CEO under investigation as two executives arrested for gross misconduct.* She scanned the end of the article again: *Reporting local news that matters to the local community since 1972. Lenore Savoie. Senior Correspondent for Local Affairs.* "Senior". She nodded, smiling. *Most thanks, Lenore.*

"Let's go, let's go!" Lewis screamed, hopping onto the bike.

Sophia shook her finger at him and tapped her head. "I know you're strong but safety first." She threw him a helmet and clicked hers on.

"Strong! Stronger than wall!" Lewis said, mimicking the taps on his head. It took a moment for Sophia to realise what he meant – that his skull was toughened by the countless times he had smashed his head against the wall.

She smiled, shaking her head. "Let's go."

As they pushed off and gathered speed, Lewis lifted his hands from the handlebar, gawking at the exhilarating sense of freedom.

"Lewis! Safety—" she started, feeling the need to reprimand him for endangering both of them, but that was the old Sophia. The new Sophia understood that it was her who needed to be protected by him.

"Faster! Faster!" he called from behind.

"Ready?" she called out.

"Go, go, go!"

She pedalled as fast as she could, as if the faster she went, the faster she could shed her old self. The past seven months had been a long and painful journey. She was battered and bruised, physically, emotionally, psychologically, and any other '-ally' she could think of.

She marvelled at the way her brother enjoyed the simple things in life. Families may not be perfect. Hers wasn't, and after trying to bend him to her will for most of her life, it was her who needed to change. Lewis, it seemed, was just the piece of the puzzle she needed, reminding her that everything would be okay in the end.

THANKS FOR READING!

PLEASE REVIEW THIS BOOK

Reviews are extremely helpful for authors.

If you enjoyed reading *Broken*, please consider leaving a review on your favourite reading platforms, share your views on social media using the hashtag *#HTPBroken* and encourage others to read the story too.

Thank you for taking the time to support me and my work.

DON'T MISS OUT

Don't forget to sign up for the *HTP Crew* newsletter to receive updates from the author, including his writing journey, writing resources and tips, tidbits about his life, info on new releases and much more.

hoitpham.com

ABOUT THE AUTHOR

Hoi T. Pham is an author with a passion for stories about the human spirit overcoming adversity. *BROKEN* is his new novel, written during weekends, after work, during family holidays and generally whenever he had a bit of time and was not sleeping.

He has been lucky to work around the world for his day job. However, no matter where he is, he still calls Australia home, having migrated to Sydney when he was a toddler with his six brothers and sisters.

When not 'doing time' behind his office desk, Hoi enjoys travelling, films, swimming, fitness and tennis – having coached his children when they were younger. He lives with his wife and two children and can't cook to save his life... though that is something he is trying to change.

To keep up with the latest or to contact Hoi, please visit hoitpham.com.